# It was all fa
## for the Exe

He didn't judge. His targe̶t̶s̶
themselves by actions so abhorrent to society tha̶t̶
simply letting them continue was a crime unto
itself.

And when society, the System, failed to purge itself
of toxic waste, sometimes the task would fall to
Hal Brognola's team at Stony Man. When the
eradication of a public enemy was urgent, and the
stakes were life or death, then Mack Bolan might be
called to intervene.

He didn't hassle tax cheats or petty thieves. He
didn't judge a target based on politics, religion,
race, gender or nationality. He stepped on vipers
that were poisoning society, perverting it for selfish
ends, and wasting lives in the process.

Most days, it felt a bit like taking out the trash.

# Don Pendleton's Mack Bolan®

## Ripple Effect

A GOLD EAGLE BOOK FROM

# W☉RLDWIDE®

TORONTO • NEW YORK • LONDON
AMSTERDAM • PARIS • SYDNEY • HAMBURG
STOCKHOLM • ATHENS • TOKYO • MILAN
MADRID • WARSAW • BUDAPEST • AUCKLAND

First edition September 2007

ISBN-13: 978-0-373-61519-3
ISBN-10:  0-373-61519-1

Special thanks and acknowledgment to
Mike Newton for his contribution to this work.

RIPPLE EFFECT

**Printed in U.S.A.**

When evil acts in the world it always manages
to find instruments who believe that what they
do is not evil but honorable.
> —Max Lerner
> *The Unfinished Country* (1959)

Wherever evil comes from, decent men are still
obliged to take a stand. The fact that it grows close to
home makes that resistance even more obligatory.
> —Mack Bolan

For Gunnery Sergeant Carlos Nathaniel Hathcock III,
USMC

# PROLOGUE

*Camp X-ray—Guantanamo Bay, Cuba*

Lieutenant Jordan Lewis hated meeting with the CIA. He knew the standard rap, of course—brothers in arms, collaborating in the war on terror, all that happy stuff—but there was still something about the Company that set his nerves on edge.

For one thing, it was flat-out wrong for spooks to give the orders—*any* orders—on a military base run for the better part of a century by the United States Marine Corps. Worse than wrong, it pissed him off.

The job at Camp X-ray was hard enough without demanding that the military personnel on-site kiss Langley's ass.

And what a job it was, containing several hundred "enemy combatants" snatched from various locales over the past six years, beginning in Afghanistan, proceeding to Iraq, and then some places the civilian public didn't even know about. Most of the hostiles caged at Camp X-ray would never face a formal charge. Hell, most of them still hadn't been *identified* to any court, congressional committee or defense attorneys. They were locked down tight and going nowhere unless Uncle Sam decided, in his own sweet time, that they were clean.

And that was where Lewis found himself compelled to share his space with cloak-and-dagger types who thought the information superhighway ran only one way. The spooks reminded him of leeches. They crept in, latched on to files and prisoners, sucked out whatever they could use, then crept away without a simple thank-you to the men and women who maintained their feeding station. It was damned elitist arrogance, no other way to read it, and it sometimes made Lewis wish that he could punch them out, beginning at the top and working down.

He could've borne their snotty attitude a little better if they got results in the real world, but after six years of interrogation, eavesdropping and fudging data, what was the result?

Nada.

Lewis heard the vague pronouncements coming out of Washington, whenever some fat cat believed his job was riding on the line. He'd blather on about the terrorist attacks that had been averted, suspects captured, lives that had been saved—and naturally, all of it was classified.

But Jordan Lewis knew the truth.

He knew that in the years of his assignment to Camp X-ray, there had been no major breaks of any kind. Osama was still out there, and funds kept flowing to al Qaeda from the usual suspects. Most of *them,* in turn, were cozily in bed with "patriotic" politicians in the States, none of their countries facing any sanctions, threats of military intervention or preemptive strikes.

It was a crazy world, and Jordan Lewis was accustomed to it. He knew that there would always be another war, as long as men could scheme against one another in the halls of power, and he understood his role in that reality. He understood that there were rules, and also times when they were set aside to serve the greater good.

No problem.

He could twist arms with the best of them when it was called for, but he didn't like some smarmy frat boy from the Ivy League intruding, telling him that he had done it wrong, suggesting that he try another angle of attack or step aside and let them do it, acting all superior while they were showing him the door.

This day, the new arrival was Bob Armstrong, or so he called himself. Lewis suspected that the name was every bit as phony as his smile. Armstrong was roughly the same age as Lewis, spoke with just a trace of a New England accent and was always groomed as if he half expected paparazzi to be waiting for him at the gates.

Some days Lewis thought about trying a change of scene, maybe a tour in Sandland, but he didn't want to press his luck.

They also serve who only sit with spooks.

To hell with it, he thought. It's what they pay you for.

And with that thought in mind, Lewis buzzed his orderly. "Corporal," he said, "show Mr. Armstrong in."

A moment later, there he was, all styling gel, bleached

teeth and Harvard attitude. Wearing a smile as phony as the spook's, Lewis walked around his desk to shake the agent's hand.

HASAM KHALED WAS WORRIED, for himself and for the great jihad. A new round of interrogations had begun, and while it had been several months since he was questioned, granting ample time for him to rest, Khaled feared that he might be weakening in custody. He had been too long out of contact with his brothers, and despite his faith in Allah to sustain him, lately there had been no answer to his prayers.

Each time the smug Americans passed by his cage, selecting someone else to grill for information, he was certain they had come for him. Someday they would, and who knew what techniques they would employ this time?

Before, they had progressed from stilted courtesy to bullying and threats, suspension of his so-called privileges. Diet could be adjusted in proportion to collaboration with the enemy, so Khaled lost weight. He didn't mind the sacrifice of flesh, content to know that Paradise awaited him.

But if he broke, what then?

The whispered rumors frightened him. In place of simple tactics—insults, threats, sleep deprivation—it was said that more effective methods soon might be employed. Torture, perhaps, or forced "repatriation" to some allied country where interrogators weren't as squeamish as Americans. Or drugs, the kind that robbed even a dedicated warrior of his wits and his determination to resist.

Hasam Khaled was frightened of the drugs. Torture was fearful, but he thought—hoped, prayed—that he could weather beatings, possibly electric shocks, without soiling his honor. Drugs, however, stole a victim's will and left him helpless, babbling everything he knew to agents of the Great Satan.

And once Khaled began to talk, how could he stop?

There had to be something he could do.

Khaled recalled his training, exhortations that prepared him to give up his life for God's holy cause. He had been lucky so far, stunned in an explosion that inflicted only minor injuries but killed his two companions and a number of civilians. The Americans weren't entirely sure whether Khaled was a combatant or a bystander, but they had shipped him to Cuba anyway. Uncertainty had given him a way to dodge their questions, up to now, but if they came at him with drugs…

There was one obvious alternative. He could become a martyr to the cause, not unlike those who strapped explosives to their bodies and then detonated them where it would do the most harm to their enemies. His self-inflicted death, while not as grandiose as an explosion in a market filled with Zionists or U.S. soldiers, still could serve the cause and bring great honor to his name, his family.

Khaled's imam had been explicit on that subject. Any death in God's service was commendable. He didn't have to kill a hundred enemies, or even one. It was enough that he *intended* to destroy the infidels, and by his death prevented God's enemies from gaining an advantage in the struggle. If by dying he could snatch salvation from the fingertips of targets marked for death by his comrades, Khaled would be a hero.

And his place in Paradise would be assured.

That vision made him strong—or stronger than he might have been without it.

Escape wasn't an option, Khaled realized, and while some other inmates of the camp had been released to satisfy the Red Cross or the media, once he was questioned under medication there would be no possibility of freedom. Once they heard his secret, Khaled might be whisked away to the American mainland for further questioning, until the heathen bastards satisfied themselves that they knew everything.

And would it be enough to save them?

Possibly.

Khaled couldn't be sure. He knew only a name, a fragment of a rumor shared by comrades in the dead of night. He had no details of the master plan itself, but once the name was given to his enemies, the rest might be superfluous. The scouring of dossiers and databases would begin, and ultimately they would have the man himself.

Khaled couldn't permit it.

There were no weapons in his cell, of course—or none, at any rate, regarded by his captors as a weapon. But the simple cotton robe he wore could serve him as an instrument of suicide.

And when he'd finished with it, they could use if for his shroud.

There was no privacy in Camp X-ray, but neither was Khaled exposed in fact to round-the-clock surveillance. When he pulled the plain white robe over his head, no one except the occupants of two adjoining cages saw him do it. Neither spoke as he stood tall on tiptoes, double-knotting one sleeve of the robe to bars that formed the ceiling of his cage.

Neither adjoining prisoner called out for help as Khaled tied a makeshift noose around his neck and pulled it tight. They offered no objection as he checked the simple hangman's rope for length, then climbed the nearest barred wall of his cage for altitude.

The bars were slippery. He almost lost his grip and tumbled back, but that wouldn't provide enough impact to stun him and prevent his hands from rising to the noose as he began to choke. In case his will to live proved stronger than his faith, Khaled was banking on a sharper drop to render him insensible.

A few more inches now. That should be high enough. The floor seemed far below him, like the bottom of a canyon. All illusion, in his present agitated state.

With one last prayer, Hasam Khaled released his grip and plummeted toward Paradise.

BOB ARMSTRONG DIDN'T CARE much for the spit-and-polish military types. He tolerated them whenever necessary, wore a smiling mask to hide his general contempt for amateurs who meddled in intelligence, and he never under any circumstances gave away the information his superiors had classified as need-to-know.

Sometimes, like now, he'd flatter certain officers with lies or slick evasions when they had to work in tandem toward specific goals, but he would no more tell a grunt in uniform what he was really thinking than he'd drop his pants and wag the weasel at a formal diplomatic function.

Some things were simply not done by professionals. Full stop. Case closed.

But sometimes you had to prime the pump, and so he said, "The truth, Lieutenant Lewis—may I call you Joseph, by the way?"

"It's Jordan."

"Ah, my apologies. Then, may I—?"

"No."

"Okay." Big smile. "The truth, Lieutenant Lewis, is that Langley's under fire right now with accusations that we overlook the little things. Nobody seems to care much if a war goes on for years with no result, but we catch hell if we don't know the dictator of the day's zip code. You follow me?"

"Not yet," the Marine said.

"My point is that we want to dot our i's and cross our t's, make sure we don't miss any little thing, regardless of how insignificant it seems."

"And that affects me…how?" the lieutenant asked.

"I've been asked to start from scratch with some of the neglected prisoners. Not *my* word, mind you. From the top, you know? Wish I could duck it. Big pain in the neck, I realize, but there it is."

"No problem," the lieutenant answered somewhat stiffly. "Do you have a list, or are we starting over alphabetically?"

"I have a list," Armstrong admitted, "but it's more like alphabet soup. They've been prioritized somehow, by someone. You can ask me how, why, who, but I don't know. God's truth."

He was about to put a hand over his heart, but thought that might be overdoing it.

"I don't require an explanation, Mr. Armstrong," Lewis said. "When did you want to start?"

"This morning, if that's feasible."

"I'll need your list."

"Of course." Armstrong retrieved two sheets of folded paper from an inside pocket of his jacket, passing them across the desk. Lewis unfolded them, blinked once, then tried to mask his surprise as he surveyed the twin columns of small, single-spaced type.

"This looks like nearly half the men in camp," the lieutenant said.

"Is it?" Armstrong cocked an eyebrow, as if mildly curious. "I couldn't say."

"And these have been prioritized, you say? Does that mean that the first, say, dozen on the list are now prime terrorism suspects?"

Armstrong shrugged, his face contorting into something that approximated puzzlement. "Beats me," he said. "For all I know, they could have ranked them in reverse order, with small-fry at the top. I really couldn't say."

"Mm-hmm." Lewis looked skeptical, to say the least. "And you want to begin with number one, meaning top left on the first page?"

"Correct."

"And work your way down column one, then back up to the top of column two? Or zigzag down the page?"

Armstrong pretended not to know that the jarhead was making fun of him. "Straight down, I think. If that's all right with you."

"Whatever," Lewis said. "These clowns aren't going anywhere. You want to start right now?"

"Ideally, yes," Armstrong replied.

"Suits me. I'll see if we have an interpreter available."

Armstrong relaxed and watched the officer go through his pantomime. In fact, as he well knew, Camp X-ray *always* had interpreters available. It couldn't function otherwise, with prisoners who spoke at least three languages aside from Arabic.

After another moment on the telephone, Lewis cradled the receiver, donned a tight-lipped smile and said, "I have a man you can use to get started this morning. Later on today, we're jammed up pretty tight."

"Where there's a will…."

"I'll see what I can do. No promises."

"Of course." He didn't feel like flexing any hidden muscles at the moment. If the jarhead still felt prickly around lunchtime, Armstrong would reach out and pull whatever strings it took to scorch his lazy ass.

"In that case," Lewis said, "we're just waiting for the interpreter. He's coming over from the barracks as we speak."

"That should be—"

Sudden rapping on the office door distracted him. The sergeant from the outer waiting room entered, flicked a distracted glance at Armstrong, then told Lewis, "Sir, we've had another…incident."

"Explain," Lewis commanded. When the sergeant looked again at Armstrong, the lieutenant added, "Sergeant, please speak freely."

"Yes, sir. It's another suicide attempt. One of the inmates tried to hang himself."

"Which one?"

The sergeant looked down at his cupped left hand, where Armstrong saw a sticky note not quite concealed. "His name's Hasam Khaled, sir. Just a nobody, as far as we can tell. One of the men on walk-through found him hanging in his cell and cut him down."

"You said he *tried* to hang himself. How badly is he hurt?" Lewis inquired, sounding as if he didn't really care much either way.

"Should be all right, sir. That's the word for now, at least. The medics have him in sick bay."

"All right. Dismissed."

The sergeant wheeled around and left the office, closed the door behind him.

"Lieutenant," Armstrong said, "I'd like to climb out on a limb here, and suggest a change of plans."

"Not sure I follow you," said the Marine.

"I'd like to reprioritize that list a bit."

"Meaning?"

"I want to put a new name at the top."

"Okay. Which one?"

"I'll have my first chat with Hasam Khaled."

"The loser who just tried to off himself?" Lewis seemed surprised.

"That's right."

"You mind if I ask why, exactly?"

As it happened, this time Armstrong didn't mind at all. "He's anxious to get out of here by any means available," he said. "That tells me that he's either cracked and lost his mind—or maybe, just *maybe,* has something to hide."

AT FIRST, HASAM KHALED believed that he had found his way to Paradise, but then he felt the harsh pain in his neck and grimaced as his vision cleared. If *this* was Paradise, then the imam had lied and there was no reward worthy of sacrifice.

Before that sacrilegious thought could take root in his head, Khaled woke to the fact that he was still alive, apparently sequestered in the camp's infirmary. He had accomplished nothing, other than inflicting needless pain upon himself.

Hoping the noose might have destroyed his vocal cords, he cleared his throat, then tried to speak. The words were hoarse and painful, but he heard them clearly, even though he whispered.

"Doctor," someone said beyond his line of sight, "this one's awake."

"Good thing," another voice replied. "I've got them breathing down my neck."

Khaled was functional in English, but he still had trouble with its slang and idioms. Why, for example, would one person breathe into another's neck, except for purposes of artificial respiration? And the second speaker clearly didn't require such treatment, since he had ability to breathe and speak unaided.

Faces loomed beside his narrow bed, one man with a white coat over his uniform, the other garbed in the fatigues worn by all guards throughout the camp. Khaled had studied rank insignia for the Great Satan's military forces, and he recognized the white coat as a first lieutenant, while the other was a corporal of the United States Marines.

His mortal enemies.

"Mr. Khaled?" The white coat peered into his face and raised a fist, the index finger pointed up. "How many fingers do you see?"

He had a normal hand. "Five," Khaled said.

The white coat raised another finger, to create a *V.* "How many now?" he asked.

"Still five."

"He's yanking you, Lieutenant," the corporal said.

"You think?"

Scowling, the officer informed Khaled, "You have some visitors. Their sense of humor sucks."

Khaled did not attempt to turn his head. He'd let his enemies do all the work, while he focused upon resisting them.

A moment later, two new faces flanked his bed. One was a sergeant in his early twenties, while the other was a slightly older man, blond haired, wearing some kind of business suit.

The suit spoke first. "Hasam Khaled?"

Khaled didn't respond. He was determined to say nothing, come what may. If later he was forced to scream, perhaps it wouldn't count against him in the eyes of God.

"That was quite an accident you had," the blonde remarked. The sergeant translated his words to Arabic.

What accident? He'd tried to hang himself. The only accident had been his failure to achieve that end.

"Escape attempts are frowned upon, you realize."

Escape? Khaled concluded that the blond man was a fool, perhaps insane.

"It adds time to your sentence, get it? And you haven't

even had your trial yet. Honestly, Hasam, what were you thinking?"

That's for me to know, Khaled thought, tuning out the voice of the interpreter.

"I'd like to help you, if I can," the American said.

Then kill yourself, Khaled answered silently. It took an effort not to smile, but even thinking seemed to hurt his injured throat.

"Of course, I can't do anything on your behalf, unless you're willing to cooperate."

Never.

"A few quick questions," the blonde said. "Nothing earth-shattering, you understand. The basic sort of thing. Name, rank and what have you."

The blonde was lying. Khaled smelled it on him.

"But if you won't help," the litany went on, "well…"

*Here it comes.* First threats, then pain. Khaled tried to prepare himself, but it was difficult, not knowing how his captors would torment him.

"I suspect," the suit remarked off-handedly, "that you could use some medicine. Sergeant?"

"I'll fetch the medic, sir."

Briefly alone, the blonde bent lower, almost whispering. "If you can follow this at all, I *really* think that you should talk to me, without the needles. Once they start…well, hey, I never knew a doctor who could say, 'Enough's enough.' Have you? Hasam? Okay. Don't say I didn't warn you."

The sergeant returned with a different white coat, this one balding and grim in the face. The new arrival carried a hypodermic syringe half filled with milky fluid.

Hasam Khaled recoiled—or would have, if his arms and legs hadn't been pinned by heavy leather straps. All he could do was wriggle, strain against the leather, as the medic with the needle swabbed his arm with alcohol, then spiked him.

Khaled was expecting pain, but in its place euphoria suffused his body. For a moment, he imagined they were killing him—some executions in America were carried out with poisoned hypodermics—but that made no sense. They couldn't question him if he was dead.

No. They were lulling him with drugs, polluting him with chemicals to make him speak. Khaled determined to resist Satan's technology at any cost, even if he was forced to bite his tongue and drown in his own blood.

That sounded like a good idea, but when he tried it, Khaled found his jaws unwilling to obey. In fact, the very notion seemed so silly that he nearly burst out laughing.

"Hasam? Earth to Hasam?"

The blonde was speaking once again, his translator echoing everything he said, like an annoying television sound track.

"Feeling better, Has, my man? That's good. Now, let's get down to business, shall we?"

*Business? I was never very good at business. You can ask my father. He will—*

"What I need to know, first thing," the rude blonde interrupted him, "is why you tried to kill yourself. Just tell me that, for starters, and we're on our way."

"Secret," Khaled whispered, not realizing for an instant that he'd spoken.

*Stop! Resist! Say nothing, in the name of God!*

"Secret? Now we're getting somewhere, Hassy. May I call you Hassy? Good. About this secret, now. What is it?"

Although Khaled had spoken English, the interpreter continued with his task.

"Too great. I must…not…tell."

"We're all friends here," the blonde assured him, smiling like a sneaky thief. "You can tell me anything. Don't be embarrassed. Hassy, I can promise you, I've heard it all."

"Not this."

"Surprise me, then. I'm always up for something new."

Khaled could feel the smile form on his face. "You will know soon enough," he said.

"Will I?" the blonde replied. "All right, then, but I'd like a little preview, if you don't mind. What we call a trailer, in the States. A glimpse, to you. How'd that be, Hassy?"

Still Khaled resisted, but he couldn't fight the drugs forever. Finally, weeping for shame and the inevitable loss of Paradise, he spoke a name.

# CHAPTER ONE

*Cocoa Beach, Florida*

Mack Bolan, aka the Executioner, walked along a quiet, nearly vacant beach at sunrise. It was *nearly* vacant, since a beach bum and his lady had apparently camped out the night before, somehow avoiding the nocturnal beach patrol to plant their sleeping bags above the high-tide waterline. They were engrossed in each other as he passed, ignoring him, waking to yet another day of—what?

Good luck, he hoped, and wished them well.

A small crab scuttled out of Bolan's path, chasing the white Atlantic surf as it retreated. In his short-sleeved shirt, Bolan was conscious of a chill wind off the ocean, but he trusted that the sun would warm him soon enough.

Right now, the chill felt good, a respite from the heat he knew was coming, guaranteed.

It was a rare day when he could escape the heat.

He'd spent the past two nights at the Wakulla Inn, taking a unit with a kitchen and more bedrooms than he needed, just to have the space. Two days of beachfront R and R had tanned him, while meandering along the main drag, two blocks from his pad, briefly immersed him in the tourist scene. He'd poked around Ron Jon's and other surf shops, happily admiring the bikinis, scowling at the baby sharks and alligators slaughtered into knickknacks for the Yankee set.

And life went on.

But not for long.

That morning, he was meeting Hal Brognola, their connection arranged on Sunday evening via sat phone linkup from Stony Man Farm. Bolan hadn't asked why Hal wanted to meet in Florida, instead of someplace close to Washington. It simply wasn't done.

As luck would have it, he'd been passing through Atlanta with some time and narcotraffickers to kill, when Hal had buzzed him to request a face-to-face. They met in person six or seven times a year, on average, but usually in proximity to Wonderland, D.C., where the big Fed held down a desk at the Justice Department, six blocks from the White House.

Bolan had never seen Hal's office. It would be a no-win situation, all around, since he had been America's most-wanted fugitive—until his death, some years ago, in New York City. Now, with a new face and several identities to spare, he did the same things that he'd done before, but with the covert blessing of his Uncle Sam.

He felt relaxed, ready to roll on whatever assignment Brognola might have for him. He didn't try to second-guess the man from Justice, having learned from long experience that it would be a futile exercise. Brognola would present the facts and arguments for intervention. Bolan had the option of refusing any job that went against his grain, in which case it would pass to other hands, but he had never exercised that right.

One reason: he and Hal were well attuned to life, society and the preventive maintenance required to keep America the beautiful from turning into something else entirely. Bolan respected the Constitution and the laws that guaranteed all citizens their civil rights, but there were times when something happened to the system and it didn't work as planned.

Sometimes corruption was to blame, or loopholes in the law that might take years to plug, while predators took full advantage of the gaps to victimize the innocent and weak. At other times, the system's built-in safeguards made the wheels of justice turn too slowly, costing lives and human misery before a verdict could be rendered, then appealed, then reaffirmed by higher courts.

Brognola found some of the targets for him. Bolan found some others on his own. Financing from the nerve center of operations came from covert budgetary pigeonholes, while Bolan's pocket money often emanated from the predators themselves. He had no qualms about relieving drug dealers or loan sharks of their blood money, and if the scumbags suffered catastrophic injuries while he was taking out a loan, what of it?

There were always more scumbags in waiting, never any shortage in the world that Bolan had observed.

Downrange, he saw a solitary figure striding toward him, hands in pockets, a fedora planted squarely on its head. He couldn't swear it was Brognola, but odds against a stranger showing up at the appointed time, in that getup, were next to nil.

Brognola called to him from fifty feet away. "Would you believe I'm on vacation?"

"Not a chance," Bolan replied.

"Okay, you're right. Let's take a walk."

They walked and talked. The basic pleasantries were brief, whatever passed for personal emotion understood between these battle-hardened warriors and beyond the reach of words. Despite a friendship so deep-seated that both took it rightfully for granted, they had business to discuss.

"Vacation," Brognola mused. "Sure, I've heard of that."

"You ought to try it," Bolan said.

"Maybe next year. And look who's talking."

"I've just had two days."

"That's two in how damned long?"

"Who's counting?" Bolan asked him.

"Right. Okay. So, what I've got is something sticky. It's a problem that I can't turn loose."

"I'm listening."

"What do you know about Guantanamo?"

"It's ninety miles that way," Bolan said, with a thumb jerk toward his shoulder. "Cuba. Big Marine base, captured from the Spanish back when Teddy Roosevelt was still a rough-rider. Maintained as U.S. territory since the Castro revolution, more or less to spite Fidel."

"What else?" Brognola urged.

"Detention blocks for terrorists and terror suspects taken in Afghanistan, Iraq and who-knows-where."

"Camp X-ray," Brognola confirmed. "It's part of why we're here."

"They need another sentry?" Bolan asked.

"I doubt it. Sentries they have plenty of. Also interrogators." Bolan caught a faint tone of distaste in the big Fed's voice, covered reasonably well. Both of them recognized that sometimes information had to be gathered swiftly, forcefully. And neither of them liked it one damned bit.

"Interrogators?" he reminded Brognola when silence stretched between them for the better part of a minute.

"Right. A few days back, one of the inmates tried to hang himself and botched it. They revived him, and decided he was worth a closer look. Why now, I'm guessing was the rationale. Why would this nobody, who claims he's innocent, decide to off himself one afternoon for no apparent reason?"

"It's a question," Bolan said.

"And they got answers," Brognola confided.

"Which involves us…how?"

"I guess you know the rule of thumb for suspects held since 9/11, right? Arrest a hundred, and you may get four or five who know a guy who knows a guy. Arrest a thousand, maybe you find one or two who *are* those guys. This guy who tried to lynch himself knows people. My guess, he got tired of sitting in his cell, ignored, and waiting for the other shoe to drop. He figured they'd be getting back to him, sooner or later, and he wanted to eliminate the chance of letting something slip."

"Too bad for him he couldn't do it right," Bolan observed.

"Too bad for him, but maybe good for us."

"How so?"

"Because he knows things," Brognola said. "Not a major player, now, don't get me wrong. His face isn't on anybody's deck of cards. They never heard of him at Langley, until three, four days ago. At least, they never really thought about him. Way down at the bottom of some list that gathered dust. No one you'd give the time of day. They might've turned him loose, another six months or a year, except for the attempted suicide."

"But now he's in the spotlight."

"Sitting right there on the grill," Brognola said. "Maybe you smell the smoke from here. And one way or another, they persuade this guy to spill his guts. Turns out, he's been around and knows his way around. Hamas, al Qaeda, PLO—little Hasam Khaled's got friends all over."

"But he's not a major player?" Bolan asked.

"Not even close," Brognola replied. "But he's the man nobody notices. Loyal to a fault, likely involved in bombings or some other shit, but mostly, he's just there. Maybe he brings the big boys tea and sandwiches, stands guard outside the tent or tags along behind them with his AK when they take a stroll. But all the while, he hears things."

"Which he's sharing with the Gitmo gang," Bolan said.

"Bingo. Some of it's history, you know, like Joe Valachi telling all about the 1930s Mafia in 1961. Khaled isn't that old, but neither are the groups he's been involved with.

What I hear, he's talking personalities and troop deployments, plans that failed, others that hit the bull's-eye, schisms in the ranks—the whole nine yards."

"That covers lots of ground," Bolan observed.

"Too much for us to think about. Except, maybe, one thing."

Bolan said nothing, waiting for it.

"There was one name that stood out," Brognola said. "I mean, a lot of names stood out, but this one was American."

"Unusual."

"In spades. You've heard about the so-called American Taliban caught in Afghanistan, and that guy with the shoe bomb that didn't go off."

Bolan nodded, still waiting.

"Well, those are the norm when al Qaeda or some rival group gets a Yank in the ranks. Disaffected young men, for the most part. They look for a cause with excitement attached. If they're rednecks, they go for the Klan or militias. Same thing. Self-improvement through hate."

"But the new name is different," Bolan said, not asking.

"And then some," Brognola replied. "This one worries the hell out of Langley, the Pentagon, maybe the White House. It worries the hell out of *me*."

"It's a congressman? Senator? What?"

"Don't I wish. If it was, we could stake out his office, tap into his phone lines, whatever. The Bureau could do it and slap him with charges from here to next Easter. It isn't that simple."

"Go on."

"First, the guy's not in-country. You've heard of free radicals? This one's the ultimate. Maybe we know where he is, maybe not. It's a toss-up, and knowing's not bagging."

"Okay."

"But he's not just elusive. He's skilled, see? He knows the guerrilla game inside and out, and it's not just in theory. He's been there, in combat, for our side and theirs. In between he was anyone's soldier if they could afford him. Turns out, some of our enemies have oil and cash to burn."

"Sounds tough," Bolan agreed.

"He's tough, all right." Brognola stopped dead in the sand, sun rising at his back. "In fact, he's you."

"Say what?"

"I don't mean *you,* you. But he's like you. Special Forces. The same training, same background, plenty of real combat experience before he took a discharge and went into business for himself."

"Who *is* this guy?" Bolan asked.

Brognola fished inside his jacket and produced a CD in a plastic case. "His file's on here, in PDF," the man from Justice said. "Long story somewhat short, his name is Eugene Talmadge. Born in 1967, joined the Army out of high school. Graduated to the Green Berets at twenty, with a sergeant's stripes. Like you."

Bolan was less than thrilled with the comparison, but kept his mouth shut, listening.

"Combat-wise, he served in Panama, the Noriega thing down there—"

Bolan supplied the operation's name. "Just Cause."

"That's it. Then, he was back for Desert Storm in 1991, followed by action in Somalia and Bosnia. Peacekeeping,

I believe they called it at the time. In 1995 there was an incident with one of his superiors. It's in the file, sort of."

"Sort of?"

"The way it reads, Talmadge had words with a lieutenant and teed off on him. The looey wound up close to brain-dead. Talmadge got a compromise verdict at his court-martial. Guilty of assaulting a superior, acquitted of attempted murder and some other stuff. The Army yanked his pension and he walked with a dishonorable discharge."

"You don't buy the verdict," Bolan said, not making it a question.

"Oh, I'm sure about the verdict," Brognola replied, "but not about the case. Transcripts are classified, but I got Aaron and his techies at the Farm to do some hacking for me, on the q.t. It turns out that Talmadge's defense was basically eradicated from the public record."

"Being?"

"Namely," Brognola said, "that he caught this officer and gentleman trying to rape a female corporal. Apparently, when Talmadge pulled him off, the looey lost it, started swinging on him, and the rest his history."

"They hung him out to dry for *that?*"

"Apparently," Brognola said. "Today, they'd probably be prosecuting the lieutenant, but the atmosphere in 1995 was different. They had adultery scandals going on, reports of sexual assaults at West Point and Annapolis. I'm guessing that one more black eye was one too many."

"And Talmadge came out pissed."

"I'm guessing yes. He shopped around for jobs, but with the DD and his lack of college training, it was pretty much a hopeless case. Before starvation hit, he started doing what he's good at, but for higher pay than Uncle Sam had ever given him."

"A merc," Bolan said. It was more or less predictable, the same course followed throughout history by soldiers of all nations who were left without a service or a war to fight.

"A merc *and* contract hitter," Brognola amended. "Once again, it's in the dossier. To summarize, we're sure of work he did in Africa, Myanmar and Brazil. That's soldiering. Talmadge is also the prime suspect in at least eleven contract murders spanning Europe and North Africa, with one in Canada. He does good work, cleans up after himself. No charges pending anywhere."

"Which brings us back to Gitmo," Bolan said.

"It does. Our songbird dropped his name last week. No, it didn't ring a bell at first, but Langley started digging, and the Pentagon pitched in. It set alarm bells ringing when they found his file."

"What's he involved in?" Bolan asked.

"Washington supposed it must be some kind of guerrilla training. Make that hoped. Sources confirmed that Talmadge has been seen in Syria, Iran and Pakistan. Also in Jordan, once or twice, hanging around the Bekaa Valley. That's dope money *and* Islamic terrorists. He could've been on tap for either, or for both. So, training, right?"

"Sounds like it," Bolan said.

"Until we started looking at his travel record and comparing it to contract hits. A Mossad district chief in Stockholm. An Iranian defector in Versailles. Two Saudi dissidents in Rome. One of Osama's breakaway lieutenants in Vienna. It goes on like that."

"He's helping them clean house."

"At least," Brognola said. "One thing I'd say about our boy, he won't discriminate. From what's on file, he likes the highest bidder while the money's flowing, and he moves on when it stops. No job too dirty, in the meantime. In Vienna, where he used C-4, the target had his wife and daughter with him. Talmadge took all three. The girl was four years old."

"Hard to believe he hasn't left some kind of trail for the forensics people," Bolan said.

"It's like I said. He's you."

"Enough with that, okay?"

"Sorry." Brognola looked contrite, or something close to it. "No offense. I mean to say that he's *professional.* Back in the day, you left a trail because you wanted to. Psy-war against the opposition, right? You rattled them by showing where you'd been, and sometimes called ahead to tell them who was next."

Brognola's first contact with Bolan had occurred while the big Fed was FBI and Bolan was engaged in a heroic one-man war against the Mafia, avenging damage to his family and rolling on from there to make syndicate mobsters an endangered species.

"It was a different situation," Bolan said.

"My point exactly," Brognola replied. "Talmadge has no cause of his own, no faith in anyone or anything except himself. He'll work for them, kill for them, but he's not committed. If he left a sign at any of his hits, it would reflect the group that hired him, not Gene Talmadge."

"But you've tracked him anyway."

Brognola shrugged. "You know how these things work. Combine the testimony of informants and survivors with the various security devices found in airports—biometric scanners are the bomb, apparently—and we can place him near the scene of various assassinations, bombings, this and that. We don't have photos of his finger on the trigger, but it comes down to the next-best thing. Besides, it isn't like we're taking him to trial."

And there it was. The death sentence.

"The action you're describing to me has been going on for—what? Eleven years?"

"At least," Brognola said.

"So why the sudden urgency?" Bolan asked.

"Ah. Because our songbird down at Gitmo didn't only drop a name."

"Go on."

"According to Khaled, al Qaeda has our boy on tap this time, to 'teach Satan a lesson he will not forget.' Khaled has no specifics on the nature of that lesson, but we didn't like the sound of it."

"That's understandable," Bolan allowed.

"So, there you are. We've got one kick-ass warrior, seemingly devoid of anything resembling conscience, working for a group that wants to take us off the map. We'd like to stop them—*him,* specifically—and do it in a way that doesn't make the Pentagon look like a nuthouse with the inmates in control. You in?"

Bolan frowned, feeling the deadweight of the CD in his pocket. "Yeah," he said at last. "I'm in."

A QUARTER OF AN HOUR LATER, back at the Wakulla Inn, Bolan reviewed the CD on his laptop. It began with all the ordinary paperwork for the induction of a U.S. Army private, with the details of its subject's early life.

Eugene Adam Talmadge had indeed been born in 1967—April 23, to be precise—in Boulder, Colorado. His high-school grades were average, except in sports, where he excelled. A college football scholarship had been on offer, but he'd turned it down to wear a uniform, and then a green beret.

Bolan was somewhat puzzled by that choice, coming in 1985, when there was no threat of a military draft and no war currently in progress to attract daredevil types. Maybe Talmadge decided that he was unsuited to a college campus, even with the free ride offered by its sports department. Maybe he was hoping to accomplish something on his own, not have it handed to him on a silver platter just because he was a jock. Trouble at home? Something so personal it didn't make the files?

Bolan would never know.

Talmadge had been a standout boot in basic training, and had taken to the Special Forces school at Benning like a duck to water, acing every course except the foreign-language training, where he struggled for a passing score in Spanish. When it came to weapons training and explosives, unarmed combat and survival, though, Talmadge had everything the service could desire, and then some.

Talmadge had killed his first two men in Panama, a couple of Manuel Noriega's gorillas who weren't smart enough to lay down their arms in the face of superior force.

There was no intimation of a trigger-happy soldier in that case, no hint of any impropriety.

In combat, people died.

In Desert Storm, Talmadge had earned a reputation for himself. On the advance from Kuwait, through Iraq, he'd personally taken out at least two dozen members of Saddam's elite Republican Guard, earning a Silver Star and a Purple Heart in the process. The citation that accompanied his Silver Star praised Talmadge for his bravery and focus under fire, resulting in the rescue of two wounded comrades and elimination of a hostile rifle squad. Details were classified, suggesting that the mission also had a covert side.

His flesh wounds didn't keep him out of action long. Talmadge had shipped out for Somalia in winter 1992, as part of Washington's attempt to regulate that nation's rival warlords and bring order out of chaos. That attempt had failed, but Talmadge scored nine more verified kills during four months in-country. His part in the rescue of a downed Black Hawk crew earned him a DSC—Distinguished Service Cross—and yet another Purple Heart.

He did all right, Bolan thought, moving onward through the soldier's life on paper.

The sutures were barely removed from Talmadge's Somalian wounds when new orders dispatched him to Bosnia-Herzegovina, land of ethnic cleansing and religious hatred spanning centuries. More warlords, more atrocities, more combat pay. Talmadge hadn't been wounded in that conflict, but he *had* logged seven kills the record keepers knew about. No decorations that time for a job well done.

The Army's standard paperwork included his record for

the next year and a half, until the bitter end. Bolan discovered that the incident in 1995 had happened at Fort Benning. A lieutenant, name deleted, was the so-called victim, with a list of fractures and internal damage ranging from his skull down to his knees. The witnesses included two civilians and a corporal, name deleted, who was almost certainly the female Brognola had mentioned in his summary.

And as Brognola had explained, the transcripts of the court-martial were missing, classified for reasons unexplained. The logic of that void was inescapable: the facts were secret. Ergo, there could be no explanation *why* they had been classified, or else the secret would've been revealed.

Catch-22.

Bolan took Brognola's appraisal of the case as valid, recognized the anger and frustration Talmadge had to have felt at being railroaded. Any remarks he may have offered to the court-martial were classified along with all the rest, leaving the slate blank. Only the verdict now remained, its stinging condemnation of a former hero sure to follow him for the remainder of his life.

Under the circumstances, Bolan was a bit surprised that Talmadge hadn't sought revenge against the Army. Then again, when he considered what Talmadge had done throughout the intervening years—what he was doing now—perhaps he had. Brognola might be wrong about the former Green Beret's coldhearted profit motive. Talmadge fought for pay, of course—he had to eat, like anybody else—but in his work for Middle Eastern terrorists, he had been striking out against the West.

And striking back at Uncle Sam.

Bolan was no armchair psychologist, but it didn't require a Ph.D. to recognize that Talmadge had his pick of causes and employers in a world where violence was the norm. He could've spent more time in sub-Saharan Africa or Southeast Asia if his only goal was money in the bank.

Instead, by working for Hamas, al Qaeda and the like, Talmadge had actually chosen sides, but with a difference. He wasn't some deluded college convert to Islamic fundamentalist extremism, or a celebrity who craved publicity at any cost. He was a soldier, and he'd made a choice.

Bolan thought he understood Gene Talmadge now, and he could even sympathize with him. Up to a point. But sympathy ran out when Talmadge cast his lot with terrorists and criminals. There was—at least to Bolan's mind—a world of difference between a mercenary soldier drifting aimlessly, involved in brushfire wars without regard to ideology, and one who set himself on a collision course with the United States and civilized society.

Whatever wrongs Talmadge had suffered at the hands of his superiors, he'd given up the moral high ground when he hired on with al Qaeda and its allies to perpetuate a bloodbath fueled by hatred and fanaticism. Bolan knew that something had to be done, and he seemed the best qualified to do the job.

Brognola's latest information placed the target in Jakarta, where al Qaeda was supposed to have a thriving outpost. Bolan's contact on the ground would be an agent from Homeland Security, who had been keeping track of Talmadge and his playmates since the news from Gitmo started making waves.

Whether the Special Forces renegade would still be there when Bolan reached the scene was anybody's guess, but every journey had a starting point.

## CHAPTER TWO

*Jakarta, Indonesia*

The city smelled of spice and death. Street vendors hawked their wares from pushcarts, many of them mobile kitchens offering the best of Far Eastern cuisine at bargain prices, while the nearby waterfront and fish market contributed aromas from the Java Sea.

Mack Bolan almost felt at home among the thousands of pedestrians and cyclists who thronged the narrow streets fronting Kelapa Harbor. It refreshed old memories of other times in Southeast Asia, when he'd gambled with the Reaper and the game had gone his way.

But Bolan always wondered if his luck would hold next time.

This time.

But while he felt at home, in some respects, Bolan was also well aware that he stood out among the locals, obviously alien. He made an easy target in the crowd, and might not see the hunters coming if they played their cards right. It was really their home, after all, and he was just a visitor with the wrong eyes, wrong hair, wrong skin.

Just like the man he was supposed to meet.

Two strangers in a strange land, who had never met each other previously, but whose movements were directed by a higher power. In Bolan's case, that power was a man named Hal Brognola, operating out of Washington, D.C. His contact also marched to drums from Washington, but had no clue that Bolan and the team he served existed.

All that was about to change, together with the contact's life, his whole conception of the world.

And Bolan's?

He would have to wait and see.

Unlike his contact, Bolan had been forearmed with a photograph to help him spot his fellow round-eye at Kelapa Harbor. If their meeting was aborted for whatever reason, they were supposed to try again that afternoon, at the Jakarta Ragunan Zoo. A hookup near the tiger pit.

For his part, Bolan hoped to get it right the first time, but he always liked to have a fallback option, just in case.

He'd come prepared, to the extent that climate and propriety allowed. With temperatures in the nineties, he could hardly wear an overcoat to cover automatic weapons, so he'd opted for a large, loose-fitting shirt, with slacks and running shoes. Beneath the shirt, he had replaced his usual Beretta with a Glock 19, a compact version of the classic semiautomatic pistol that retained its firepower—two rounds better than the Beretta Model 92—while eliminating the external hammer and safety. Two extra magazines weighted his trouser pockets, with a folding knife that re-sembled a Japanese *tanto*.

Bolan had purchased those weapons, and some others that he couldn't sport in public, from a local dealer recom-mended by Brognola, who acquired the name and address from an unnamed source. That suited Bolan, since the source wouldn't know *his* name, either, or the reason why Brognola needed guns in Indonesia, several thousand miles beyond his legal jurisdiction.

Bolan didn't know if his contact was armed, or if he had been trained to any serious degree in self-defense. The U.S. war on terror, winding down its first decade with no clear end in sight, had thrown together many strange bed-fellows with a mix of capabilities, knowledge and skills that was almost surreal. Homeland Security, for instance, was neither restricted to the continental U.S.A. nor limited in operations to securing airports, borders and the like. Its agents might be anywhere.

Even Jakarta, on a steamy morning when the city smelled like spice and death.

Bolan had memorized a photo and description of his contact, and he had a name. Tom Dixon. He could pick the man out of a crowd, particularly on these streets, but find-ing him was only step one of the job at hand.

Bolan preferred to work alone, whenever possible, but there were times—like now—when he required assistance from a local or an agent with specific background, skills, intelligence. Tom Dixon was supposed to fit that bill. And if he didn't?

Once again, Bolan would have to wait and see.

TOM DIXON DAWDLED at a newsstand, checking out the tabloids while he tried to spot a tail. The hairy monster known to locals as *orang dalam* had paid another visit to Johor, one paper told him, leaving twenty-inch footprints and scaring hell out of coffee plantation workers in the process. Other headlines clamored about rebels in the countryside and government attempts to crush them, while the price of oil was going up again, no end in sight.

Dixon had drawn the Indonesian posting mainly because his language skills included fluency in French, Bahasa Indonesia and Cantonese. It helped to speak the native tongue, of course, but as a white man in an Asian world, there still were times when he felt totally alone.

Like now.

He'd thought the job sounded exciting when he started. Cloak-and-dagger stuff in an exotic setting, very double-0 and all that rot. He even had a pistol, which he'd qualified to use under instruction from a grizzled combat veteran who looked as if he'd been used for target practice by the Red Chinese back in the day.

He'd rolled into Jakarta thinking it would be a piece of cake—or, at the very least, something to tell the kids about, assuming that he ever married, settled down and got around to siring children. Then the truth had slapped him like a wet towel in the face, and Dixon realized that he might never see the U.S.A. again. Might never make it to his thirtieth birthday.

That understanding hadn't come upon him all at once, of course. First, Dixon had begun to recognize that learning different languages didn't make him a native of the world at large. No matter how he honed his accent, he was still a white-bread boy from Mason City, Iowa, at heart. And he had much to learn about survival in a society where life was cheap and might made right.

He'd managed well enough at first, in terms of following instructions and collecting certain information his superiors required, but then he started feeling as if everyone was watching him. At first, Dixon had chalked it up to a first-timer's paranoia, but he soon discovered that he was, in fact, under surveillance.

Fine.

It could've been the government, although Indonesia was a theoretical ally in Washington's attempt to save the world from all free radicals. Or maybe it was someone else. In which case, Dixon thought, he might be well and truly screwed.

There'd been no move against him yet, but maybe they were waiting for a certain time and place in which to strike. Now, with another agent coming from the States to help him out—or do the dirty work, why kid himself?—he wondered if the other side had finally decided to eliminate him.

All his contacts with Homeland Security so far had been securely routed through the U.S. Embassy, and while he didn't think there was a leak inside, Dixon was wise enough to know he could've tipped his hand a hundred different ways while chasing leads on foreign soil. He spoke the language, but he didn't know the people well enough to tell if they were working both sides of the fence, scheming to bait a trap that would destroy him and his faceless, nameless ally from America.

How's that for trust? he asked himself, leaving the news-stand with a last glance back along the street he'd traveled moments earlier. No one immediately hid his face or ducked into a doorway, nothing to betray a clumsy tail.

And that was the point, Dixon thought. No one said the enemy was clumsy, stupid or inept.

It was a part of the established Western mind-set, he supposed, but it was clearly wrong. In Vietnam, peasants in black pajamas, armed with weapons left behind from World War II, had fought the mighty U.S. Army to a standstill after eight long years of war with no holds barred. On 9/11, zealots armed with supermarket boxcutters had seized four high-tech airliners and scored the single most destructive hostile raid on U.S. soil in all of history.

Long story short, it didn't pay to underestimate the enemy, especially when operating on their enemy's native soil. Dixon had spent the past two nights without much sleep, trying to figure out where he'd gone wrong, and he still had nothing to show for it.

Maybe the new guy from the States, this Mr. X, could put things right. If not, then, what?

James Bond would never take this lying down, Dixon thought.

He was smiling when he hit the fish market, then caught a whiff of what was waiting for him, and his face went blank. Dixon had walked the same ground yesterday, getting familiar with the turf, and knew exactly where to go for his anticipated rendezvous. Along the way, he stopped at different stalls, chosen at random, checking out the fish and casting sidelong glances at his backtrack.

Nothing. Zip. *Nada.*

Which reassured him not at all.

The pistol underneath his baggy shirt, a .40-caliber Smith & Wesson, felt heavier than usual this morning. He supposed that it was nerves, and hoped he wouldn't freeze if he was forced to use the gun for once, instead of simply hauling it around with him.

He saw the stall with squids and octopuses heaped in baskets, countless arms entangled as if someone had prepared a latex sculpture of Medusa, daubed with slime. Dixon was almost there when strong hands gripped his biceps from behind and someone aimed a solid kick behind his right knee, dropping him into a crouch.

He felt rather than saw the keen blade drawn across his throat.

BOLAN WAS THIRTY FEET from Dixon when it started going down. He'd made a positive ID on Dixon, had the password turning over in his mind, when suddenly two wiry Asians came at Dixon from behind, out of the crowd.

Each man clutched one of Dixon's arms, one kicked his right leg from behind, to put him on his knees and, as he dropped, the man on Dixon's right had drawn a long knife from its hidden sheath, whipping the blade across his target's throat.

Instinct let Bolan draw the Glock 19 as Dixon's legs were buckling. By the time that his attacker had the knife in hand, Bolan was leaning into target acquisition, with his lightweight autoloader braced in a two-handed combat grip.

He didn't fire a doubletap, for fear of sending one round

wild into the crowd. Instead, he stroked the trigger once and slammed a Parabellum hollowpoint round into the knife man's chest. Before it had a chance to flatten, chewing through a mangled lung, he was already tracking toward his second target, hands rock steady on the Glock.

Without a sound suppressor, the shot was loud. A wailing cry went up from somewhere close at hand, joined instantly by others, but the racket didn't mess with Bolan's aim. He had his target zeroed, even as the second would-be killer raised his eyes from Tom Dixon to glimpse the face of death.

The second round drilled through a startled eye, scrambled the dead man's brain and flattened up against the inside of his skull. Bolan was moving as his gunfire echoed through the fish market, stooping to clutch at Dixon with his free hand, meanwhile checking out the crowd for any further enemies.

He spotted three within two seconds, give or take, identifiable by their reaction to the shots. While normal vendors and their customers recoiled from the explosive sounds, ducking for cover where they couldn't flee, these others jostled *toward* the sound, fighting their way upstream against the human tide. One of them had a pistol in his hand, and Bolan didn't think the other two would be unarmed.

"Come on!" he snapped at Dixon, giving him a yank to put him on his feet and moving in the right direction, which was anywhere away from there. A solid shove for emphasis got Dixon jogging, ramping up into a sprint after the first few yards.

Bolan was close behind him, following and guiding all at once. They had to reach his car somehow, and hopefully without the bloodbath that would follow naturally from a full-scale shootout in the crowded market.

Dixon, running, called across his shoulder, "Christ, I hope you're who I think you are."

"I don't care much for octopus," Bolan said, giving him the first half of the pass code.

"On the other hand," Dixon replied as he should have, "I'm fond of squid. Thank God!"

"Pray later," Bolan said. "Run now. That way!"

They ran, and someone in the crush behind them risked a shot. It missed both fleeing targets, struck a woman off to Bolan's left and dropped her with a spout of crimson from her neck.

Bolan ducked lower as he ran, his shoulders hunched, braced for the impact of a bullet at any second. Somewhere behind him, whistles started to blow, indicating that police had joined the chase. That meant, in turn, that he and Dixon now had twice as many enemies. If they were honest cops, they'd go for everyone with guns, likely shoot first and ask their questions later.

Bolan and his sidekick neared the eastern exit from the fish market. This time, a burst of automatic fire tore through the crowd, leaving at least four persons wounded, but again the shooter missed his primary targets.

A moment later, they ran out of fish stalls, but the street beyond was every bit as crowded as the marketplace, with bikes and cars thrown in to make progress more treacherous.

"Go right!" Bolan commanded, satisfied as Dixon made the turn and kept on running.

Bolan, for his part, glanced back in time to see an Asian shooter aiming at him with some kind of automatic weapon. As he fired, Bolan lunged forward, pushing through the crowd.

"WHERE ARE THEY?" Kersen Wulandari barked into his handheld radio. "Report!"

Instead of the immediate responses he expected, Wulandari heard more shooting from the fish market, this time a submachine gun's ripping sound, and he could feel his stomach clenching painfully.

"Report at once!" he shouted, noting but not caring that his driver winced. It made no difference to Wulandari if pedestrians outside the car heard what he said. They wouldn't understand it, and they'd never volunteer to testify against him.

After several seconds more, with shots, police whistles and screaming from the fish market, a breathless voice came back to Wulandari.

"Targets moving east on Laks Martadinata. Hard to see with crowd."

"Close in!" Wulandari barked. "Stop them!"

To his driver, he added: "Hurry! You heard the street."

The black sedan surged forward, winding through a maze of slow and stationary vehicles, cyclists who seemed suicidal and pedestrians who made a game of stepping into traffic without looking either way. Such traffic was one of the main reasons why Kersen Wulandari hated cities. That and the police.

Given the choice, he much preferred escorting rural drug convoys, but Wulandari would do any job that paid him well enough. This one paid very well indeed, but now he worried that it was about to end in failure and rejection of his claim for payment.

Maybe worse.

The people who had hired him didn't—what was the American expression?—mess around. Upon receiving word of failure, they might kill him as an object lesson to the next shooters in line.

The good news was that his employer hadn't specified live capture of the two round-eyes. That would've made Wulandari's task a hundred times more difficult, and killing them was hard enough already.

They reached the intersection of Hajam Wuruk and Laks Martadinata, where his driver turned left into more abominable traffic, leaning on his horn to clear oblivious pedestrians out of the way. Seething with anger and frustration, Wulandari held the radio close to his ear, as if proximity alone could make the others speak to him.

And to his great surprise, it worked.

"Crossing the street," one of his soldiers blurted out. "I see!"

Which was a damned sight more than Wulandari could assert. Somewhere ahead of them, he heard more gunfire, sounding like a string of fireworks in the middle distance. His foot soldiers were outrunning Wulandari, yet another reason for his anger to be spiked at fever pitch.

"Catch up with them," he told the driver.

"But—"

"Just do it! Now!" As Wulandari spoke, he reached into a canvas satchel set between his feet and lifted out a Skorpion machine pistol.

"Yes, sir!" the driver answered smartly, giving one more bleat of warning to pedestrians and all concerned before he swung the steering wheel and stepped on the accelerator.

In front of them, three teenage boys, their faces stamped with childish arrogance, slowed down in answer to the driver's horn, one of them fanning a rude gesture toward the driver. Wulandari smiled at the resounding thump of metal striking flesh, saw one youth cast aside as if he had weighed nothing, while the seeming ringleader was sucked beneath the car. More satisfying sounds emerged from underneath it as the driver floored his gas pedal and caromed into traffic, gaining ground by fits and starts.

It wasn't easy going, even with a nervous madman at the wheel. They still had to negotiate around the bulk of other vehicles, while scattering pedestrians and cyclists. Wulandari didn't care how many peasants suffered injury or worse, as long as he wasn't included in the final tally of the dead.

And if he completed this job, if the men behind it then refused his payment or tried playing any other kind of dirty game with Wulandari, he would make them all regret it to their dying day.

Ahead, he glimpsed men running pell-mell in the street, one brandishing a pistol overhead. He also heard police whistles, their shrill notes grating badly on his nerves.

The targets were to be eliminated, not delivered to the law for questioning. If they were jailed alive, it meant an even greater failure than if they escaped completely. Wulandari didn't understand the reason for the contract, but he knew that much with perfect certainty.

The targets had to be silenced. That was paramount in the instructions he'd received.

"Get after them!" he shouted at his driver. "Never mind this rabble. Go!"


AS THEY WERE CROSSING Laks Martadinata, dodging bikes and cars, Bolan turned back to catch a quick glimpse of his enemies and gauge their progress. They were gaining, he discovered, and it came as no surprise.

The hunters knew these streets, and they had no compunction about firing in to the crowd to clear a path. Although denied that option, Bolan still had choices, and he chose to exercise one now.

The nearest gunner, lank and wiry, carrying a small machine pistol, unleashed a burst that fanned the air a yard above his targets, peppering an office block directly opposite. Before he had a chance to fire again, Bolan made target acquisition, stroked his trigger once and closed the gap between them with a single hollow-point round.

The shooter's head snapped back and he went down,

dead index finger clenched around the trigger of his SMG and spraying bullets toward the sky. A driver coming up behind him tried to stop but couldn't make it, thumping hard over the twitching corpse.

Bolan spun and sprinted after Dixon while the traffic snarled behind him, several cars slamming into one another after some kind of homemade pickup truck rear-ended the small sedan that had flattened his enemy. Cyclists swerved to miss the pileup, several of them toppling from their two-wheelers to the pavement.

Confusion was good.

It would slow the police and maybe the shooters still fit to pursue him. As curious spectators rushed toward the accident scene, Bolan's stalkers would find it more difficult bucking the tide. With any luck, he thought, the small delay might let him reach his car.

Maybe.

And maybe not.

No choice, he told himself as he began to overtake Tom Dixon. There were limits to how far the pair of them could run, and while Dixon might be familiar with Jakarta's streets, he wouldn't know them as well as the natives who hunted them. Sooner or later, fatigue and superior numbers would spell defeat for Bolan and the contact he had barely met.

The parking garage was just three blocks away. If they made it that far, if they could reach his rental wheels, they had a chance.

Bolan refused to entertain defeatist thinking. Catching up with Dixon now, he called out, "Left. Two blocks." His contact turned at the next intersection, ducking as a bullet struck the wall above him, spraying concrete chips into the crowd.

Another backward glance showed Bolan two shooters when he could readily identify, and he had no good reason to believe they were alone. If even one of them was in communication with a mobile team, somewhere ahead or even running parallel, then Bolan's race could end in seconds flat with blazing automatic weapons.

He ran on, goading Dixon from behind, and saw the tall, ugly shape of the parking garage up ahead. They'd have to cross the street again, through traffic, but it was a risk they could afford, compared to the alternative.

They covered another block, with no more shots behind them, and he called to Dixon, "The garage. Across the street."

"Okay," the young American replied, and with the briefest glance to either side, he plunged into the flow of bikes and cars.

The guy had nerve, at least.

Bolan pursued him, dodging vehicles, ignoring tinny protests from a dozen horns. Behind him, another brief crackle of SMG fire made him dodge to the left, using an ancient panel truck for fleeting cover as the bullets struck a windshield and a motorcyclist to Bolan's left.

Collateral damage, and he couldn't do a thing about it in his present situation. Bolan hated it when bystanders were sucked into his war, but in each case where that occurred, the choice belonged to someone else. One of his enemies. To Bolan's certain knowledge, he had never injured a civilian noncombatant beyond minor cuts and bruises, in the most extreme of situations. Shrapnel did its own thing, and to hell with consequences, but he specialized in strikes of surgical precision, taking out his targets without any street-gang drive-by nonsense that was typically a waste of time and ammunition.

Clearly, those pursuing him had other views on how a battle should be fought.

The hell of it was that they still might win.

Dixon had reached the other sidewalk now, and Bolan joined him a second later, shoving him for emphasis when Dixon slowed to see if he was keeping up.

"Third level," Bolan rasped at him. "A gray Toyota four-door, backed into space 365."

"Got it!"

They'd passed the stairs already, which meant running in a long, slow zigzag pattern up one sloping ramp after another, to the third floor of the vast parking garage. There were at least a hundred parking spaces on each level, overhead fluorescent lighting casting pools of shadow between cars that could conceal an army of assassins, if they knew where he had parked.

They don't, he thought. Why chase us, otherwise?

That logic got them to the third level, but Bolan half imagined running footsteps just below them. Shooters catching up? Maybe a rent-a-cop who'd glimpsed his pistol as they entered?

Bolan palmed the rented vehicle's keys and thumbed the button to unlock its doors. The dome light flared, helping direct Dixon to the car. While the agent threw himself into the shotgun seat, Bolan slid in behind the wheel, cranked the ignition and released the parking brake.

"They found us!" Dixon told him as the gray Toyota leaped out of its parking space.

"Hang on!" Bolan said to his passenger. "It's all downhill from here."

# CHAPTER THREE

Three shooters formed a fragile skirmish line across the exit ramp as Bolan's hired car hurtled toward them, gaining speed with an assist from gravity. The middle man carried some kind of Uzi submachine gun knockoff, while his flankers brandished shiny semiautomatic pistols. When they saw that Bolan wasn't slowing, the bookends dived for cover, while their seeming leader opened fire.

Too late.

His first round cracked the gray Toyota's windshield, two or three more struck the window frame and roof with glancing blows and all the rest were wasted as the bumper clipped his knees and rolled him up across the hood, then tossed him high and wide over the speeding car.

Wild pistol shots rang out behind them, none finding their mark, and Bolan's vacant rearview mirror told him that the bookends had decided not to mount a hot pursuit.

He slowed when they were out of range, hoping to pass the exit booth without another incident, but then he saw the cashier craning a look from his window, obviously trying to pinpoint the source of gunfire. Bolan floored the gas then, surging forward as the clerk ducked backward, out of sight. They hit the flimsy wooden barricade at fifty, smashed on through it and were gone.

More damage to the rental, there, and Bolan knew he'd have to ditch it soon, or else risk drawing more attention from police. Before he thought about new wheels, however, there was still the matter of escaping from their present trap.

They weren't clear yet. He was prepared to bet his life on that.

To prove his point, a navy-blue sedan bearing two or three men raced head-on toward Bolan's vehicle, when he had barely cleared the gate of the municipal garage. The grim-faced driver seemed intent on ramming him, but Bolan called his bluff.

Another terse "Hang on!" to Dixon, and he held down the accelerator, holding steady on the steering wheel. Most hit men, in his experience, lacked the fanatic's common urge toward martyrdom. In short, they shied away from suicide whenever possible—but there were always rare exceptions to the rule.

With thirty yards between them, Bolan wondered if the other driver had the grim resolve to take him out at any cost. A head-on collision at their current rate of speed meant almost certain death, regardless of the built-in air bags or the safety harness that he hadn't taken time to buckle as they fled. No vehicle created for the world's civilian markets could save its occupants if they were doing sixty miles per hour and they hit another car doing the same. That made the terminal velocity 120 miles per hour.

And the operative word was *terminal*.

"Jesus!" Dixon blurted out. "What are you—?"

"Doing," or whatever else he meant to say, was swallowed by an incoherent squeal of panic, just before the chase car's driver swerved to save himself, jumping the curb and scattering pedestrians as it decelerated brutally, tires smoking on the pavement.

Bolan took advantage of the lag, however brief, before his enemy could turn and follow him. Accelerating toward the nearest busy cross street, he decided slowing for the turn would be a costly waste of time, more likely to produce an accident than to avert one. It was all-or-nothing time, and Bolan's life was riding on the line.

"Hang—"

"On, I know," Dixon finished for him, clutching at the plastic handgrip mounted just above his door. "Just do it."

Bolan did it, swerving into northbound traffic with a chorus of protesting horns and overheated brakes behind him. He was looking for police cars now, as much as shooters, hoping that it wouldn't turn into a three-way race.

The press of traffic slowed him, but he still made fairly decent speed. Jakarta's drivers didn't dawdle unless they were stuck in traffic jams, and some of them were daredevils in their own right. He watched for hunters, heading either way, and warned Dixon to do the same.

"I'm on it," the agent replied, his voice sounding more normal than it had a moment earlier. "Sorry about all that back there."

"It may not be your fault," Bolan said, knowing even as he spoke that Dixon probably had missed some sign that he was being followed to the meet, and likely well before.

But, then again, it could've been *his* fault. They'd likely never know unless the trackers overtook and captured them.

How many in the hunting party? Bolan couldn't say. He'd dealt with three men on the run, a fourth in the garage, with two more seen on foot and two or three in the chase car. Beyond that, he'd be guessing, which was usually a waste of time and energy.

If Bolan couldn't count his enemies, he would assume they had him covered, both outnumbered and outgunned. He'd act accordingly, and put a damper on whatever latent cockiness he might've felt after a hell-for-leather getaway that left him and his contact more or less unscathed.

They weren't clear yet.

And if he needed any proof of that, his rearview mirror gave it to him, framing a blurred image of the navy-blue chase car.

"Incoming," Bolan told his passenger. "Get buckled up."

Bolan followed his own advice, knowing the safety harness wouldn't save him from a bullet, any more than it would help him walk away from sixty-mile-per-hour crashes into other speeding vehicles. Still, it was something, and he needed any small edge he could get right now.

To stay alive and find out what the hell was going on.

KERSEN WULANDARI CLUTCHED his Skorpion machine pistol so tightly that his fingernails and knuckles blanched, the weapon's wooden grip printing its checkered pattern on his palm. He didn't feel it, kept his index finger off the trigger only with an effort, craning forward in his seat and staring at the target up ahead.

"Get after them!" he snarled. "Don't let them get away this time!"

His driver didn't answer, fully focused on the street and the traffic that surrounded them. They were already well above the posted speed limit and still accelerating, but the other cars around them made a straight run at their prey impossible.

Wulandari couldn't fault his driver for not crashing into their opponents' vehicle outside of the garage. He had no wish to die for what he had been paid to do, the present job, although that risk was always present in Wulandari's line of work. The trick, he knew, was making sure that other people died, while he survived to joke about their final, agonizing moments with his friends over a round of drinks.

Unfortunately, these damned Westerners weren't the kind of targets he was used to. They were quick, courageous, deadly. He'd already lost at least three men pursuing them, and now Wulandari didn't know what had become of those who'd chased the targets into the garage. The building's steel-and-concrete structure interfered with messages after they ran inside, and there'd been nothing more since the Americans escaped.

All dead?

Wulandari didn't know, nor, at that moment, did he care.

The men he'd chosen for this day's assignment had proved adequate on other jobs. All ten were killers, tested under fire in gang wars with the triads and the Yakuza. They hadn't failed him yet, but once was all it took to make a corpse out of a street soldier.

Three corpses. Maybe six, for all Wulandari knew.

And three more shooters still at large, somewhere, presumably attempting to make contact with the targets.

Scooping up a walkie-talkie in his free hand, Wulandari keyed the button for transmission, snapping at the air, "Car Two! Where are you? Answer!"

Agonizing second later, came the answer. "Passing the art gallery, westbound. Over."

That had to mean Jakarta's Fine Art Gallery, below Merak Expressway. They were headed in the right direction, anyway.

"We're near the Puppet Theater," Wulandari told his second chase car. "Target fifty meters up ahead. Hurry, before you lose us!"

"Coming!" the tinny voice said before the radio went dead.

Wulandari should've felt relieved, with help rushing along behind to join him, but his anger and frustration banished any positive emotion. Even as the fury raged inside him, he was fully conscious of his cardinal mistake.

*Don't get involved.*

Killing and kidnapping for money was a business, he understood, and businessmen who let personal feelings cloud their judgment soon went *out* of business, losing everything they had.

In this case, that could mean Wulandari's life.

He didn't plan to die that afternoon, but neither had the

men he'd lost so far. Wulandari guessed that all of them had counted on another night of drinking, sex and restful sleep after a job well done. For three of them, at least, those plans were rudely swept aside and cast onto the rubbish heap.

Wulandari didn't care to join them.

"Speed up, damn you!" he grated, striking at his driver's shoulder with the hand that clutched his radio. The wheelman grunted, flinched, his jerky move reflected in their auto's swerving progress.

"Hold steady!" Wulandari barked, but he recognized his own irrationality, refraining from another blow.

The car surged forward, somehow finding still more power underneath the hood. They brushed against a slower vehicle, passing too closely on Wulandari's side, but he dared not complain. His driver was obeying orders, narrowing the gap that separated them from their appointed targets.

Wulandari found the power button for his window, held it down until the tinted glass was fully lowered and a rush of wind filled up the car. He propped his elbow on the windowsill, bracing the Skorpion, but hot wind made his eyes tear, blurred his target as he tried to aim.

He couldn't tell the driver to slow down, but if he couldn't see…

Wulandari reached into his shirt pocket, heard fabric rip as he retrieved his sunglasses and slipped them on. It was a little better when he again poked his head outside the speeding car. Not perfect, but at least he had a chance to aim.

And have his head ripped off or shattered, if his driver brushed against another vehicle.

"Be careful now!" he shouted, words torn from his lips by rushing wind.

Sighting as best he could, Wulandari pulled the trigger, spraying five or six rounds from the Skorpion's 20-round box magazine. A march of bullet holes across the gray Toyota's trunk rewarded him, before his weapon's muzzle rose and sent the last two rounds hurtling downrange, wasted.

"Closer!" Wulandari shouted, reaching with his left hand to extend the Skorpion's wire shoulder stock.

His driver muttered something unintelligible in the roar of wind, but he produced another surge of speed. Wulandari smiled, lips drawn back over crooked teeth, and steeled himself to try again.

"THAT'S TOO DAMNED CLOSE," Dixon said, his shoulders hunched against the prospect of a bullet drilling through his seat.

"Tell me about it," the grim man at the wheel replied.

Dixon had drawn his Glock but knew he couldn't make a decent shot under the circumstances, swiveled in his seat and leaning out the window where he'd have to fire left-handed. He was in this stranger's hands, with killers rolling up behind them, spraying the Toyota with machine-gun fire.

Terrific.

"There's more company," his wheelman said.

Turning so quickly that he sent a bolt of white-hot pain searing along the right side of his neck, Dixon picked out a second chase car gaining on the first. He knew it wasn't just another crazy native driver, from the way it swerved through traffic, breaking all the rules to overtake the dark sedan bristling with guns.

We're toast, he thought, but kept it to himself, as if afraid that saying it would realize his fears.

"Hang on," Bolan said.

"Right."

It had become their litany, damned near the only conversation passed between them since their mad race from the drab parking garage. He wondered if the man they'd struck was dead or dying, mildly startled to discover that he hoped so.

One less to come back and bite them in the ass, he thought.

But there were still enough behind them to kill him and the man he knew as Matt Cooper. All the men and guns they needed were in the two chase cars. He didn't know if Cooper could evade them, doubted it, and doubted even more his own ability to come through any kind of urban gunfight with body and soul intact.

Dixon had trained for this, after a fashion, but he'd never really taken any of it seriously. No one in his graduating class believed that they'd be shooting anyone. They were paper pushers, marginal investigators, only dubbed field agents out of courtesy. Even the posting to Jakarta, with the various advisories upon departure, hadn't driven home the point.

But he was thrashing in the deep end now, and no mistake about it. Under other circumstances, Dixon might've said he had a choice—to sink or swim—but as it was, his choices seemed to be preempted by the driver of the vehicle in which he sat, and by the killers burning up the road behind him, shooting as they came.

"You know this neighborhood?" Bolan asked.

"More or less," Dixon replied.

"I need some kind of cul-de-sac or parking area where I can get some combat stretch, maybe to turn around."

Dixon thought hard enough to give himself a headache, which was no great trick just then. "Okay," he said. "You're heading for a turnoff to the lake. Penjaringan. It's on your right. Take that and go down toward the water. There's a parking lot for tourists. Shouldn't have too many cars, this hour on a week day."

"Let's find out," Bolan said, as the sign rushed at them. This time, when he made the screeching turn, there was no warning to hang on. Dixon was ready for it anyway, and gripped the handle overhead as if he'd been aboard a subway train racing at top speed through the dark.

"We've got at least four guys behind us," Dixon noted when his driver had the gray Toyota running straight and true again. "There could be twice that many."

"Right."

"You plan to take them all?"

"I'm working on it," Bolan said. "But if you have a plan, I'm open to suggestions."

"Nope. Not me. Just wondered how you meant to pull it off." The sinking feeling in his gut told Dixon that he was about to die.

"When you're outnumbered," Bolan said, flicking another quick glance toward his rearview, "there are three things you can do. I doubt our friends back there are interested in negotiation or surrender."

"What's the third option?" Dixon asked.

"Fight like hell."

"Uh-*huh*."

"You're not a pacifist, I hope?" Bolan asked.

"No."

"All right, then. If you get a chance to use that Smith, remember what they taught you on the range."

"Center of mass. Don't jerk the trigger. Double tap, if feasible."

"Sounds like the ticket," Bolan said. "And here we are."

They roared into a spacious parking lot with fewer than a dozen vehicles in sight, all clustered at the far end, near an area of restaurants and gift shops. Lake Penjaringan was popular for boating, fishing and assorted other water sports, but weekends were its busy time.

"I bluffed their wheelman once," Bolan said, his eyes locked on the rearview now. "I don't know if he'll tumble twice, but it's the only chance we have right now." And then, "Hang on!"

Dixon couldn't be sure exactly what the stranger did next, but he seemed to stamp down on the brake and the accelerator simultaneously, meanwhile spinning the wheel rapidly to his left. The net effect included squealing tires, a revving engine and a dizzying 180-degree turn that left rubber scorch marks on the sun-bleached asphalt of the parking lot.

Dixon was still recovering from the bootlegger's turn, trying to get his stomach back in place, when Cooper floored the gas again and charged off toward their enemies.

This time, two chase cars were approaching, side by side and barreling ahead at sixty miles per hour. Dixon wondered if the drivers were prepared to lose their second game of chicken to this brash American.

"Ready?" Bolan called as his window powered down, right arm extended with his Glock clenched in his fist. "Okay, then. Give 'em hell!"

BOLAN WAS COUNTING on surprise and sheer audacity to give him an advantage over his pursuers, but it was still a gamble. Repetition of a tactic could be perilous, yet Bolan's options were distinctly limited. He couldn't drive around Jakarta with the shooters on his tail until his car ran out of gas, nor did he care to bail out in the middle of a crowded thoroughfare and take the battle back to urban infantry maneuvers.

Barring reinforcements, which he didn't have, the chicken run would have to do—but with a twist this time.

The chase cars were advancing side by side, with several feet of empty space between them, giving the shotgun riders and whoever occupied the back seats room to aim and fire their weapons. Bolan's angle of attack meant that, unless they rammed him, he would pass along the driver's side of the vehicle on his right, while Dixon faced the front- and back-seat guns of its companion, on their left. Bad luck for Dixon, but if he had nerve enough, they just might make it work.

Bolan began to fire his Glock when they were twenty yards from impact, three rounds out of eighteen gone before he sighted on the left-hand chase car's windshield. Two shots drilled through the driver's side, and then he saw the black sedan begin to swerve off target.

He had a glimpse of someone in the back seat, leveling a weapon larger than a pistol, flinching from the windshield hits. Before the shooter could recover, Bolan triggered two more shots and punched him backward, out of view. A jagged muzzle-flash spit bullets through the right-hand chase car's roof.

To Bolan's left, Tom Dixon's .40-caliber pistol was hammering away, while a Kalashnikov erupted, chattering defiance. Bolan heard a couple of the rifle's slugs strike home, like hammer blows against the hired Toyota's flanks. They apparently missed the tires and engine, but Bolan flinched when Dixon grunted, wondering if he'd taken a hit.

They roared on past the chase cars, Bolan's eyes pinned to the rearview mirror as he asked, "Are you all right?"

Dixon was swiping at his cheek with bloody fingertips. "I think so. Caught a splinter, maybe."

Lucky.

"Here we go again," Bolan warned. "This time, don't expect a break."

"I'm ready," Dixon said.

Swerving through the turn, Bolan saw one carload of his assailants stalled, its lifeless driver slumped behind the wheel, the shotgun rider scrambling out on foot. The other car was swinging back around to make another run, with the AK protruding from a window on the driver's side.

The other side could make a sieve of his Toyota with the Kalashnikov, he knew, chewing him and Dixon into hamburger. The rifle was a killer at three hundred yards, three times the theoretical effective range of Bolan's Glock, ten times its practical effective range.

He couldn't duel the rifleman, but he could seize the moment to his own advantage.

If he dared.

Bolan stamped down on the accelerator, hurtling toward his enemies. "Be ready when I make another turn, and brace for impact," he told Dixon.

"Impact. Jesus."

Bolan tore across the parking lot, directly toward the second chase car, locked on a collision course. At the last moment, when it seemed explosive impact was inevitable, he swung through another tire-scorching one-eighty, starting so close to his adversaries that the swerving rear of his Toyota struck their front end like a half-ton slap across the face.

The Executioner was out and running, even as the aftershocks of impact shuddered through both vehicles. He saw Tom Dixon moving on the other side, pistol extended as he raced back toward the chase car, his face etched in a snarl.

Then Bolan started firing, pumping Parabellum rounds into his shaken enemies at point-blank range. The AK handler took one through his left eye socket, and another through his gaping mouth for safety's sake. Up front, the shotgun rider had to have dropped his pistol, fumbling on the floor between his feet as Bolan turned and shot him once behind the ear.

Dixon took out the driver, blasting rounds into his neck and chest. Behind him, Bolan saw the last man from the other chase car hobbling toward them, lining up a shot, and called a warning to his contact.

Dixon turned, fired once and missed, then nailed it on the second try, even as Bolan helped him with a rapid double tap.

And they were done.

Around them, only corpses shared the battleground.

"We're out of time," Bolan told Dixon, "and we need fresh wheels. Tell me your story on the way."

"WHAT KIND OF BACKGROUND do you need?" Dixon asked when they'd cleared the killing ground.

"Start from the top," Bolan replied, "but don't go back to Genesis."

"Okay. I've been on-site for just about a year. Before that, I did two years stateside. Nothing relevant. You may know that al Qaeda and some other groups with similar potential have had cells in Indonesia since the nineties. Not surprising, when you think about it, since the population's mostly Muslim. Eighty-odd percent. And they've got reasonable access to material support from China, too."

Bolan had known that going in. He waited through the appetizer, for the main course.

"Now, this Talmadge character's been in and out of Indonesia for the past three years, I understand," Dixon continued. "We hear rumors that he may've been involved with some of the activity in East Timor."

*Activity* presumably referring to the genocidal action instigated by Indonesian rulers in 1999, when East Timor's population voted to secede from its parent nation and enjoy self-rule. By the time UN peacekeepers restored a semblance of order and supervised East Timor's first election in April 2002, an estimated three hundred thousand persons were dead, East Timor's meager infrastructure lay in ruins and the mostly agricultural economy was belly-up.

"Which side?" Bolan asked.

"Hard to say. The rumors go both ways," Dixon replied. "Since then, our boy has mostly been a gun-for-hire and part-time training officer for outfits like Hamas, al Qaeda and the Islamic Jihad. No Muslim background that we know of, but he likes those petrodollars. Has three bank accounts, one each in Switzerland, the Caymans and Sri Lanka."

"It's a small world, after all," Bolan remarked.

"And getting smaller all the time, apparently," Dixon said. "In the past eleven months, Talmadge has logged close to a half a million frequent-flyer miles. We've tracked him back and forth to different parts of Europe, to Australia and New Zealand, Pakistan, South Africa, and once to Canada—B.C., specifically. He's literally all over the map. Some of it's visits to his banks. The rest, we're guessing meets with his employers and some contract jobs that just coincidentally occur when he's nearby."

"Has anybody thought of handing him to Interpol?" Bolan asked.

"Thought about it, sure. But on what charge? His bank deposits are straightforward, nothing to suggest a laundry operation. He's not moving contraband, as far as anyone can tell. The people we can prove he's spoken to aren't fugitives—at least not in the countries where they're living at the moment. On the hits, we can't prove anything beyond proximity."

"And now, this Gitmo thing," Bolan said.

"Right. He's up to something for the AQ crowd, but what? We've covered his apartment in Jakarta. Bugs and taps, the whole megillah, but he doesn't use the telephone for anything important, and his only visitors are hookers. Once a week, like clockwork, he gets laid if he's in town. Tonight's the night."

"Maybe we ought to crash the party."

"It's a thought. Take flowers, maybe?"

"Maybe lilies. But we need another car, first thing."

"You won't be trading this one in, I take it," Dixon said.

"I don't think so."

"Okay." The younger man considered that, then said, "I've never hot-wired anything before. I mean, they didn't teach car theft or anything like that in training."

"I'll take care of that," Bolan said. "What we need right now is somewhere we can drop this one and not be noticed while we switch the plates to something suitable."

"My first thought would be HPK," Dixon replied. "Halim Perdana Kusuma. The airport."

Bolan thought about it, judging distances. It meant driving three miles or so, across Jakarta, without being noticed by police. "What's closer?" he inquired.

"There's Kemayoran, formerly the local airport," Dixon said. "They've turned it into some kind of outlandish shopping mall, but there are parking lots."

Closer, the warrior knew, from memorizing street maps in advance. "Okay. Let's try that first."

"Suits me. You know the way?"

"I've got it," Bolan said. "But just the same, correct me if you see I'm heading off toward Borneo or something."

"Right." It was the first time he had seen Tom Dixon smile. "About just now...in case you couldn't tell, I've never killed a man before."

Bolan could have replied, "First time for everything," but that would be both flippant and a lie. Most people never killed another human being. Soldiers, cops and criminals were those most likely to take lives, but even then it was a relatively rare event. Millions of soldiers served their tours of duty in peacetime and never fired a shot in anger. Most cops never pulled the trigger on a suspect, making those who did so more than once immediately suspect in the eyes of their superiors. Even most criminals had never killed, restricting their activities to theft, white-collar crimes or petty drug offenses.

Without planning it, Tom Dixon had been drafted into a fraternity whose members shared a single trait: the rare experience of canceling another human being's ticket to the great arcade of life. Some members of that clique enjoyed it; others never quite forgave themselves. The rest, who spilled blood in the line of duty forced upon them by their times, their conscience or their personality, learned how to live with it.

Bolan couldn't predict which kind of killer Dixon might turn out to be. In fact, he didn't care, as long as Dixon managed to perform his duties adequately for the next few hours or days.

Once Bolan left, he could break down and weep, become a raving psychopath or simply go back to his paper-pushing job. It wouldn't matter to the Executioner.

This day, this job was all that mattered.

But they had blown their cover big time. Everything beyond that point would be a catch-up game.

And Bolan feared that they were running out of time.

# CHAPTER FOUR

Jakarta's Kemayoran district, formerly the site of a major airport, lies in the city's eastern quadrant, two miles distant from the cooling breezes of the Java Sea. It swelters from the wicked combination of a tropic climate and an overdose of asphalt topped by concrete towers rising toward the humid sky. Pedestrians sweat through their clothes while traveling a block, and those blessed with the miracle of air-conditioning are prone to let it run full blast.

Finding the former airport was no problem. It appeared on Bolan's maps, and Dixon knew the mall by reputation, while denying that he'd ever shopped there. Bolan cruised the spacious parking lot until he spotted a Toyota the same year and model as his bullet-punctured ride, then parked as close as possible.

It was that hazy time of dusk, between late afternoon and early evening, when floodlights set on timers hadn't flared to life and mall employees tasked to watch security monitors were thinking more about the night ahead than what was happening on any given one of twenty smallish screens. Bolan was grateful for the hour, but he wasn't leaving anything to chance.

"You're watching, right?" he asked Dixon.

"Affirmative."

Reaching into a bag behind the driver's seat, Bolan withdrew a foot-long strip of metal and a large screwdriver, both of which he tucked beneath his floppy shirt. He left the car with Dixon, his companion staking out a point midway between the two Toyotas and pretending that he had to tie his shoe while Bolan went ahead.

Another moment placed him in the parking slot beside the target vehicle. He took a final searching look around, then slipped his shim into the narrow gap between the driver's window and its frame. He found the catch in something like ten seconds, slipped it and was in the driver's seat a heartbeat later, thankful that the car had no alarm installed.

The screwdriver came next, applied with brutal force to wrench the round ignition keyhole mechanism from the steering column. Once that obstacle had been removed, Bolan's screwdriver doubled as the missing key itself; a simple twist was all that he needed to revive the sleeping engine.

Bolan left it running as he found a switch beside his seat, opened the trunk and exited. Dixon kept watch while Bolan palmed another tool, removed the rental's license plates, then claimed his various belongings from the now abandoned car: his small toolkit, a slightly larger bag for clothes and shaving gear, a heavy duffel bag that clanked and rattled when he picked it up or set it down.

The latter earned a blink from Dixon, but he didn't ask. Instead, he settled in the shotgun seat as if the car belonged to him and always had.

Two points for cool.

The second-worst part of stealing any car was exiting the crime scene proper without being spotted. Once they reached a public street, they would become invisible. A second stop, to switch the license plates, would make the switch complete. From that point onward, only a direct comparison of vehicle registration numbers would prove that the plates on their car were mismatched.

A quiet place to park, no witnesses, nothing to make a round-eye draw attention while he touched up small details about his vehicle. Bolan was looking for the perfect spot when Dixon asked, "What will you do with Talmadge?"

"That depends on him," Bolan replied. It wasn't quite a lie.

"Because I had a briefing on the Justice ruling, back in 1990-something, authorizing federal agents to arrest suspected terrorists on foreign soil, without a warrant from the local courts. We're clear on that."

Bolan suppressed a smile as he replied, "You think the Indonesians might consider that kidnapping? Did they get the memo? Does an order signed in Washington trump local law out here?"

"It does in my book," Dixon answered. "We're at war."

"You'll get no argument from me on that score," Bolan told him, "but it didn't start on 9/11, and it won't end if and when we bag Osama. As for orders out of Justice, *please* refrain from telling any local cops or soldiers that you got your go-ahead from the attorney general of the United States. You'll only make them laugh before they put a bullet in your head."

"So, what you're saying is—"

"We're not in Kansas anymore. This isn't U.S. soil and never has been. People here salute a different flag, and they're not bound by anything the President or members of his cabinet may say. We're fugitives right now, and most of what we do from this point on will be illegal."

"In the strictest sense, of course, but—"

"In the only sense that matters," Bolan interrupted him. "We've killed nine men. The penalty for murder here is death by hanging or by firing squad. You get a choice, but no appeal. Maybe you think the embassy will intervene if you're arrested."

"No," Dixon said, sounding more subdued. "They made a special point of clarifying that."

"We're clear, then," Bolan said. "You have to watch your step. Forget about what some attorney general said ten years ago, and focus on surviving, here and now."

"I hear you."

"Good."

He found a residential lane where streetlights were in short supply and parked the car. Five minutes later, they were on the move again, wearing the license plates from Bolan's rental.

It was still a problem, but at least he'd bought some time. Their new car would be flagged as stolen when its owner finished shopping at the mall, but with so many Japanese compacts thronging Jakarta's streets, its tags would be the main identifier. Those were gone, and by the time some clerk at Bolan's rental agency decided to report the other car missing, he hoped his work in the vicinity would be completed.

"Next stop," he said to Dixon, "Talmadge's apartment."

"It's across town," Dixon told him. "On the west side, off Tomang Raja, near the Banjir Canal."

"Okay." A careful U-turn got them headed back in the direction they had come from.

"But I'm still not clear," Dixon said, "on what you—what we—intend to do with Talmadge."

"We intend to question him, ideally," Bolan said.

"And if the circumstances aren't ideal?"

"Our bottom-line assignment is to stop him doing any further favors for his latest batch of clients. Period."

"Kill him, you mean."

"It's possible," Bolan allowed.

"Because he's dangerous. To the United States."

"He's dangerous to everyone right now," Bolan replied. "Al Qaeda and Hamas don't limit their attacks to the U.S. or Israel. They've bombed London, Spain, Kenya and Tanzania. They're full-service murderers."

"That's good." Dixon was nodding like an athlete getting pumped up for the big game of the season. "Right. That's very good."

"Just keep your eyes and ears open," Bolan suggested. "You've already proved yourself. You didn't freeze. Whatever happens next, you'll be all right."

"I'm good," said Dixon. "We're the good guys, right?"

"That's what it says on my white hat," Bolan replied.

THEIR TARGET'S SMALL apartment house off Tomang Raja stood among a hundred others that were more or less the same, distinguished by their faded colors more than anything unique about their architecture. They reminded Bolan of a minicity he had seen at LEGOLAND in Europe, on another job. Instead of plastic pieces, though, these lookalike apartment houses had been built with lath and plaster, cheaply painted, then abandoned to begin their slow decomposition in the tropic climate.

Sun and rain would do the rest, assisted by the tenants who cared nothing for a landlord's property, and sometimes precious little for themselves.

Bolan wasn't surprised that Talmadge would've chosen such a neighborhood in which to live. He wouldn't fear the neighbors—quite the opposite, in fact, if they were wise—and living in a downscale area helped to preserve his anonymity. He would desire a low profile, waiting to make a bigger splash when he retired.

And Talmadge would have enemies, like any other mercenary who had shopped his skills around the troubled planet. There was never time or opportunity to kill them all, as Bolan knew from personal experience. No matter how he tried, regardless of his scorched-earth tactics, there would always be survivors hungry for revenge.

Still, with a new address, new name, new face, new history, he just might pull it off.

Somehow. Someday.

"Garage stalls in the back," Dixon explained, "along a kind of alley fronting the canal. No parking lot."

"It's not a problem," Bolan said. He'd noticed empty

parking spaces on the street and didn't mind a short walk back from wherever they had to leave the car.

"So, what's the drill?" Dixon asked.

"We go in and knock," Bolan said. "Say hello and ask if he can spare a cup of java."

"Like Jehovah's Witnesses?"

"Without the Bibles," Bolan said.

"Okay with me," his contact said. And then, "You sure?"

"What were you thinking?" Bolan asked him. "Climb a drainpipe? Go in through the bathroom window?"

"I don't know what I was thinking," Dixon granted. "But it seems to me, he may be waiting for us. Well, not us, but someone. He's a killer, right?"

"A soldier," Bolan said.

"Ex-soldier. And a *terrorist*."

"You're thinking he may shoot us," Bolan said.

"It crossed my mind. Suppose he's sitting on an arsenal up there? Then what?"

"Has anybody looked inside? The team that bugged his place?"

"They didn't want to risk it. Went in through the neighbors' flats and put mikes in the walls."

Which meant that Talmadge could be sitting on an arsenal—or nothing. Bolan didn't think he'd be unarmed. It went too much against the grain, against his lifelong training and experience, but there were countless levels of preparedness. It was a waste of time to sit and speculate.

He parked the stolen car a block west of the target, locked its doors and took the slender shim along with him, for when they doubled back. It might look strange, him fiddling with the window when he wanted to get back inside, but Bolan chose that option over leaving it unlocked and trusting thieves to stay away.

Losing a stolen car was one thing, but he wouldn't risk the hardware in its trunk until he'd had his money's worth out of the mobile arsenal.

"Just pistols?" Dixon asked him as they left the car and crossed the street.

"If we need more than that," Bolan replied, "our plan is seriously flawed."

"About this knocking thing…"

"It's how they play it, in polite society."

"Is that what this is?" Dixon asked.

"Hope springs eternal."

"Right."

He had a point, of course. Maybe they should've loaded up for bear and smashed through Talmadge's front door with automatic weapons blazing, but the job—at least in Bolan's mind—was more than simply taking out a soldier who'd gone bad.

They were supposed to find out what Talmadge was doing for his latest sponsors, what their move was meant to be against the country they called Satan. Simply dropping Talmadge in his tracks might stall the plan, but on the other hand, there was a decent chance it could proceed with other personnel and reap the same results.

Whatever those were.

Count on chaos and destruction, maybe catastrophic loss of life, or else selective murders of specific targets carried out with surgical precision. Either way, the zealots who were renting Talmadge and his expertise would want the most bang for their bucks. And at the moment, only Talmadge could reveal who his employers were.

Only the man they'd come to see could give them details of the plan.

Assuming they could make him talk.

That would be easier if he was breathing when they started asking questions, but in games like this the target often literally called the shots. If Talmadge chose to make a fight of it, resisting with the same skills Bolan had and using any weapons within reach, taking the man alive might not be possible.

And if he forced their hands, what then?

Where did they go for answers?

Wait and see. Don't count him out.

Not yet.

They walked around the block, came in behind the building, with the broad canal exuding stagnant odors on their right, stucco and curtained windows on the left. Bolan counted the buildings, picking out the paint job, and the back door opened at his touch.

So far, so good.

Stairs just inside, and Bolan led the way, knowing that Talmadge had a flat on the third floor. The stairs were solid, maybe concrete under threadbare carpet, so they didn't squeak.

On three, Bolan let Dixon take the lead, moving along a narrow hallway redolent with smells of cabbage, pork and something else he didn't want to think about. Maybe a version of despair.

Talmadge had found a place to hide where no one would expect to find him.

No one but the Executioner.

Dixon stood off to one side of the door and nodded.

Bolan reached across to knock.

NOTHING. THE RAPPING ECHOED back at them but brought no answer from inside the flat. No shuffling feet, no verbal challenge. No gunfire.

Nothing.

Dixon watched as his partner reached around the jamb and knocked again, more forcefully. They waited half a minute.

Still nothing.

"Keep watch," Bolan said as he knelt before the door, extracting something like a wallet from one of his pockets. Dixon saw him open it and withdraw slender lock picks, then turned his full attention to the undemanding task of covering the hallway.

No one had emerged from any of the other flats to catch a glimpse of who was knocking on their neighbor's door. He guessed it was that kind of place, where people minded their own business and resented nosy neighbors. Even so, he paid attention to the stairs and to the other doorways, keeping one hand on his Smith & Wesson in its belt holster.

Ready to shoot at the first sign of a hostile move.

What a day it had been, and not over yet!

In training, back at Quantico, Dixon and some of his classmates had talked about what they would do if they were ever placed in killing situations, where the only rule worth mentioning was do-or-die. With one exception, Dixon reflected, they'd been young males, full of piss and vinegar. Without exception, all of them had vowed to tag and bag all enemies of the United States if given half an opportunity.

Now Dixon had been graced with such an opportunity, and he'd surprised himself. He wouldn't say the killings had been easy necessarily, but neither did he have the sickly feeling he'd expected, like an overdose of early childhood guilt. The shootings had been self-defense, beyond a shadow of a doubt, involving criminals or terrorists. He hadn't started it, and he was definitely glad to be alive.

"You ever face a situation where it's them or you," his range instructor had remarked on one occasion, "make damn sure it's them."

Amen.

But he was nervous, like a restless sleeper waiting for his upstairs neighbor's second shoe to drop before he dared to close his eyes. And Dixon couldn't shake it.

Was it simple fear of getting caught? Of what came next? What if he—?

Click!

He turned and found the door open, Cooper crossing the threshold with his Glock in hand. A beat behind the action, Dixon drew his Smith & Wesson and followed, covering the left side of a smallish living room while Cooper took the right.

Gene Talmadge wasn't home.

Dixon inferred it from the silence, then confirmed it

with a hasty room-to-room search that left no piece of furniture unturned. He checked the tiny bathroom, while Matt Cooper scoured the closets and looked underneath the bed.

Their man was gone, with roughly two-thirds of the clothing from his bedroom closet. In the bathroom, Dixon found no toothbrush, no shampoo, no comb, no mouthwash.

"Should there be luggage here?" Bolan asked.

"I couldn't say," Dixon replied.

"How's that?"

"This was an ELINT job," he said. "Electronic—"

"Intelligence. Got it. You're telling me no one was detailed to eyeball our man?"

"My supervisor at the embassy considered it 'unnecessary and unwise,'" Dixon said, sketching air quotes with his fingers. "He was worried Talmadge might pick up on physical surveillance, or the local cops might take offense. Between the two, I think the cops carried more weight."

"So, we have no idea how he keeps house," Bolan replied. "If he's packed up and split, or if he just hates buying clothes. Maybe his hygiene's not the best, but I'd say that the bathroom looks cleaned out."

"Agreed."

"He's gone, then. Any way to check on phone traffic or visitors before he hit the road?" Bolan asked.

"I can make a call about the tapes and taps. If someone came to see him," Dixon said, "we may have caught some conversation with the bugs."

"Do that. Meanwhile, what does he drive?"

"The last I heard, a Honda Civic." Dixon rattled off a license number.

Bolan nodded, looking pleasantly surprised. "Okay. If he was just an ordinary fugitive, we'd want an APB. Can't do that here, but we can keep an eye peeled. First for Talmadge—second for the car. Bearing in mind that he can switch like we did, maybe even go legit."

"There must be something else," Dixon said.

"Well," Bolan said, "we can always tear the place apart."

"Sounds good to me."

And so they did, but quietly, avoiding any racket that would make the neighbors think of burglary in progress. They went through the small apartment like a dose of salts, Dixon remembering his training as he lifted cheesy artwork from the walls, slit cushions on the furniture, emptied the kitchen cupboards and reviewed the contents of the small refrigerator in the kitchen.

Bolan started in the bedroom, opening the flaccid mattress with a knife blade, disappointed by its contents. Likewise pillows, stuffed with musty-smelling rubber. Talmadge's remaining clothes, castoffs, he slit along the seams to check for any hidden articles. Found none.

Dixon attacked the bathroom, checked the grungy toilet tank, then pried loose the medicine cabinet, leaving a hole in the wall. Nothing there. He left the boxlike cabinet with its mirrored door lying across the toilet bowl.

Back to the living room. His partner had disemboweled the sofa by the time Dixon arrived. Together, they pulled up the carpet, watched the roaches scurry before letting it fall back in place. There was nothing left to do unless they started tearing out the walls, and nothing even hinted at the presence of a safe.

Dixon could never say the flat was clean, but it contained no evidence of any criminal activity.

"What about a forwarding address?" Bolan asked as he washed his hands in Talmadge's kitchen.

"You think?" Dixon asked.

"No. Not really, but it's possible. We ought to ask."

"And show the manager our faces?"

"Your face," Bolan said, correcting him. "A round-eye, nameless. Something tells me we all look alike."

"But—"

"Anyway, you speak the language. I'll go get the car and meet you out in front."

Dixon experienced a flash of paranoia, thinking maybe Cooper had devised a plan to ditch him, but he couldn't think of any reason for the newcomer to do so.

"Right," he said at last. "I'll go and find the manager."

"You owe him money and you need to reach him. It's a buddy thing. Maybe mention a small reward for anyone who hooks you up."

"Okay. I'll see you in a couple minutes, then?"

"Sure thing."

Still grappling with uneasiness, Dixon retreated from the flat they'd trashed and started toward the stairs.

BOLAN DROVE once around the block, slowly, and spied Tom Dixon on his second pass. The young agent held up a hand, as if he was flagging down a taxi, and jogged out to meet the car.

"Nothing," Dixon said as he settled in the shotgun seat. "The manager had no idea Talmadge was gone. Rent's paid up for the month, and Talmadge never gave him any headaches. He was more or less invisible."

"Okay." It figured, after all. Talmadge had not selected that apartment, in this crappy neighborhood, in hopes of drawing more attention to himself. He would've been a model tenant, paying all his bills on time and making no complaints about the flat if he could help it. Roaches wouldn't bother him, and nothing else would prompt a squeal unless raw sewage started pumping out of his commode to flood the place.

So he was gone, without a trace. Unless he surfaced someplace where the embassy had watchers, Bolan had no realistic hope of tracking him.

Unless…

As if attuned to Bolan's thoughts, Dixon asked him, "What now?"

"We have two options," Bolan answered. "One, we wait and see if Talmadge shows himself. It could take time, and he may be long gone before he surfaces again."

"That sucks. What's option number two?" Dixon inquired.

"I go to see his friends."

"Meaning?"

"You said al Qaeda has a local cell. Maybe Hamas, on top of that?"

"Correct." Even as Dixon nodded, he was filled with dread.

"And Talmadge has had contact with them."

"Right again."

"Okay. Maybe they've sent him on another mission.

Maybe he's just on vacation. Either way, my guess is that if one group or the other has him on retainer, Talmadge won't leave town without supplying contact information. They won't let him slip the leash."

"Makes sense," Dixon said, grinning. "On the other hand, you can't just walk in there and ask them if he left a forwarding address."

"Why not?"

Dixon half turned to stare at him. "Jesus, you're serious."

"Hey, listen, if you have a better plan for tracking Talmadge, I'm all ears. Let's hear it."

"No. I mean, I don't have anything. Sorry."

"No reason to apologize. In my opinion, we've exhausted all but one of the available options."

"Okay, I hear you," Dixon said. "But damn, for you to walk in there alone—"

"Did I say that?" His turn to smile.

"Oh, hey, now! Hold the horses, pardner. I'm most definitely not the guy you want for anything like this. Uh-uh. No freaking way."

"You did all right this morning," Bolan said.

"You drove the car," Dixon protested, "and you did most of the shooting. I believe I hit one guy. Well, maybe call the second half-and-half."

"Still, for the first time, you were cool," Bolan said. "And you speak the language."

"Al Qaeda's men aren't Indonesian," Dixon said.

"You speak Arabic. It's in your file."

"Oh, right. But look, I've got no training for a gig like this. No military background, anything like that. You want some kind of SWAT guy, rigged for climbing walls and jumping over barricades. Helmet and flame-retardant uniform. That kind of thing."

"I'll take what I can get," Bolan replied.

"I don't think I can do it."

"You surprised yourself this morning," Bolan said, catching the agent's startled blink. "You may again."

"It will surprise me when they blow my head off," Dixon said. But he was weakening. Bolan could hear it in his voice.

"I'll do the hard part," Bolan told him. "Clear the road for you to follow. When I bag a prisoner, you'll question him. Get what you can."

"If he resists?"

"We'll improvise."

"Jesus."

"What do you say?"

"I hate this," Dixon answered.

"That makes two of us," Bolan said.

"I'm scared shitless."

"Only natural."

"And I don't want to die."

"That's not the plan," Bolan replied.

"Damn it! Okay, I'm in."

"I have some addresses for the al Qaeda operation in Jakarta," Bolan said. "Do you have anything?"

"A mosque and an apartment. Taps and bugs on both," Dixon said. "At the mosque, their imam rants about America. At the apartment, we get bits and pieces, but they mostly play it cool."

"Like Talmadge."

"Right."

Bolan gave an address for the apartment, drawing on his memory of Hal Brognola's file.

"That's it," Dixon confirmed.

"How many people in the flat?" Bolan asked.

"Hard to say. They come and go like it's Grand Central Station over there. Full-time, I'd guess there's four or five in residence."

"Any with jobs?"

"They all have jobs, of one kind or another. Day work, mostly. Leaves them free at night to hatch their plots."

"But not where any of your microphones can pick it up."

"I wish."

"Okay," Bolan said. "I guess we'll have to drop in for a chat. Surveillance?"

"Intermittent, on the flat," Dixon replied. "We can't afford to trail them all, 24/7."

"Your thoughts on any weapons they might have?"

A shrug from Dixon. "Sorry, no."

"Do you have a Kevlar vest, by any chance?"

"I wasn't issued one," Dixon admitted woefully.

"It shouldn't be a problem," Bolan said. *Unless you're shot.*

"Goddamn it."

"Going in, the main thing's not to worry. Stay cool. Watch your back. Watch everything. Don't panic."

"Sounds like good advice. I'll take it, if I don't freeze up and get my ass shot off."

"If you were prone to freezing," Bolan said, "it would've been this afternoon."

"You think so?" Dixon asked him. "It seems different. They were chasing me. This time, I'm chasing them."

"And you'll have the advantage of surprise."

"You do this kind of thing a lot?" Dixon asked.

"Now and then. Nobody likes it, but when there's no choice, we go with what's available."

"I guess it's too late," Dixon said, "to call in sick."

"Remember, when we get inside, the mission is to bag a prisoner. If we can catch one with his guard down, wrap him up for takeout, that's the way to go."

"And leave the rest?" Dixon inquired.

"Not functional," Bolan said. "Talmadge on the move means they may have an operation in the works, or else may think he's running out on them. In which case, there may be a certain sense of...desperation."

"Desperate terrorists. Terrific."

"Are there any other kind?"

"Listen, if I get killed—"

"Don't think about that now," Bolan replied. "Look on the bright side."

"I'm looking for it," Dixon said. "I'm looking hard."

# CHAPTER FIVE

The safehouse, or apartment, was located in Jakarta's low-rent Halim district, near the terminally noisy Halim Perdana Kusuma Airport. It wasn't the typical East Asian slum, where civilized life takes a nosedive, but rather a district where working men and women scrabbled hard each day to make ends meet at jobs with no potential for advancement. Halim's residents, by and large, were Jakarta's maids and janitors, laundry and factory workers, taxi drivers and bicycle messengers.

It was the perfect place to hide a cell of Muslim terrorists who kept odd hours, lived in crowded rooms and didn't socialize with neighbors. No one in Halim had time for minding anybody else's business. Some could barely manage to conduct their own.

Although the neighborhood wasn't a slum per se, Bolan had qualms about leaving their hot Toyota on the street, with military weapons in the trunk. Instead, he stopped before they reached the target zone, along a darkened street, and parceled out the hardware he suspected they would need. Dixon had blinked at the assortment and demurred at taking hand grenades, for fear that he might bring the building down, and them along with it.

When they were adequately armed, Bolan drove past the target to an all-night fast-food take-out establishment, where he sent Dixon in to parlay with the clerk. Money changed hands, and Bolan saw the Indonesian smiling as he cheerfully agreed to watch their vehicle for half an hour, tops.

If they were gone that long, Bolan supposed, they likely wouldn't make it back at all.

They walked back to the three-story apartment house, a short block from the store, both wearing jackets now against the nighttime chill and to hide their weapons, talking over strategy along the way.

"Remember with that Uzi," Bolan said. "Short bursts. Don't hold the trigger down unless you plan on taking out a wall. Two-handed grips, or it'll climb on you."

"I've got it. We spent half a day in training with the different SMGs. Not minis, but the full-sized models. This feels like an Ingram."

"It's got better accuracy," Bolan said, "and roughly half the Ingram's cyclic rate of fire, but it won't jam on you. At least, it shouldn't."

"Right."

Two white men stood out in the Halim neighborhood at night more than they had by daylight in the marketplace at Sunda Kelapa. Bolan felt eyes tracking them but couldn't help it. Apprehension would keep any but the worst locals from challenging their presence.

And the very worst were who they'd come to see.

An alley separated Bolan's target from the next apartment house immediately to the west. Bolan and Dixon entered there and made their way through stinking darkness to the building's rear. A door stood ajar, and with a final breath of what passed for fresh air, they slipped inside.

The smells reminded Bolan of the odors he'd experienced at Talmadge's apartment house, compressed and multiplied by ten. People got used to it, he guessed, but it was still depressing to consider that some Halim residents considered it a step up on the ladder of their lives.

The men they hunted had a second-floor apartment, definitely shared by eight, and possibly by ten or twelve. They were confirmed al Qaeda, at least two of them acquaintances of men who'd gone to flight school in the States and used their skills to wreak havoc on 9/11. Strangely, Bolan felt no greater animosity against them than he did for any other human predator who tormented and killed the innocent.

Beyond a certain point, he'd found, it was extremely difficult to quantify evil. Killing a hundred or a thousand helpless people had to be worse somehow than killing five, but Bolan didn't hold the scales.

And he would stop both killers if he could.

On two, he hesitated for a heartbeat, glancing one last time at Dixon, waiting for the nod that signaled he was going all the way. It came, and they advanced to stand before the door labeled 24. It was a corner flat, identified from floor plans as including three small bedrooms and a single bath.

Because the door might be secured by something other than a simple lock and chain, and since it had no peephole, they went straight into Plan A. Dixon rapped sharply on the door, and in a fairly decent singsong accent, called out the equivalent of "Landlord! Open up!"

It shouldn't spook their targets like a visit from the cops, but there was still enough presumed authority behind to get past the several locks.

A voice responded, unintelligible to the Executioner, but Dixon snapped an answer, reaching out to knock again, more forcefully this time. The inner voice, placating, moved up closer to the door.

Bolan reached inside his jacket, hauling out the Spectre SMG he'd chosen for himself. No safety to release, thanks to the double-action trigger, and he held it ready, pointed at the door.

ALI WASSAL WAS INSTANTLY suspicious of the rapping at the door. Why should the landlord come at night, and in the middle of the month, when rent was paid through the thirty-first? It was unusual, and that made him unhappy.

As appointed leader of the cell, it was his duty to assess potential threats and deal with them as he saw fit, bearing in mind that he couldn't expose the cell unnecessarily. Overreaction was as great a danger as the failure to react in time.

Killing their landlord on a routine errand, for example, would be bad.

Wassal answered the knock and call. "A moment, please. We're praying."

God would forgive the lie, as He forgave all minor sins committed in defense of the jihad. Even as he was speaking, Wassal used hand gestures to direct his men toward various positions. Guns were never far away in the apartment, but if it turned out the landlord's visit was legitimate, they also had to seem at ease, as if nothing was wrong or out of place.

The knocking was repeated. "It's important, I'm afraid," the outside voice insisted. "There's a gas leak in the building."

Gas leak?

Wassal pointed young Asad Matalka toward the door, nodding permission for him to release the locks. At the same time, Wassal called out, "I'm coming. Just another moment, please."

Matalka had an automatic pistol in his waistband, hidden by the long tail of his shirt. Wassal retreated to a nearby closet, opened it and reached inside to grasp a folding-stock AKSU assault rifle, already cocked and locked.

Matalka reached the door, opened the simplest lock, began to turn the knob without releasing the security chain. Wassal thumbed off the safety switch on his Kalashnikov and stepped behind the closet's open door, where he would be obscured from view immediately as the landlord entered.

If there was no problem, he could simply put his gun away and close the door.

With a resounding crack, the door flew open, ripping loose the slender chain that would've blocked its opening. It struck Matalka in the face and knocked him sprawling on his back, no time for him to reach his pistol as a pair of white men armed with submachine guns burst into the room.

Ali Wassal fired through the closet door without aiming, then poked his head around the door to find out what was happening and glimpsed chaos within the small space designated as a living room.

Matalka, masked with blood that flowed from nose and lips, was struggling to all fours and groping for the pistol in his belt. A bullet found him as he reached it, raised another spurt of crimson from his left shoulder, and flipped him over on his back once more.

The two white men had both found cover of a sort, one crouched behind a ratty-looking easy chair Wassal had purchased from a local thrift shop in a bid to make the small apartment livable. The other lay behind a mismatched sofa and was presently invisible.

None of the furniture was bulletproof, but padding, springs and wooden frames still helped to slow incoming rounds. Meanwhile, the two unknown intruders weren't simply lying still and waiting for hot rounds to find their flesh. Instead, both men were milking short bursts from their automatic weapons, seeking targets of their own.

Wassal, aiming this time, triggered a burst into the couch, then scuttled backward toward the bedroom that he shared with Butrus Bari. He could fight from there as well as from the closet in the living room, and if the battle went against them, he could slip out through the window, down the fire escape into the night.

Unless the whole house was surrounded.

No. He doubted that. Clearly, the white men weren't police, and they appeared to have no backup in the outer cor-

ridor. Why should he think that there were any more of
them below, watching the streets?

Kill first, he thought. Think later.

And with that in mind, Wassal triggered another burst
from his Kalashnikov, in the direction of his hidden enemies.

FROM HIS PLACE behind the musty-smelling sofa, Bolan
tried to find an unobstructed target, wriggling first one
way and then the other, as he huddled under fire. At least
two AKs were unloading now, the other targets firing pistols, but he reckoned there'd be other weapons stashed in
the apartment, waiting for a terrorist with nerve to make
the break from cover and retrieve them.

Dixon fired another short burst from his roost, behind
the bulky armchair, and his bullets made a slapping sound
as they punched through a stucco wall. Wasted, but it was
difficult to aim under the circumstances, all the more so
with their targets crouched behind odd bits of furniture or
firing from the doorways of their bedrooms.

Bolan thought, Time to shake things up a bit, as he
palmed a frag grenade and hooked the pin loose with his
other thumb. Precise delivery was probably impossible
under the circumstances, but he guessed that anything he
did to rattle their opponents had to help.

"Fire in the hole!" he warned Dixon, and pitched his lethal egg in the direction of the nearest bedroom doorway
on his left. If it fell short, he was protected by the couch
from flying shrapnel. If it scored—

The blast was louder than anticipated, rattling walls that
once had been erected swiftly, on the cheap. A rain of

plaster from the ceiling mixed with smoke and dust to foul the air. Downrange, someone was coughing, while another voice cried out in pain.

It could've been a trap, but Bolan knew he had to take the chance. If he did nothing, the grenade was wasted and he'd likely never move from where he lay behind the bullet-riddled couch.

He rolled instead of rising to his feet, thus minimizing target value for his shaken enemies, and caught one of them standing in the nearest bedroom doorway, slumped against the jamb and coughing violently. A three-round burst from Bolan's Spectre let more air into the target's aching lungs, but not in any way that nature had intended.

One down and out beyond all possibility of conversation. Even as the first man dropped, Bolan was seeking other targets, angling for a way to bring one down without a mortal wound. They didn't make it easy, riddling the apartment walls with bullets, and he knew that even in this district of Jakarta, some neighbor was bound to summon the police.

Which meant that he was running out of time.

As if to prove that point, a burst of AK fire sliced through the couch, a foot above his head, spraying the Executioner with tattered stuffing. Bolan hugged the floor but knew it wouldn't save him from concerted fire. He had to make his move, and soon, before the home team finished him and Dixon where they lay.

Bolan clutched another frag grenade and freed the safety pin. He warned Dixon once again—"Fire in the hole!"— and lobbed the bomb toward the second bedroom, pitching blind from memory this time. It didn't have to be a perfect hit, as long as it created adequate confusion for his purposes.

The second blast produced sufficient dust and smoke to cover Bolan's move. He rolled clear of the couch, squeezed off a short burst toward the site of the explosion, then immediately vaulted to his feet and rushed toward the first bedroom doorway he had cleared. A corpse obstructed him, but Bolan hurdled it and landed in a crouch behind the doorjamb, with a new perspective on the flat.

Gunfire still hammered at him from the third bedroom, and Bolan saw a solitary muzzle-flash wink at him from the second, spitting short bursts through the smoky pall. He guessed that they had cut the hostile force by half, but couldn't say if any of their downed assailants were alive or fit for questioning.

To answer that, he'd need a closer look.

He heard scuffling noises coming from the first bedroom, where his grenade had detonated moments earlier. Turning, he saw a broken figure, lurching forward on one knee and one elbow, straining for a weapon in the middle of the floor. the man's jaw hung loose on one side, shattered.

Bolan leveled his SMG and put a mercy round between the scarecrow's hate-filled eyes.

Two rooms left to clear, and if he didn't get a talking prisoner from one of them, he'd count the raid a failure.

Time to go.

He glanced at Dixon's hiding place, wished there was some way to alert him of the move that Bolan had in mind.

Even as that thought took shape, he saw the young Homeland Security agent burst from cover, firing as he ran.

DIXON HAD NO REAL PLAN to speak of, simply knew that he was sick and tired of crouching behind an easy chair and waiting for some stranger to get lucky with a hit that killed or crippled him. If he was going out, at least he'd try to take a couple of the bastards with him, count for something in the final moments of his life.

Cooper was lobbing hand grenades, rattling the walls and ceiling, shrapnel added to the storm of bullets flying all around the flat. Dixon tried to imagine how it sounded to the neighbors, plaster raining on their heads downstairs, slugs punching through the walls on either side. He hoped there were no children present, then dismissed the thought. There was nothing that he could do about it either way.

After the second blast, he caught a glimpse of Cooper moving, rushing from his place behind the couch to gain the middle bedroom's doorway. That was progress, he supposed, trying to catch the bad guys in a cross fire, but his own position didn't offer much by way of contribution to the effort.

He was nearest to the bedroom on the far right, as they entered, presently the one untouched by Cooper's hand grenades. Judging by sound and strobing muzzle-flashes from the doorway, Dixon guessed there were three shooters in that bedroom, fully focused for the moment on Matt Cooper. Dixon didn't think they had forgotten him, but if he took advantage of their momentary lapse—

Don't think about it. Do it!

Mouthing silent curses, painfully aware that he would soon have to reload, Dixon lunged from the marginal protection of his cover, charging toward the open doorway of the third bedroom.

He fired a short burst from the mini-Uzi on the run, most likely wasted, though he heard a startled cry from somewhere in the shadows there. Then he was down and sliding on the bare floor, like a baseball player stretching for home plate, thumping against the wall with force enough to make him bite his tongue.

Someone in the bedroom sprayed his wall with automatic-rifle fire, but they were aiming high, the bullets drilling abstract patterns where he would've been if he was kneeling. In another second, his assailant would catch on—or other guns would join the fusillade—and he'd be dead.

Matt Cooper saved him, leaning out from cover with his SMG and triggering a burst to rattle Dixon's enemies. A heartbeat later, Dixon raised his own weapon and started firing through the wall, blindly, tracing the bullet patterns etched a moment earlier by AK fire.

It felt good, making noise and spitting out the shreds of stucco that cascaded over his face, but Dixon's ammo was exhausted in two seconds, give or take. He blinked dust from his eyes, ejected the spent magazine and fumbled for a spare.

If anyone was still alive inside the third bedroom, this was the time for them to finish him. They had to know where Dixon was by now. A trigger stroke from the Kalashnikov, and he was history. If only he—

The loaded magazine clicked home, the Uzi's bolt snapped shut and Dixon scrambled from his prone position to an awkward running crouch. It wasn't anything he'd ever learned in training, just a reflex, trying to remain below the hostile line of fire as long as possible.

He made it to the bedroom door and ducked across the threshold, firing. On the floor in front of him, a bloody face stared wide-eyed at him, unprotesting. Farther back, two other men were huddled in a corner, weapons lying close at hand. One of them twitched, and Dixon fired again, stitching them both. Remembering too late that he had wanted one of them alive.

He swore, frustration purged by the obscenities as rage had flowed out through his trigger finger seconds earlier.

You blew it, said the small voice in his head. Again.

ALI WASSAL WAS in a panic, torn between an impulse to remain and die fighting, a guaranteed ticket to Paradise, or to escape and fight again another day. Honor played no part in his hasty calculations. He thought only of the damage he could wreak against the enemies of God if he lived another month, another year.

The single window of the bedroom where he crouched, pinching his nose with one hand to prevent him sneezing in the haze of dust and smoke, opened onto a fire escape. By now, with the explosions, he supposed some of his neighbors had already fled the building. If he chose to live, the way was open to him.

Probing gunfire from the second bedroom fanned the air

above his head. Wassal's two enemies were edging closer to him, and he had no soldiers left to halt their slow advance. Perhaps police would come before they reached him, but what benefit was that? He'd be arrested, charged with terrorism and a list of other crimes, condemned to life in prison if they didn't kill him outright.

No. Better to flee and fight again.

Retreating toward the window, he thought briefly of the mercenary, hoped that no ill had befallen him and that he would fulfill their contract. If he failed, God would punish him, but that would be small consolation to the faithful praying for a great victory in their long war against America and all its works.

Death to all enemies of God! May they burn in Hell!

He almost spoke the curse aloud, then caught himself and beamed it silently across the smoky apartment toward his opponents as he reached the bedroom window. Wassal reached up blindly for the latch, keeping his eyes and weapon trained upon the bedroom doorway, flinching as another burst of gunfire raked the ceiling overhead.

Poor shots, he thought, and almost smiled.

He found the latch, released it and was forced to face the window for a moment as he pushed it open. He couldn't gain proper leverage reaching backward and above his head, and required both hands in fact to raise the window, creaking in its frame.

He reached out toward the night and touched a rusty window screen. Of course, he'd known that it was there, had peered through it a hundred times, but now it threatened him. Wassal lashed out with a clenched fist, dented and bowed the screen with his first punch, then tore it free and sent it spinning from its frame.

A furtive backward glance showed no one gaining on him—yet. Snatching his AKSU from where he had left it on the floor, Wassal lunged through the open window, scraped one shoulder in his haste and grimaced as his first steps sent metallic echoes up from the fire escape.

The frail suspended staircase shuddered as he got his footing, peered inside his former bedroom for the last time, then began descending toward the darkened alley-way. Sirens warbled in the distance, fire brigades and armed police responding to the battle scene. They might prevent him getting to the old, cheap car shared by the members of his cell, but he could still escape on foot, find someplace to conceal his weapon safely while he reached out to his contacts in Jakarta and arranged another place to stay.

It wasn't time for him to leave the city yet.

But soon, perhaps, now that the hired American had gone.

The fire escape wobbled more violently, produced more clanging sounds than were accounted for by Wassal's scrambling passage down its steps. He paused, looked up-ward and beheld a dark shape closing in pursuit.

He angled for a shot, but couldn't trust his rounds to penetrate the metal steps directly overhead. Cursing, Was-sal clutched at the narrow railing, braced one hip against it, and leaned far out over empty space to aim his rifle in a tremulous, one-handed grip.

One shot was all he needed. Just one decent—

He was barely conscious of it when his fingers lost their

purchase on the railing. Gravity reached out to claim him, and he tumbled backward, plummeting some fifteen feet to earth. It was a fluke that Wassal landed on his head, bright fireworks flaring in his brain before the darkness swallowed them and him, consuming all.

"It's lucky that he didn't break his neck," Tom Dixon said.

"Lucky for us," Bolan replied. "I'm not so sure he'll feel the same."

"Should he be coming out of it by now?"

"Ready or not," Bolan said, reaching out to slap their captive's cheek, first lightly, then with greater force.

The prisoner awoke by stages, grudgingly. His first response, like that of nearly everyone who's knocked unconscious, was to vomit on himself. The smell repulsed Bolan until he took the dented bucket filled with rust-brown water from a nearby tap and doused their hostage, cleansing him and finishing the wake-up process.

Their man sat on a concrete floor, inside an old warehouse Dixon had located along Jakarta's waterfront. His hands were tied behind him, back and shoulders braced against one of the pillars that supported the abandoned structure's roof. He sputtered at them, gasping, grimacing through what had to have been a killer headache, while he craned his neck, trying to glimpse their faces.

"Ready?" Bolan asked his comrade.

"As I'll ever be," Dixon replied.

"Do you speak English?" Bolan asked the prisoner, evoking no response. He glanced at Dixon. "Okay. Translate. We're looking for a man, American, who's spent some time with you during the past few weeks. A mercenary. If you tell us where to find him, you can live."

Dixon produced a rapid-fire harangue in Arabic. The terrorist appeared to listen, but didn't respond.

"Tell him he has two choices," Bolan said. "He either gives us what we need, in which case he survives intact, or we can take the information. If we have to draw it out by force, there's a good chance that he'll be left insane."

"Say what?"

"Tell him!"

Frowning, Dixon delivered Bolan's ultimatum to their prisoner. If he was frightened by the threat, it didn't show.

"Tell him that if we steal his senses," Bolan said, "he'll lose his love of God and his dedication to the cause. He'll never get to Paradise."

Dixon complied. This time, the hostage rattled off an answer, looking smug despite his circumstances.

"He says God sees all, knows all, and he won't be held responsible for anything we do to him. A martyr's guaranteed a place in Paradise."

"Explain to him once more that we don't plan to kill him," Bolan said. "I have a drug that will compel him to betray his fatwa, and will change his brain forever. When I'm finished with him, he won't be a martyr. Just a drunk, pork-eating infidel."

Dixon translated. Once again, the hostage spoke with evident disdain.

"He says to do your worst."

"Okay." Bolan retreated to a nearby gym bag, resting on the warehouse floor, and rummaged briefly through its contents. He returned a moment later with a hypodermic syringe and a rubber-stoppered bottle of clear liquid.

"Should I ask what that is?" Dixon queried.

"The fulfillment of a promise," Bolan answered.

Studying the prisoner to gauge his weight, Bolan half filled the syringe and pocketed the tiny bottle. If he needed more to do the job, it was available. Crouching beside the captive, who now snarled at him and tried in vain to pull away, he raised the left sleeve of the Arab's soggy shirt and found a vein, delivering the needle's payload.

"Give him five," Bolan said, "then we'll start again."

The prisoner berated them in angry tones—no need to translate that—but after several moments, he began to slump against his bonds, head lolling, chin on chest. His eyes were open, but he still looked half-asleep.

"What now?" Dixon asked.

"Ask him about Talmadge. Where he's gone, the details of his mission, how they keep in touch. We need to know whatever *he* knows. All of it."

Dixon began again. It was like pulling teeth, but he was getting answers, nodding as he went along, saving the English version for the moment when their prisoner ran out of words and Dixon had no more to ask him.

"So?" Bolan inquired.

"If you can trust the mojo juice," Dixon replied, "our boy here has no way to get in touch with Talmadge. It's security, whatever. Talmadge has some phone numbers for contacts here and there—in Europe, Canada, the States."

"Where is he going?" Bolan pressed.

"First stop, Vancouver. Not the one in Washington. British Columbia. He's meeting someone there. Taking delivery."

"On what?"

Dixon looked bleak as he replied. "A dirty bomb."

# CHAPTER SIX

*Airborne over the Pacific*

The Learjet 35A was a comfortable ride, on loan from a friend of a friend who…whatever. Jack Grimaldi didn't ask a lot of questions in regard to where a plane came from. His main concerns revolved around where it had been and where it was going, with him at the controls.

This particular Learjet had spent its working life on trans-Pacific runs from California to Hawaii and Tahiti, mostly shuttling those who passed as VIPs in high society, but who didn't maintain a private set of wings. Grimaldi hadn't asked how Hal Brognola had obtained use of the Learjet on short notice, didn't care what favors were exchanged, as long as all the maintenance records checked out and the bird could perform.

So far, no sweat.

His flight plan was Jakarta to Oahu, fueling there, then onward to Vancouver. He was flying light, two passengers instead of eight, himself the only crew aboard. It was no problem cruising at an altitude of twenty thousand feet, on autopilot, with a helpful tailwind boosting the Learjet's standard 529 miles per hour closer to 550.

Grimaldi was scanning his radio channels, amusing himself, when movement in the cockpit doorway brought his head around. Instead of Bolan standing there, it was the other guy. Tom Dixon, he'd been told, a youngster from Homeland Security who'd lately received his baptism of fire.

"Permission to come aboard, Captain?" Dixon asked.

"You're already aboard," Grimaldi reminded him.

"Right. Can I join you, in that case?"

"Feel free." Grimaldi nodded toward the empty copilot's seat, and Dixon settled into it.

"Smooth ride," he said for openers.

"The way I like it," Grimaldi replied.

Dixon surveyed the vast Pacific through the Learjet's windshield for a moment, then said, "Can I ask you something?"

"Feel free," Grimaldi said. "I'll have to hear the question, first, before I know if I can answer you."

"Seems fair. Have you known Cooper long?"

Grimaldi had become accustomed to the cover names that Bolan used. Since he had died—at least officially—in New York City, the warrior and top-ten fugitive known as Mack Bolan no longer existed. Surgery had changed his face, twice, while every copy of his dossier within the Western Hemisphere had been stamped Closed—Deceased. The man who had emerged used a variety of names. The latest of them was Matt Cooper.

"We've been around the block together once or twice," Grimaldi said. "Why do you ask?"

"Just curious," Dixon replied. "I mean, here *I'm* supposed to be some kind of covert agent, but the first time things get sticky, here comes Superman. I didn't see him changing in a phone booth, but the rest of it… How did he learn all that?"

"By doing, mostly. And he isn't Superman. He's just… superior."

"You mean stuck-up and all? He doesn't come across that way."

"No, no," Grimaldi said. "I mean superior according to the basic Webster's definition. When it comes to jobs like this, they don't get any better. But he's human. Bet on it."

"Okay, when you say that the two of you have been around the block—"

"I can't say any more on that," Grimaldi interrupted him. "It's classified."

"I get it. Need-to-know and all that."

"Right. It's not important, anyway," the pilot said. "The two things you should keep in mind are, first, that he's the best you'll ever work with. Second, he'll never let you down or leave you hanging. That's a guarantee."

"I'm not sure what you know about this thing we're doing," Dixon said.

"Enough to get from Point A to Point B."

"The thing is, when it started, I was pretty green. I mean, I'm still green, when you calculate time on the job. But all the shit that we've been through the past few hours, and the things I've done…"

"Try not to let it worry you."

"It doesn't," Dixon said. "That's just the thing, you see?"

"Not quite."

"I'm worried that it *doesn't* worry me. I'm worried that I like it."

Grimaldi said, "You're probably just psyched up by the action, first time out and everything. It's natural. Sometimes you take a newbie, no offense—"

"None taken."

"—and you drop him in the deep end of the shark tank, it can be a scary thing, but still exciting, too. First time a fighter pilot solos, or a jarhead hits the beach. The action ramps you up, adrenaline starts pumping, all the stuff that helps you stay alive. Some people get a little high on that, while others crash and burn."

Dixon looked vaguely troubled. "I don't know. In training, when we used to talk about it, everybody put up fronts, you know? *'I have to shoot somebody, I won't hesitate,'* and all that crap. But when it came down to the crunch, I didn't hesitate."

"And here you are," Grimaldi said. "Alive and thinking through it, with your body parts intact. You win."

"That's how I feel," Dixon replied. "I won. But part of me keeps thinking that it shouldn't be that way. I should be all strung out and guilty, like those TV cops who agonize over a shooting like they wish the other guy had capped them. Get it?"

"I hear what you're saying," Grimaldi replied. "And I've known guys who felt that way. Working through what the shrinks call a survivor's guilt complex. Hey, it's a fact of life for some, and I don't question that. But is it normal? Are we all supposed to feel bad for surviving close encounters with the Reaper? I don't think so. Hell, no."

"That makes sense," Dixon said. "But I can't stop thinking that I liked it too much. Like, I've just been waiting all my life to—"

"What? Become an instant psycho-killer? Trust me, I've known some of those, too, and they don't just pop out of the closet. Nothing like that happens overnight. You get the buildup, see the warning signs."

"Such as?"

Grimaldi shrugged. "I'm no psychologist, okay? But from my personal experience *and* what I've read in my spare time, your basic psycho gets the yen for pain and killing when he's still a little kid. He tortures animals, sets fires, beats up on smaller kids. Does any of that sound familiar, from your personal experience?"

"No. I'd remember that."

"Well, then, I think you're safe. As for the rest, don't sweat it. You could go the rest of your career, put in the twenty years, and never see another job like this."

"Or anybody else like Cooper?"

"That's for damned sure," the pilot agreed. "When they made him, they broke the freakin' mold."

*Vancouver, British Columbia*

"So, what's the urgency about this American we're looking for, do you suppose?" Rudy Howell asked.

"I got the same briefing that you did," Chester Ettinger

replied. "Some kind of flap from Washington. Homeland Security hiccoughs and we're supposed to run in place."

The sergeant didn't try to mask his cynicism. Twelve years with the Royal Canadian Mounted Police had taught him that his country's neighbor to the south was often pushy, begging—no, *demanding*—favors when it had little to offer in return. And it had only gotten worse since 9/11's horror show, with every minor fugitive promoted overnight to ten-most-wanted status, labeled a potential terrorist.

The latest, he supposed—this Talmadge character— would be another load of crap, but he still had orders to be carried out, and the young corporal to assist him.

"The briefing said he's armed and dangerous," the corporal reminded him.

"They *always* say that," Ettinger replied. "One reason is, the Americans have so damned many guns floating around down there, they reckon everyone must have at least two pistols on his person at all times. Mind you, the murder rate suggests they aren't half-wrong."

"But here he's forty-something, eh?"

"Just forty-two," Ettinger said.

"All right, then. Forty-two. But what I mean to say is, most old-timers start to slow down in their forties, don't they? It's a funny time of life to go all armed and danger-ous, I'd say."

Motoring south on Granville Street, Chet Ettinger glanced over at his passenger. Howell was a fresh-faced twenty-three-year-old who seemed to think that thirty was the hump and forty meant the end of life.

"Listen and learn," he said tersely. "You're making several mistakes, and any one of them could get you sliced and diced if you're not careful. First, I have to tell you forty-two's not old. It may be nearly twice your age, but many men—most men—are fit and hearty at that age. They've more experience than you do, and more street smarts, most of them. Which brings me to my second point."

"I'm listening," Howell said. He didn't sound at all contrite.

"If you were half-awake during the briefing, then you know this Talmadge is a former Special Forces man. That means they've trained him seven ways from Sunday how to kill and stay alive in any situation you can think of—plus a hundred that you can't. Try cuffing him alone, he'd likely tear your arm right off and hit you with the wet end."

"I reckon they're overrated, anyhow," Howell said.

"Who is?"

"Those Green Berets. And if they can't mind their own elite soldiers, what is it coming to?"

"That's not for me to say," the sergeant answered, though he had some thoughts along those lines himself. Why was the FBI and Homeland Security looking for a decorated Green Beret who'd fought his country's battles overseas?

Oh, well. It took all kinds. Soldiers went bad sometimes, just like policemen, lawyers, judges, dentists—any occupation he could think of. There were bad apples in every barrel, festering to spoil the rest if they were given time and opportunity.

Chet Ettinger was proud to be a member of the RCMP, even though he didn't talk it up. Of the top-flight law-enforcement agencies in North America, he'd picked the one least prone to scandal and embarrassment. The Mounties might not *always* get their man these days, but they gave it a damned good try.

Now, here he was, seeking an American the FBI and Homeland Security couldn't find. And best of all, he had a lead.

The canvass of apartment buildings in Vancouver had produced three hits on tenants by the name of E. or G. Talmadge. Chet Ettinger wasn't convinced their man would put his own name on a lease, but God knew stranger things had happened. He and Howell had checked on the first candidate already, eyeballing a sixty-something black man, George Talmadge, who bore no vague resemblance to their fugitive.

One down and two to go.

Their orders put him off a little, most particularly the "do not approach" command, but Ettinger could live with it. If Eugene Talmadge was as dangerous as some folks seemed to think he was, then Ettinger had no desire to be up close and personal. Better to let his weapon do the talking, from a nice safe range.

"Who's next?" Howell asked.

"E. Talmadge, at the Waterford Apartments, Fraser Street."

"Seems like we could've phoned ahead and spoken to the managers. That would've saved some time, I think."

"Or tipped off the bastard, maybe," Ettinger said.

"Not likely, is it? Why'd they want to help a wanted man, when all he means to them is monthly rent?"

"Loose lips," Ettinger said.

"How's that?"

"Forget it," he replied. "We brace the manager in person, as instructed, and we go from there."

"Do not approach," Howell echoed their commander.

Don't remind me, the sergeant thought. But he said, "That's right. Do not approach. Remember that, my son, and you'll be fine."

*Vancouver International Airport*

BOLAN HAD SLEPT enough during the flight to get him through another day, and then some, if he had to push it. Rest was where he found it, and no dreams to trouble him this time. Dixon was dragging, but the chill air of a brisk Vancouver sunrise seemed to bolster him.

"What now?" he asked.

"Collect our things, pick up some wheels," Bolan replied. "Touch base, if anyone has anything to tell us."

"Right."

The best thing about charter flights was their exemption from the normal routine of airport security. Private charter planes loaded and departed from different terminals than commercial aircraft. Their passengers and crew didn't pass through metal detectors, weren't frisked or commanded to take off their shoes for inspection. Their baggage was loaded without any kind of preflight inspection by anyone wearing a uniform.

Charter flights were the great blind spot of post-9/11 aviation, and for reasons Bolan didn't fully understand, no one in Congress or the FAA yet seemed inclined to plug that glaring loophole.

Criminals with money flew in private jets because they weren't subjected to examination. They could transport drugs, weapons, explosives, steamer trunks chock-full of blood money, and no one in authority had any clue what they were moving on domestic flights or internationally. While commercial passengers were lining up and emptying their pockets for the Man, a motley crew of gangsters, rich eccentrics and filthy-rich felons were free to come and go unsupervised.

Because?

Blame it on influence in Congress or a blind spot on the part of conservative lawmakers where their financial angels were concerned. Rank had its privileges, and one of them, apparently, was thumbing noses at the rules applied to most Americans on any given day.

It was a wild and wacky world, but on a day like this, it worked to the Executioner's advantage. There was no one to insist on poking through his duffel bag of military hardware, or to check the Glock holstered beneath his jacket. No one to inquire why he was violating half a dozen laws, just standing there, armed to the teeth.

It was a short walk to the car-rental office, where a young redhead confirmed his reservation of a four-door Honda Civic. Bolan hadn't made the reservation, trusting that to Stony Man, but he was ready with a passport and a driver's license in the name of Matthew Cooper, corresponding to the information on the rental contract.

He waived the standard insurance, trusting "Cooper's" Platinum Visa credit card to cover any damage suffered by the vehicle, and palmed the Honda's keys.

Outside the terminal again, with Dixon trailing him, he

found the Honda in its numbered slot, opened the trunk and stowed his baggage. Dixon climbed into the shotgun seat, while Bolan took the wheel.

"Where's Jack?" Dixon asked, catching Bolan with his key in the ignition.

"He stays with the plane," Bolan replied, "on tap in case we need another airlift in a hurry."

"Ah. We're all set, then?"

"Not exactly," Bolan said. "We're short one target."

"Damn it!" Dixon shook his head. "I must be jet-lagged. You've got something working with the locals to find Talmadge, right?"

"Let's hope so. Without leads, we're all dressed up with nowhere to go."

"Is there a number you can call?" Dixon asked.

"Somebody on this end has my cell."

"So, then…?"

"We wait." As Bolan spoke, he gave the key a twist and revved the Honda's engine. "But we don't wait here."

"Suspicious, right? Just sitting here too long?"

"I'd say."

He wound his way out of the airport parking lot, an exercise on par with tracing mazes in a children's magazine. A few more turns, tracking the flow of traffic, brought him to Marine Drive and his first glimpse of Vancouver proper.

"We just drive around and wait?" Dixon asked.

"Pretty much," said Bolan.

And the cell phone in his pocket purred.

"So, LET ME GET this straight." Staff Sergeant Albert Hotchkiss of the RCMP didn't try to hide the fact that he was ill at ease. "Officially, you do not exist."

"Officially," Bolan said, "that's affirmative."

"But you're in Canada to handle 'something big,' I'm told, by my superiors. Something of 'vital interest' to both our countries."

"That's about the size of it."

"You need the RCMP's help to find a man—this Eugene Talmadge—but you won't say why."

"Can't say," Bolan corrected him. "It's classified."

"Of course it is. That was explained to me. I'm crystal-clear on how this is supposed to be a one-way street, no questions asked."

"It's not my choice," Bolan replied. "We all take orders."

"Right. You'll understand, though, I've no doubt, if this all sounds a little strange to me."

"I do."

"More than a little, if the truth be told."

"Completely understandable," Bolan said. "I appreciate your candor."

"From the background information we were granted on this Talmadge fellow, sketchy as it was, he's obviously one of yours. A military man, I mean. Someone considered…dangerous."

"We're looking into that," Bolan said.

"Right. But not at home, on your own patch."

"He's traveling. We're playing catch-up."

"It's too much to ask, I realize, but exactly what do you think he's doing in Vancouver?"

"If I knew that," Bolan answered honestly, "we wouldn't need the RCMP's help to pin him down."

Hotchkiss forged ahead. "We may assume, I take it, that he's not in town for any purpose that would benefit the city or the province. Nothing beneficial, may I say, to any decent person you could name."

"Again, the details, if I had them, would be—"

"Classified. Of course." A frown carved lines in the staff sergeant's face. "While under orders I may be, you understand that my first duty is to the protection of our citizens from any danger that I may have knowledge of, regardless of the source?"

"That's clear," Bolan said.

"And it happens that your Mr. Talmadge is a person known to us, although I'll be quite frank in saying that we've overlooked him, for the most part, until now."

"Meaning?"

"Assuming that he's here, in fact, this won't be Mr. Talmadge's first visit to Vancouver," Hotchkiss said. "He keeps a flat in Gastown, just off Hastings. Nothing ostentatious, mind you. Just a tidy home-away-from-home, wherever home may be."

The RCMP wouldn't know him solely from a street address. "He's in your files," Bolan said.

"That he is, but in a minor way, as I've explained. It isn't him we've studied, up to now, but some of his associates."

"And they would be…?" Dixon asked, speaking up for the first time since he was introduced to Hotchkiss.

"Quite a motley bag, I must say. We have gentlemen of the Chinese persuasion, for a start. Triads, in fact, if you'll permit me to be blunt. We keep a routine eye on their activities. Your Mr. Talmadge sometimes dines with them when he's in town."

"But you don't think it's strictly social," Bolan said.

"What is, these days?"

"Who else?" Dixon asked. "In the motley bag."

"Some gentlemen of Arabic descent," Hotchkiss replied. "Not residents. They come to town on business, once or twice a year. Your Mr. Talmadge has been seen with them on two occasions."

"And you track them—why?" Bolan asked.

"Ah." The Mountie smiled. "If I was half the bastard some people think I am, I'd tell you it was classified. But in the spirit of cooperation, call it being neighborly. We're paying more attention to the visitors from the Middle East since your President declared a global war on terror."

"Who are they supposed to be?" Bolan asked.

"Oilmen—on the surface, anyway. The one in charge, Nasser Asad, has Saudi diplomatic papers to his credit. We can't nick him, even if we wanted to."

"Why would you?" Dixon asked.

"His travel history suggests familiarity with certain radical Islamic fundamentalists whose names might ring a bell, young man. Some you might find on wanted posters, or a deck of cards."

"And who's the other?" Bolan prodded.

"Ahmed Zero, if you can believe it. I had trouble with it, let me tell you, but our linguists tell me it's a proper name in Arabic. Another Saudi, by the way. Nothing against him on our books, except you never find him more than two steps from Asad."

"Would you know whether they're in town at present?" Bolan asked.

"Nothing suggests it," Hotchkiss answered. "Should they be?"

"Beats me," Bolan replied. And told the Mountie honestly, "I never heard of either one before today."

"But you suspect?"

"I'm interested. But getting back to Talmadge and his flat—in Gastown, was it?"

Hotchkiss nodded. "I have people watching it, discreetly. Someone's home, apparently, although they haven't seen the man himself. Whoever's there, it seems they're entertaining guests."

"And they would be…?"

"Some of the Asian gentlemen I mentioned earlier. Known for investments in our finer shopping malls, golf courses and some products that you won't find listed on the corporate balance sheet."

"Triads," Dixon said.

"Not for me to judge," Hotchkiss replied, "but if I *had* to say, I'd guess you're not far off."

"The address?" Bolan asked.

Hotchkiss supplied it. "If you need an escort—"

"We can find it on our own, thank you."

"And my officers?"

"You're better off relieving them."

"Are you about to cause a ruckus in my city, Mr. Cooper?"

"Not if I can help it," Bolan said.

"Just dropping by to pay respects, I take it."

"More or less."

"I hope you're welcome, then. We have enough untidy business on our plate already, without adding any more."

"You've been a help, Staff Sergeant," Bolan told him. "If we don't meet up again—"

"I have a feeling," Hotchkiss interrupted, "that it may be for the best."


"GASTOWN," Dixon said as they passed Thornton Park, northbound on Main Street. "What's that all about?"

"Maybe there's something in the guidebook," Bolan said. Dixon was nervous. Bolan understood that, even sympathized, but it was time to focus on the job at hand.

"It's not important," Dixon answered. Then, after a silent block, he asked, "How do you want to play this?"

"It depends on what we find," Bolan replied. "The layout. Who's at home. How many visitors, and who they are."

"Feels like we're flying blind," Dixon said. "I'll know Talmadge, if we see him, but the rest are ciphers. Just because a Mountie says they're triads, do we…I mean…."

"Every situation is unique," Bolan replied, "but we follow certain steps, regardless. First, a threat assessment. Second, calculation of the force required to yield desired results. Third, application of the force deemed necessary, within situational constraints."

"Sounds like a lecture that I slept through back in high-school chemistry," Dixon said.

"Just the basics of survival," Bolan said. "Assessment

means we eyeball everything we can. The field, the players, any hardware visible. It's simple preparation."

"How's that work," Dixon asked, "if they're up in his apartment doing whatever it is they do, and we're out on the street?"

"I'll have to see the place before I answer that. There may be access from another building, from a fire escape. Something."

"And if there isn't?"

"Then we improvise."

"Just wing it?"

"As a last resort."

"So calculation of the necessary force is also flexible, I take it?"

"Within situational constraints," Bolan repeated.

"That's my next question."

"He's in a public residential building, not a hardsite or a free-fire zone," Bolan explained. "We can't sit back and plaster him with heavy weapons. Even if we could do that, it wouldn't get us where we need to be."

"Because we don't know what he's up to," Dixon said.

"Exactly right. If taking Talmadge out would solve the problem, we could do it. *I* could do it. But we don't know that. He may just be a conduit or middleman. Right now, there's too much blank space on the map. We aren't prepared to find our way."

"You need to ask him."

"That would be ideal," Bolan replied.

"Like with the Arab, in Jakarta," Dixon said.

"I doubt that it will go that way."

"Because he's Special Forces?"

They were coming up on Chinatown, with another mile or so before they reached the district known as Gastown and began to look for Talmadge's address.

"Not strictly speaking," Bolan answered Dixon. "Green Berets are taught resistance to interrogation, but that's mainly torture. Toughing out the pain and psychological assaults. There's no training for drugs. Unless you go in saturated with an antidote, the juice will break you down."

"What, then?"

"He may not let us take him. Probably won't let us," Bolan said.

"He'll fight, you mean."

"At least."

"You're losing me."

"It all depends on how committed Talmadge is to whatever he's doing. If it's just the money, sure, maybe he'll take the cease-fire option if his situation's hopeless. But if he has other motivations working *with* the greed..."

"Hold on. You think he'd off himself?"

"Unknown," Bolan replied. "If he's committed to a cause beyond the payday, if he's got that kind of motivation—hate, revenge, whatever—then it's possible."

"And if he's dead—"

"We won't know if we've solved the problem," Bolan said, "until it turns out that we haven't."

"Sounds like we need a SWAT team and negotiators," Dixon said.

"That's not an option. This is all q.t."

"It won't be, if we drop the ball," Dixon stated.

"We can't afford to drop it, then," Bolan told him.

"No pressure. Great."

"No more than usual," the Executioner replied.

"You always live like this?"

"Jobs come and go. They're rarely by the numbers."

Dixon sighed and shook his head, turning to scan the sights of Chinatown. "I thought I had a handle on this deal, you know? Professional responsibility and all that. Turns out I've been clueless all along."

"Wrong place, wrong time," Bolan said.

"If you said 'Wrong man, wrong job,' you might be closer to the truth."

"You've done all right so far."

"I talked to Jack about that, on the plane, while you were resting."

"Oh?"

"Nothing specific, like. I didn't blow our game."

"Jack's in the loop," Bolan said.

"Either way. The more I think about it," Dixon said, "I think I should've stuck with law school. I could have a tiny office with no windows, work a solid hundred-hour week, maybe make partner by the time I'm forty. Never have to think about somebody blowing out my brains."

"So where's the fun in that?" Bolan asked.

Dixon laughed, then couldn't seem to stop it for a moment. Finally, he got a grip and said, "Hysterics. That's exactly what I need."

"Save it," the Executioner replied. "Here's Gastown coming up."

# CHAPTER SEVEN

*Gastown, Vancouver*

"Okay," Gene Talmadge said. "We all know why we're here tonight, and all this food—delicious as it is—is not the reason."

Nods around the spacious dining table told him that the others were prepared to talk business. He scanned the faces, wondering again why triads always brought so many people to a sit-down. Did they really think the numbers would impress him?

Anyway, they'd brought the food, so Talmadge wasn't money out of pocket—yet.

What happened on the business side still remained to be seen.

"Right, then," he said when no one raised any objections to proceeding with the business at hand. "What kind of weapons are you looking at this time, and in what quantity?"

The delegation's spokesman held his fork poised over

spicy shrimp and noodles as he spoke. "Type 56 assault rifles," he said. "Five hundred. Type 79 sniper rifles, fifty."

Talmadge made the automatic translation in his mind. China's Type 56 autorifle was a direct steal from the Russian AK-47, with the addition of a hinged bayonet. The Type 79, likewise, was a carbon-copy of the old Soviet Dragunov SVD sniper rifle, complete with a factory-standard 4X scope that copied the Russian PSO model, with the same infrared capability.

Sometimes he wondered if there was one original thinker in all of the People's Republic of China. But, then again, he wasn't being paid this night for wit and wisdom.

Just results.

"What destination?" he inquired.

"Los Angeles," the triad mouthpiece answered.

He didn't question why the residents of gun-happy L.A. would need or want more deadly weapons. Motives weren't his business. Talmadge was a mover and a shaker, and he based his fees on risks entailed by different shipments.

"Both guns," he told his dinner guests, "are classified as assault weapons under the Clinton-era legislation banning importation, sale and ownership of same. On top of that, the state of California has a few laws of its own in place, concerning automatic weapons, this and that. It all adds up in court, say ten to twenty for a solid bust. It won't matter, in those quantities, if it's a first offense."

"How much?" the leader of the group inquired.

It galled Talmadge a little that they took his help for granted, at a price. But, then again, why shouldn't they? He'd never turned them down before, never refused a shipment or a deal, as long as someone in the gang met his demands for cold, hard cash.

He ran some numbers in his head before replying. It was cool to keep the tough guys waiting, sometimes, put them in their place, but subtly, without risking anything.

"A shipment of 550 pieces," he said at last, "at two thousand per, the current going rate, will bring no less than 1.1 million on the street. My fee is ten percent, which covers use of my connections in Los Angeles and transport from the docks within a two-mile radius. In the event of any mishaps while the guns are in my hands, you get a full refund, of course."

"But lose the weapons, yes?" a second triad member asked him from across the table. This one hadn't spoken earlier, though Talmadge had no trouble translating the frank suspicion on his face.

"In the event of confiscation by authorities, of course you lose the guns. I guarantee no leaks on my side of the operation. As for all your hundreds of employees, relatives and what have you…"

He left the sentence dangling, punctuated with a lazy shrug.

The triad gangster who had challenged him was fuming, but he kept it to himself. The mouthpiece shifted narrow eyes between them, finally announcing, "We accept your terms, Mr. Talmadge."

"And I thank you," Talmadge said, offering the slightest inclination of his head as if bowing. It never hurt to grease the Asian egos, after all.

Better to keep a friend than make an enemy—unless

he had a chance to make the enemy drop dead and disappear.

"When will the shipment be—?"

A strident buzzing interrupted him, a harsh insectile
sound. The downstairs intercom, announcing someone
who demanded his attention.

"Not more food, I hope," he joked with his assembled
guests, rising. "I'll be right back."

And he was halfway to the door when something
crashed behind him. Glass. Wineglasses?

No. A window.

Gene Talmadge was halfway to the floor, diving headlong, when the grenade exploded and his little dinner party
went to hell.

BOLAN HAD SCOPED the place on his approach, making a
slow drive-by, confirming what he saw by standing briefly
on the sidewalk, down below. There was a fire escape,
with access from the roof, and he could reach *that* roof in
turn from the apartment building immediately to the left,
or west, of his intended target.

Perfect.

Sketching out his final plans in sixty seconds flat, he'd
left Tom Dixon watching the front door, counting ten minutes on his synchronized wristwatch before Dixon began
to ring the buzzer up in Talmadge's apartment from its button down below. While that distracted Talmadge and his
guests, Bolan would make his entry from the fire escape,
and Dixon could proceed upstairs to close the vise.

Because he wanted Talmadge talking, even if the mercenary's guests would end up on morgue slabs, Bolan didn't start the square dance with a frag grenade. Instead, he used a special flash-bang with a kicker: blinding light and thunder for the shock-and-awe effect, plus scores of black hard-rubber balls the size of buckshot, a nonlethal brand of shrapnel that could knock a man sprawling.

The pitch was perfect. Bolan couldn't ask for better, with cascading glass and then the fat grenade, arcing across a smallish living room and bouncing once on impact with a low-slung coffee table, dropping to the floor from there and spinning in the no-man's-land between the living room and dining area, as if it were the pointer in some hard-core game of spin the bottle.

Bolan didn't see the flash. He had retreated far enough to spare himself its impact, but before the echoes reached buildings across the street, he was already clearing jagged glass out of the window frame, ducking inside.

The haze of mingled smoke and dust was long familiar to his eyes and to his nostrils. Plastic goggles kept his vision clear as Bolan circled slowly through the living room, toward the dining room. He'd find the triad gangsters there, or close at hand.

Someone cut loose at Bolan with an SMG. The first rounds whispered overhead and stitched an abstract pattern on the living-room ceiling, maybe punching through to give the upstairs neighbor a hot foot.

Instead of dropping to the floor, Bolan sidestepped and let the apartment's layout protect him. Six feet to his right, he was covered by a wall that screened the kitchen from the living room. It wasn't much, just lath and plaster, but he hoped the triad gunners wouldn't waste their ammunition if they couldn't spot a target.

Two shots from a pistol, drilling through the wall, made Bolan question his decision, but it stopped then, no great volley ripping everything apart. Half-crouching, with the Spectre in his hands and ready for all comers, Bolan shifted his attention toward the entryway, where Talmadge ought to be if the flash-bang had caught him moving toward the intercom beside the door.

Nothing.

Where was he, then?

Bolan was on a stranger's turf, and this time he was up against an enemy who shared his training, discipline and skills.

Plus six or seven angry Chinese mobsters.

It was Talmadge, though, who gave him pause. The need to bring him in alive for questioning.

Bolan heard Hal Brognola's haunting words again.

*"He's you."*

GENE TALMADGE WRIGGLED on his belly like a lizard, powering himself across the floor with fingers, elbows, knees and feet. He stayed below the thickest of the smoky haze that way, sparing his eyes, letting his iron-willed discipline suppress a hacking cough that would've led his unknown enemies directly to him.

Flash-bangs could've meant police, but Talmadge didn't think that was the case. Cops wouldn't wait this long, after the first icebreaker, to come smashing through the door in their Darth Vader uniforms, all guns and jackboots, bellowing instructions with the speed and clarity of auctioneers.

But if no cops, then who?

The problem with a mercenary's lifestyle, traveling year-round and dealing with a host of clients prone to violence, many of them raving paranoids, was that Talmadge never had a shortage of potential candidates who might desire to kill him.

Arabs, mobsters, someone from one of the countries where he'd fought and killed for money in a civil war or revolution. Any one or all of the above might have a motive for eliminating Talmadge.

Then again, he might not even *be* the target.

There were seven Chinese gangsters in his dining room—or had been, anyway, before the blast—whose syndicate fought ceaseless holding actions against rival triads, Russian mobsters and the Yakuza. For all that Talmadge knew, his apartment might've been chosen for a hit against his visitors. Nothing to do with him at all.

Fat chance.

The time to hit his guests, for maximum effect, would have been on the street, when they were piling out of cars and walking single-file up to his door. A shooter could've strafed them then. Two shooters could've caught them in a nifty cross fire, cutting them to ribbons on the sidewalk, without taking extra pains to destroy Talmadge's apartment.

No, they were after him, Talmadge acknowledged.

Which brought him back to who, but at the moment, Talmadge didn't give a damn. Survival was his top priority. Payback could wait.

He reached the narrow hallway leading to the bedrooms, one of which he occupied, the other being set aside for gear useful in situations like the present one. Talmadge had given up on praying as a child, but now he offered up a silent supplication to the god of fighting men, for help reaching his cache of gear in the guest room.

Behind him, more gunshots. Full-auto, followed by a pair of handguns, popping off in syncopated rhythm, too disorganized for anything resembling precision fire. He couldn't tell if anyone was firing back at the Chinese and didn't care.

Their deal was off, his fee a fading memory. The only payoff Talmadge wanted from this wasted evening was his life.

He reached the guest-room door and had no choice from there. He had to rise, crouching, and make a larger target of himself to open it, a vulnerable moment there, before he slipped inside and softly closed the door behind him. He locked it, buying himself at least a little time.

In retrospect, he should've worn the Kevlar vest to greet his dinner guests, but coulda-shoulda bullshit wouldn't save his life.

Safe for the moment, as brief as it might be, Talmadge shed his jacket, slipped into a vest, then back into the jacket. From the closet arsenal, he chose a SIG-Sauer P-226 self-loading pistol with a 20-round box magazine and wedged it down inside his belt, then pocketed spare magazines.

His next choice was a Steyr AUG assault rifle with forty-two rounds in its see-through plastic magazine, and two spares for his jacket pockets, balancing the load. He had a lockback folding knife already, and it felt like time to go.

Nothing in the apartment now was worth dying for. No cash in any serious amount, and Talmadge always kept his several active passports on his person or within arm's reach. As for his guests in their extremity…game over, man.

He jacked a round into the Steyr's chamber, thumbed the safety switch and turned his full attention to the nearby window.

Time to go.

TOM DIXON POUNDED UP the stairs, four flights to reach the second floor, passing a pair of tenants who recoiled and cowered from the mini-Uzi in his hand. He blurted something that he hoped would pacify them for the moment, nonsense with "quiet" and "police" to dissuade them rushing to a telephone.

But what did quiet matter, with the racket going on upstairs? Even if he could silence those two, who would stop the building's other tenants—or its neighbors—telephoning the police?

Dixon had no idea how many guns were firing now in Talmadge's apartment. Cooper had to have barged into a hornet's nest, and the grenade obviously hadn't served its purpose of subduing them. Now *he* was charging into that, with no idea what he should do upon arrival, other than attempting to survive.

He moved toward Talmadge's apartment, dodging tenants who were rushing toward the stairs, some of them barely dressed. More of them saw his weapon, women crying out or sobbing while the men tried to protect them, putting on a semblance of brave faces as they fled.

The door to Talmadge's apartment opened just as he arrived, a slender man framed in the opening with smoke or dust curling around him. Dixon dropped into a crouch, remembering Cooper's instruction not to kill the former Green Beret, but then he saw the figure in the doorway was Chinese.

One of the triad gunners, blinking at him now, was leveling a shiny automatic pistol.

Dixon fired a short burst from his SMG and saw the bullets strike his target, watched the man's silk shirt ripple with their impact, flushing crimson in a heartbeat as the man went down.

Dixon advanced to reach the threshold, where his adversary's body kept the door from closing. He remembered just in time to take the dead man's pistol, reach around and slip it underneath his belt, in back.

Cooper had told him not to leave a weapon for the enemy, and it made good sense. Besides, if he ran out of ammunition for the Uzi and his Smith & Wesson, now he would have a few more rounds to use in self-defense.

The apartment had seemingly been decorated by an individual who didn't give much thought to luxury and knew his time within those walls was limited. Not quite a crash pad, but it clearly wasn't home. The furniture was cheap, utilitarian and nothing Dixon hadn't seen a hundred times before.

A bullet whispered past his face, and Dixon hit the floor behind a low, square sofa, crawling toward the other end while slugs ripped through the cushions overhead. Someone had marked him coming in, but Dixon couldn't say if it was Talmadge or the triad gunners.

Either way, he had to do something—and soon—before they took him out.

There was an alcove ten or fifteen feet beyond the couch, some kind of spindly-legged table in it, holding up a telephone. He bolted for the niche, backhanded the flimsy table out of his way and dropped into a huddled crouch as bullets chipped the walls around him.

Christ! He would've traded damned near anything for one of Cooper's hand grenades just then, but having turned them down when there'd been time to pocket two or three, he'd have to do without.

One thing he knew for certain from the fusillade: if several men were firing at him, only one of them could possibly be Talmadge. That meant he was free to kill the rest in self-defense, if that proved possible.

But doing that, he realized, could get him killed.

JOHN LEE HEAPED SILENT CURSES on Talmadge, on his ancestors and on the day Talmadge had first made contact with the 14K Triad. If Talmadge hadn't fled to save himself, if he'd been standing there in front of Lee, Lee would have gunned him down without a second thought.

But Talmadge wasn't there, and now, two of Lee's four companions—his friends—were dead.

For what? To plan a shipment that would never happen, thanks to Talmadge and his unknown enemies.

Lee knew the shooters hadn't come for him because he'd glimpsed them both, a pair of round-eyes, and his triad had no quarrel with any of the white gangs in Vancouver or beyond. Their last clash with the Russians had been fourteen months earlier, and Lee knew that the truce was holding strong.

Which meant these gunmen came for Talmadge, catching Lee's small delegation in the cross fire. It was terminally unprofessional for Talmadge to convene a meeting at a time and place where he might be attacked. If Talmadge's opponents hadn't finished him already, John Lee meant to do the job.

He owed it to his triad brothers, to himself and to the bastard who'd betrayed them.

Lee fired the last two rounds from his first magazine toward a round-eye huddled in a corner of the small apartment's living room, then dumped the empty clip and took a fresh one from his pocket, slapping it into the grip of his Heckler & Koch P-7 pistol. Remembering to pocket the spent magazine with his fingerprints on it, Lee moved around behind the upturned dining table, edging past his two surviving comrades.

"Cover me," he ordered, speaking Mandarin in the assurance that his adversaries wouldn't understand it, even if they somehow heard his voice. His comrades nodded, poised with weapons ready for his move.

Lee didn't warn them, simply rose and rushed from cover toward the doorway where he'd last seen Talmadge. It was closed, locked from the inside when he got there, leaving him exposed to gunfire from his enemies. Crouching, he fired one of his pistol's thirteen rounds into the knob, then rushed the door and kicked it open, charging through to find his host.

Talmadge was halfway through the window, stepping

out onto the fire escape. Lee's sudden entry made him hesitate, turn awkwardly to face the doorway. As the round-eye turned, Lee saw the automatic rifle in his hands.

Lee fired instinctively, pointing instead of aiming, and he saw his first shot strike Talmadge with jolting impact, saw the white man grimace, but he still kept turning, as if pain and crippling injury weren't enough to stop him.

Lee fired two more shots, a hit beneath his target's left arm and a miss that gouged the window frame behind him. Even with a second mortal wound, however, Talmadge still controlled his automatic rifle, bringing it to bear on Lee.

Too late, Lee turned to run, and when the storm of 5.56 mm rounds broke over him it was too much. The bullets cut Lee's legs from under him with searing pain, then plunged him into darkness everlasting.

TALMADGE CURSED THE PAIN of bullet strikes against his Kevlar vest, and in the same breath blessed the fabric that had kept Lee's pistol shots from crippling him. He didn't give another thought to Lee, already dead or dying on the bedroom threshold, but the open door told him that time was wasting and he couldn't hang around to watch the show.

How many triad members remained alive? He didn't know and didn't care.

How many *others*? Never mind.

Who were the others?

That was something Talmadge had to answer for himself, before he found himself in trouble that he couldn't wriggle out of quite so easily.

But first he had to get away from there and save himself, while time remained.

He hustled down the fire escape, a short run down to ground level, with no one on his heels. Lee's men were good for something, even if he'd never see the color of their money on the arms deal he had been negotiating with the 14K Triad.

That was unfortunate, but there were always other weapons, other sources, other buyers. Violence made the world go 'round and kept Talmadge from going hungry in the process.

Out in front of his apartment building, neighbors he had never met were milling on the sidewalk, speaking excitedly. Some of them spilled into the street, obstructing traffic, but they didn't seem to notice Talmadge moving in the shadows, on the west side of the house.

His way was clear, if no one challenged him or glimpsed his weapon and alerted the police. Talmadge could hear a whoop of distant sirens, but he guessed the first patrol cars were at least five minutes out. He should be long gone by the time they reached the scene, unless his enemies had someone staking out his vehicle.

Slowing, Talmadge approached the parking area he shared with other tenants of the building. There was no one covering the vehicles, as far as he could tell, but Talmadge still moved cautiously to reach his Saturn four-door. Nothing flashy, just a car that took him where he had to go and back again reliably.

Right now, he needed it to take him out of Gastown and away from his enemies.

No challenge came as Talmadge neared his vehicle, keeping the AUG well down against his leg and out of sight from any passersby. He had the parking lot all to himself, while tenants from surrounding houses ran around in front to watch the action.

Morons, he thought. One day, before too long, reality would swing around and bite them all on their collective lazy ass.

And he would be a part of it.

He palmed the Saturn's key, thumbed the door-opener and heard the latch pop on the driver's door. Another moment put him in his seat, behind the wheel, and he relaxed a little when he heard the engine purr. Easing the Saturn into motion, Talmadge put the parking lot behind him, watched his speed along the alley and merged with traffic on the nearest side street.

Sirens were closer now, and plenty of them, but they'd come too late to trap him. Maybe they'd do him a favor and corral his would-be killers, take them out with SWAT teams and let Talmadge read about it in his morning paper.

Either way, the flat was lost to him, and he'd be forced to fall back on one of his alternate identities. It had been careless, using his own name to rent the place, but at the time there'd been no reason to believe that anyone was looking for him.

Who? And why?

Two questions Talmadge knew he'd have to answer, if he hoped to stay alive and carry out his mission.

And he didn't plan on letting anybody stop him.

Not while he had strength enough to pull a trigger.

BOLAN WAS WATCHING when the leader of the triad group bought it, dropping in the doorway of the bedroom where he'd burst in shooting, seconds earlier. Since neither Bolan nor Tom Dixon occupied that room, Bolan surmised that Talmadge and his dinner guests had undergone a sudden falling-out.

Sorry to wreck the party, boys, he thought, and darted toward the open doorway where the Chinese mobster lay.

But the survivors in the dining room had something else in mind for him. They started firing at him when he broke from cover, both of them with semiauto pistols. Bolan ducked and rolled, with no place to hide once he began his run, and came up firing with his Spectre, set for three-round bursts.

His weapon had a fifty-round box magazine, and Bolan reckoned he was ten or twelve rounds down when he began to duel the shooters in the dining room. His first burst from the floor was simply meant to drive them under cover, stitching holes across the upturned table where they hid. Since he was loading military rounds, full-metal jackets, they punched through and slapped the wall beyond, keeping the gunners down.

Bolan was on his feet again before they dared to risk another volley, ready for the enemy as they showed themselves. He triggered two more bursts, watching the table sprout new holes, while both of the Chinese gunners were pumping desperate rounds his way. One of them took a hit, staggered, but kept on firing as he clutched his chest. The other ducked and dodged, then recoiled in surprise as Dixon started firing at him from his right.

Bolan and Dixon had the last triad survivors in a cross fire now, blasting away with everything they had. Bolan unloaded on the nearer of them with another three-round burst, aiming, and saw a portion of his target's skull detach with crimson mist exploding from his hairline.

Swinging toward the last man up, he was in time to see Dixon drop his man, two shockers from his Smith & Wesson ripping through the triad gunner's chest to drop him in a lifeless heap.

"Talmadge?" Dixon asked as he closed in toward the dining room.

"In there," Bolan said, moving toward the open bedroom doorway.

There was no one left to stop him this time as he peered around the doorjamb, standing over Talmadge's late dinner guest. As Bolan scanned the room beyond, he saw no sign of life, but marked the open window that admitted wailing siren sounds.

Dixon came up behind him, careful not to stand too close. "Where is he?"

"In the wind," Bolan said as he crossed the threshold, probing corners as he verified his first impression. He found weapons in the open closet, ammunition boxed on shelves by caliber, but Talmadge had already taken what he needed from the place.

"Goddamn it!" Dixon swore behind him. "Not again!"

Bolan shared his frustration, leaning through the open

window, peering down the fire escape. A corner apartment
had its advantages. Talmadge had clambered down the
metal staircase Bolan had rejected for his means of entry,
since it offered no view of the dining or living room.

"Gone," he said. "And so are we."

"We've got the law downstairs," Dixon remarked.

"No time to waste, then. Follow me and keep your
weapons out of sight."

He left the apartment as Talmadge had, hearing the
clang of metal steps beneath his feet. Anger teamed with
frustration, gnawing at his nerves, while Bolan scanned the
alley in both directions, watching out for cops.

Another miss, and he was running out of freebies.

If they didn't collar Talmadge soon, they might not have
another chance.

"Okay, what now?" Dixon asked when they were on
level ground and moving toward their car.

"We look for help," Bolan replied, "where East meets
West."

## CHAPTER EIGHT

*Chinatown, Vancouver*

Joseph Lee was ninety seconds late. He walked into the conference room alone, after the other delegates were seated, and his tardy entrance struck the others dumb.

So many things to talk about, and now they were afraid to speak.

The godfather of Chinatown was never late. None of the dozen men seated around the polished hardwood table could recall a single incident where Lee had kept them waiting. Each of them had rushed from home or from their social functions instantly, when they were summoned to the midnight meeting.

None of them was late, and when their leader missed his self-imposed deadline by ninety seconds, none of them felt any sense of triumph or superiority.

Instead, they were afraid.

Whatever caused a ripple in their master's schedule, even ninety seconds' worth, had to be severe indeed.

The dozen men who greeted Lee with silent bows were all "red poles," lieutenants, in the 14K Triad. Among them, they had some four hundred years' experience of smuggling drugs, weapons and human beings; slaying enemies and hiding corpses; bribing politicians; gambling; and whatever else went into managing a criminal empire. All had survived brutal gang wars, emerging with blood on their hands and scars on their souls.

But none was certain he would live to see another day.

When Lee was comfortably seated, a carafe of water at his elbow, he began. "My brother was assassinated," he informed them, "at approximately 9:18 this evening."

The news caused a collective gasp, but no spoken response. None of the red poles questioned the precision of Lee's "approximate" time.

"With John, at my request," Lee forged ahead, "were six more brothers. All are dead now, murdered while performing duties for the clan."

This time a low-pitched murmur made its way around the conference table. Lee waited until it had made the circuit, coming back to him, and then stopped short because the man immediately to his left had no one else to tell.

"Some of you know the man our brothers went to meet," Lee said. "His name is Eugene Talmadge. He's American. For those who don't know it already, we have—or, rather, *had*—a mutual interest in movement of weapons from China, through Canada to the United States. Tonight, John and the rest were meeting Talmadge to arrange the details of another shipment. Now, our brothers have been slaughtered and the round-eye is missing."

The muttering grew louder, each red pole attempting to outdo the others with his show of indignation, promises of long, slow retribution against any man who dared to harm the 14K, much less eliminate Lee's brother.

If the situation had been different, some two or three of them talking among themselves, secure in private, their attitudes might have been different. But none of them would dare to tell the godfather of Chinatown that his late brother was an arrogant and overbearing ass who likely got what he deserved and took some good men with him to the grave. Among the triad members present, eight or nine at least were glad to see John Lee removed from access to the seat of power, while the rest were secretly indifferent.

Six other deaths, however, meant something to all of them.

"Do you believe this Talmadge killed all seven?" Thomas Cho inquired. He was the oldest man present and a personal adviser to the godfather.

"It is logical to think so," Lee replied, "since they were murdered at his home. However, the police say that the killers used at least three different guns—and that they threw a stun grenade into the flat from outside, on the fire escape."

"Perhaps a ruse," Cho said, "diverting our attention from the round-eye."

"Possibly," Lee said, "but Talmadge telephoned me to deliver his condolences, and to explain that he is innocent. His call delayed me from arriving here on time."

That news produced a babble, silenced only when the godfather of Chinatown raised his hand, commanding their attention.

"I anticipate your questions and objections," Lee pressed on. "It is entirely possible that Talmadge lied and was responsible for murdering our brothers, though his motives at the moment are obscure. He has earned money with and from our family. The new transaction would have benefited all concerned. If he betrayed us, we must find out why."

"He is a round-eye," Robert Ng observed. "They can't be trusted."

"Talmadge is a thoroughly corrupt round-eye," Lee said. "As far as I can tell, he has no loyalty to his homeland or to anyone except himself. If he betrayed us, it means he received a better offer from one of our enemies. We need to find out who has hired him, in that case, and punish them accordingly."

A rumble of agreement greeted that decree.

"He told me something else, as well," Lee stated. Silence descended on the table as he said, "Talmadge described the killers as two round-eyes, strangers he had never seen before. If that is true, we must identify them, find out who employed them, what they want."

"And if he lied?" Cho asked.

"We'll find out when we question him. For that, he must be found and kept alive. Hear me! The man who kills Talmadge without my order takes his place for punishment. A thousand cuts will only be the start of what he suffers. Are we clear on this?"

The red poles nodded, mumbling assent like members of a ragtag chorus. Pinning each in turn with hard eyes, Joseph Lee soon satisfied himself that all had heard and understood his message.

"Go, then," he commanded. "And let no man sleep until our brothers are avenged!"

"YOU'RE KIDDING, right?" Tom Dixon asked.

Bolan responded with a slow shake of his head. "I'm absolutely serious."

"So, let me get this straight. We've already got Talmadge and al Qaeda on our plate, but now we're taking on a triad, too?"

"Unless you've got a better way to locate Talmadge," Bolan said. "If so, I'm listening."

"A better way? Is there a worse way? We just killed six triad hardmen at his place. Talmadge shot one himself. I don't think he'll be on the best of terms with them right now."

"Better for us," Bolan replied.

"How do you figure that?"

"Simple. The triad was in bed with Talmadge, business-wise, until we blew their gig tonight. They must've had some way to get in touch with him, when he wasn't at home."

"Likely a cell phone," Dixon said.

"Which beats what we have now."

"The problem with that logic," Dixon said, "is that they either want to bury him right now, or at the very least grill him to find out what went down. In either case, I doubt they'll want to share."

"Don't underestimate the power of persuasion," Bolan said.

Dixon went through a little pantomime of turning in his seat, looking around the inside of their rented car, before he said, "It doesn't look like we've got anything to trade right now."

"We will have," Bolan told him.

"Oh? Like what?"

"Security and peace of mind. They'll be in short supply among the triads of Vancouver pretty soon."

"So, that would be your plan?

"They'll tell us what we want to know," said Bolan, "when they've lost enough and hurt enough."

"And this has worked for you before?"

"I've never seen it fail."

"You're talking just the two of us, I take it? Against— what? A couple hundred triad gunners in Vancouver?"

"I'm not planning pitched battles," Bolan said. "Hit-and-run does the trick more often than not."

"And they fold? Guys like this?"

"When they're broken, they fold."

"What's Talmadge doing while we run around Vancouver taking on the Chinese?"

"Whatever brought him here *besides* the triads," Bolan said. "That's why we need to pin him down ASAP."

"After the set-to at his place," Dixon replied, "I don't think we'll be getting any more assistance from the Mounties, never mind the local cops."

"I've got it covered," Bolan said.

"That call you made?" Dixon asked.

"Right."

If Hal Brognola couldn't get the names and addresses he needed, via Stony Man, they could be up the creek.

"It's funny," Dixon said. "I don't know whether I should

hope your source comes through or not. One way, we're in hot water with the triads, and the other—"

"We lose Talmadge," Bolan finished for him.

"Damn. I wish that guy back in Jakarta could've given up a name for Talmadge's contact."

"That's need-to-know in action," Bolan said. "Somebody cut him from the loop for just that reason, and it's slowed us down accordingly."

"Goddamned al Qaeda," Dixon grumbled. "Always inconsiderate, that way."

"Don't give up yet," Bolan replied. "With any luck, I'll have the information that we need in half an hour, maybe less. Then we can introduce ourselves and start negotiating. Any luck at all, we'll have a link to Talmadge in the next few hours."

"He could be down in the States by then," Dixon pointed out.

"Not without whatever he was sent to pick up in Vancouver," Bolan countered. "If he doesn't have it yet, smart money says he won't leave town without it."

"And if it was waiting for him on arrival? Then what?"

"Then I have to ask myself why he was spending time with triads at his apartment, when he had other work to do."

"I hadn't thought of that," Dixon admitted.

"It's just a thought," Bolan said.

"Something, anyway."

Bolan refrained from saying that he had his fingers crossed, hoping that he was right and Talmadge hadn't fled Vancouver in the wake of the firefight at his apartment. Losing him again could put a fatal crimp in Bolan's plans, if Talmadge had the weapon he'd come looking for. If he was off and running with the dirty bomb, there was no realistic hope that they could stop him short of entry to the States. No reason to suppose that Talmadge wouldn't detonate the bomb as planned by his employers.

When and where?

Only the man himself could tell them that, assuming they could find him, pin him down before he triggered a device that made the 9/11 raids seem like a minor inconvenience for America.

Bolan had given up on wondering what would provoke a former Green Beret to turn against his nation and his people. The Oklahoma City bombers had been U.S. soldiers, too, but service to the flag hadn't prevented them from loading up a Ryder truck with fuel oil and fertilizer, parking it outside a federal building back in April 1995.

That blast, propelled by racism and paranoid obsession with the New World Order, had destroyed more than 160 lives. The kind of bombing Eugene Talmadge had in mind would number victims in the tens of thousands—maybe higher, if the bomb was large enough, dirty enough, strategically located for its drift to do the maximum potential damage.

Armageddon in a suitcase, coming to a shopping mall near you.

Unless the Executioner could stop it.

And doing that meant taking on a triad, in a city where the Chinese syndicate had deep, malignant roots.

No problem, Bolan thought. All he and Dixon had to do was stay alive, somehow, and beat the odds.

Before the clock ran down and there was no time left.

*Washington, D.C.*

HAL BROGNOLA CHECKED the wall clock in his office and subtracted three hours for Pacific Standard Time. It was getting late, no matter how he calculated it, but he was known at Justice as an officer who sometimes burned the midnight oil and gave the cleaning people fits because he wouldn't let them in his office while he worked.

Like now.

Brognola didn't care if they were hovering or having coffee, checking out or rolling up the overtime. His work was classified by definition, and he wouldn't have cleaners barging in when he was on the telephone with Bolan, running down a lead from Stony Man, issuing orders to the men of Able Team or Phoenix Force.

The carpet and trash could wait.

But he'd collected all the answers Stony Man could give him at the moment, working from its files and any covert hack jobs Aaron Kurtzman's whiz kids had performed on data banks belonging to the FBI, the CIA and Interpol.

Brognola now knew more about the triads in Vancouver and environs than he'd ever wanted to. What was it Sherlock Holmes had said to Watson on their first meeting, when Watson told him Earth revolved around the sun?

"Now that I know, I shall have to forget it," or words to that effect.

Like Holmes, Brognola only had so much room in his mental files for information he might never use again. He likely wouldn't need to know the addresses or the unlisted phone numbers of Joseph Lee and his assorted red poles, or the name and address of the strip clubs owned by triads in Vancouver, where the tough guys spent their nights away from home, when they weren't smuggling heroin or killing someone for the hell of it.

Brognola would be just as happy to forget all that, assuming he could pull it off.

There was one positive note, he decided: once Bolan received the addresses, odds were fair to good that some of the triad gangsters, their houses and watering holes would no longer exist. Brognola knew that Bolan wasn't beefing up his Christmas list, but rather choosing targets. His brief explanation on the telephone, an hour earlier, had answered all the big Fed's basic questions on the change of focus in his mission, but Brognola worried all the same.

He was afraid that Talmadge might've given Bolan and his pal from DHS the slip.

And with him, possibly, had gone the dirty bomb.

It was the nightmare of the new millennium, though terrorists and those who stalked them had been fretting over suitcase nukes for thirty years or more. One man with knowledge and resources, one man with the determination to succeed, could visit Hiroshima's curse on any major city of the world, for any reason that excited or amused him. The technology had been available for decades, as had quantities of weapons-grade materials required to make the bombs and guarantee a catastrophic wave of fallout.

Brognola spoke from time to time with experts in the field, and most of them were surprised that it hadn't happened already. The Soviet Union's collapse had put weapons, technicians and soldiers on the black market at prices an oil-rich sheikh or a drug-cartel ruler could easily afford. In this age of creeds and causes run amok, why hadn't someone, somewhere, gone all the way to Hell on Earth?

When others posed that question, Brognola could only shrug, make sympathetic noises and attempt to steer the conversation in a new direction. He couldn't explain that several groups and individuals had come close to triggering an outlaw nuke and setting off the catastrophic chain reaction that was bound to follow any such event.

Because a dirty blast would never be the end of it. Suspects would be identified, accused and hunted down. The aftermath of 9/11 would seem positively puny by comparison. If someone in authority identified—or *mis*identified— the culprits as, say, Russians or Chinese, the end result could be a global holocaust.

That's why the Nuclear Emergency Search Team responded to fifteen or twenty calls per year, the vast majority of them patently bogus. That's why Stony Man Farm was on constant alert for the first hint of WMDs in the hands of rogue nations or terrorist groups.

And that's why Bolan was in rainy Vancouver, getting ready for a deadly game of Chinese checkers that, with any luck, would tell him where to find his missing quarry.

Soon, rather than later, was the key.

They knew—or *thought* they knew, based on the declaration of an Arab terrorist—that Talmadge was in Canada to take delivery of a dirty bomb. It seemed unlikely that a die-hard mercenary would deliver that package himself, and that in turn meant that their target had another contact somewhere down the road.

Maybe a middleman. Maybe the "righteous martyr" who would walk the package into some government building, crowded shopping mall or downtown public park.

Like Central Park, for instance. Or the Mall, in Washington, D.C. Why not Grand Central Station or Times Square?

Hell, why not anywhere?

If they lost Talmadge, then they lost the bomb. And that would mean they lost the game.

And Brognola wouldn't permit that kind of tragedy to happen on his watch.

Dialing the number of an old friend's sat phone, with the urgently requested information spread in front of him, Brognola hoped that he wasn't too late.

*Chinatown, Vancouver*

"OKAY," TOM DIXON SAID, when his partner broke the sat link to his headquarters, wherever that might be, and pocketed his telephone. "What now?"

"As planned," Bolan replied, "I have another call to make. Depending on how that one goes, we'll either get the information that we need or else we won't."

"I'm guessing won't." Dixon tried not to sound as glum as he was feeling at the moment, or to show the tingling undercurrent of excitement, either. "What's the drill when the Chinese won't play along?"

"If that's the case," Bolan said, "then we'll have to shake some people up, rattle their cages, maybe blow their houses down."

"You got a list of targets on the phone just now?" Dixon inquired.

"Potential targets. Right."

"I noticed you weren't taking any kind of notes."

"I have a fairly decent memory," Bolan said. "Anyway, you never know when notes will fall into the wrong hands, maybe cause more trouble than they're worth."

"So how much information are we talking here?"

"Not much," Bolan replied. "Say half a dozen names, addresses, phone numbers."

"Not much, eh?"

"We can get more as we go along," the Executioner assured him.

"Do we plan to make this a crusade, by any chance?"

"That's not our call. The other side can nip it in the bud. Just give us Talmadge or a way to find him, and we're out of here."

"You think they'll play?" Dixon asked.

"Only one way to find out."

"Okay, then. Who's on first?"

"I'm starting at the top. The leader of the local triad clan is Joseph Lee, from Hong Kong. He'll have the authority to finger Talmadge, if he wants to play. There's no point messing with a middleman."

"So, you just call him up and—"

"That's the plan," Bolan said, dialing as he drove through traffic in the heart of Chinatown.

Dixon sat staring at the lights and people on the street, eavesdropping on Cooper's one-sided conversation.

"Put me through to Joseph Lee," the tall man said. A

brief delay, then, "Tell him I'm the one who crashed his Gastown dinner party earlier tonight." Another second passed. "Just *tell* him, or get ready to explain how you decided he should miss this one-time-only call."

A longer stall this time, dead silence in the car until Dixon surmised that Joseph Lee was on the line.

"My name isn't important," Bolan said. "The one you need to focus on is Eugene Talmadge.... No? I thought you'd be familiar with him from your business dealings. He was at the dinner bash this evening, but I missed my chance to say hello.... That's *your* concern because I can't leave town until I've met him."

Dixon had a fair idea of what the triad leader must be saying on the other end. Cooper's replies seemed to confirm it.

"My offer's simply this," he said. "Give me the contact information I require, and life goes on for you as usual. If not…"

Something made Cooper frown then. When he finished listening, he said, "Your call," and broke the link.

"No sale, I take it," Dixon said.

"We hit a snag," Bolan told him.

"Something in particular, besides you calling up to threaten him?"

"Lee's brother."

"What about him?"

"He was one of the triad gunners at Talmadge's apartment."

"Oh." Dixon experienced a sinking feeling in his gut. "So it's a blood feud, then?"

"Whatever," Bolan said. "It doesn't change our plans."

Except that now the triad will be working overtime to take us out, Dixon thought. But he said, "We'll need to watch our backs, then."

"Always." Bolan took his eyes off traffic for a moment, glancing over as he asked his passenger, "Are you still up for this, or would you rather take a pass?"

"I'm on assignment," Dixon told him.

"That's no answer."

"If you knew my boss—"

"My boss can get you reassigned. Trust me on that."

"No, thanks," Dixon replied so quickly that he half surprised himself. "I've come this far. I'll see it through."

"Be sure," Bolan said. "After we commit on this one, you won't get another chance to bail."

"I'm in. That's it."

"Okay. Your call."

"Who are we hitting first? This Joseph Lee?"

"He'll be mobbed up," Bolan said, "sitting in a hardsite somewhere, waiting for it. I'd prefer to hit him where he least expects it. Take him by surprise, as much as possible."

"We blew that, calling him," Dixon said. He felt charitable, using *we,* when it was Cooper's plan. His show.

"I had to try it," Bolan said. "Give him a chance to wrap it up the easy way."

"And now?"

"We scan the list of targets and decide who gets the ax."

# CHAPTER NINE

*Richmond, British Columbia*

Gene Talmadge parked on Cambie Road and walked a long block south to Richmond Park. His drive across the north arm of the Fraser River hadn't really helped relax him, but the jangling nerves felt good, reminding him of the run-up to battle, when he always felt truly alive.

Moving through early-morning darkness, Talmadge kept his eyes peeled for an ambush and for Richmond's nosy cops. He wasn't in the mood for any field interrogations, and the Steyr AUG beneath his jacket guaranteed that any interview with the police would be a brief one, terminated at his own discretion.

Losing his Vancouver apartment and the triad munitions deal annoyed him, made him wish that he could punish someone for the rude intrusion. Maybe later, when he had been able to identify his enemy. Meanwhile, he had important business to conduct and little time to spare.

The pass was scheduled for that afternoon, the merchandise already safe and sound, so Talmadge had been able to revise the time and place with a quick phone call. Word of the blowout at his apartment was already a topic of discussion in the local underworld, and while his contact was initially suspicious, Talmadge spoke a code word that confirmed nobody had a pistol pointed at his head.

And so the meeting time was changed, nine hours cut from the schedule, bringing up forward from noon to 3:00 a.m. Instead of meeting on the ferry, as originally planned, Talmadge had picked the park entirely on a whim. If guns were waiting for him, at least he wouldn't die alone.

This was the tricky part—or, rather, one of them. Taking delivery of the first component left him vulnerable for the rest of his forthcoming journey, but he'd minimize the risk by driving, shunning any form of public transportation until he had made the drop in Minnesota. After that, it was a waiting, watching game, and maybe he'd have time to think about the bastards who had trashed his apartment.

His call to Joseph Lee had been perfunctory, a mixture of the truth and lies designed to spare himself from being hunted by the triad when he needed space and privacy the most. He had explained to Lee about the two round-eye intruders, leaving out the part where *he* had shot Lee's brother in the bedroom doorway, but he got a feeling that the triad leader didn't really give a damn. Once family had been insulted, much less killed, there was a certain vengeance ritual to be observed.

Good thing I'm getting out of town, Talmadge thought, as he neared the park. A few more minutes, and with any luck he would be driving eastward, leaving B.C. and its angry triad behind him.

Not that his departure would prevent Lee looking for him far and wide. The triad had long arms and longer memories. But Talmadge would burn that bridge when he came to it, after he'd carried out his primary mission.

After that, nothing would ever be the same again.

His name might be forgotten in the chaos that ensued, or someone might remember and come looking for him, if they had the wherewithal. In either case, Talmadge would be prepared.

And they would have to find him first, before they could attempt to punish him.

On entering the park, he moved directly toward the reserved children's area. There, among the swings and teeter-totters, Talmadge waited patiently, allowing his contact to study him and verify that he had come alone. At last, a low-pitched whistle from the shadows pooled beneath a nearby copse alerted Talmadge to his contact's presence and position.

He responded with a hand sign, whereupon a slender man of middle age and Arabic descent emerged from darkness to approach him. His contact, Aman Nadir, was carrying a bulky case, its normal shiny surface painted matte-black in a bid to make it less conspicuous. Talmadge could see that it was heavy, from the way it dragged Nadir's left shoulder down and threw his body out of balance.

Even now, Nadir still kept his right hand free to reach the pistol tucked inside his belt.

As if a gun could help him now.

"That's it?" Talmadge asked as his contact set the bag down on the grass.

"As ordered," Nadir replied.

"And we're all square on payment?"

"This is for the cause," Nadir reminded him. "I take expenses only."

"Right. And the lead shields are all in place?"

That made the Arab smile. "Don't fret about your unborn children. Someday, they may thank you for your service to God."

Talmadge, who had no wish for children, was concerned about survival if the contents of the case hadn't been insulated properly. Eyeing Aman Nadir, however, he supposed the Arab hadn't taken any chances with his own life or his procreative capacities.

"All right, then." Talmadge stepped up to the bag and hefted it. The steel framework and leaden lining easily outweighed the two-pound payload locked inside. Talmadge was ready for the weight and gave no outward sign of feeling it across his shoulders, in his lower back.

"In case we do not meet again—" Nadir began.

"We won't."

"—may God bless your enterprise and lay his enemies before you, dressed for slaughter."

"Amen, brother."

Talmadge turned and walked away without a backward glance, leaving Nadir to watch him if he chose, or to retreat and let the shadows swallow him. He stayed alert during the walk back to his car, and stowed the case inside its trunk. A moment later, he was at the wheel and rolling toward the airport.

In another hour, he'd be airborne, flying eastward.

Toward the sunrise.

Toward a day of reckoning.

*Winnipeg, Manitoba*

MUHUNNAD HASHIM SAT in a borrowed car with stolen license plates and waited for the man who had been sent to help him change the world. The car was borrowed from his nephew, therefore safe. The license plates, six months in storage since they had been stolen from a minivan outside the Unicity Mall, were likewise "cold" and safe. None of the passersby appeared to notice Hashim or his vehicle as he sat waiting in the parking lot outside the Fort Whyte Nature Center, near the junction of McCreary Road and McGillivray Boulevard.

Hashim had chosen the meeting place well. The nature center hosted steady streams of tourists, school field trips and local families with children on the weekends. There was never any trouble at the center, and security was light, the uniformed attendants more familiar with lost children than with desperate fugitives.

They wouldn't know about the trouble in Vancouver— or, if some of them had listened to the news on television overnight, they wouldn't draw a link to Winnipeg, some fourteen hundred miles due east from where the gang-related killings had occurred.

Why should they?

What connection could be drawn between a pack of

Chinese gangsters on the coast and Hashim's mission, even if the fools around him knew of his affiliation with al Qaeda? To the best of Hashim's knowledge, there *was* no connection, other than his contact's tendency to overreach himself.

Talmadge was loyal to the cause. If Hashim doubted that, he would've been prepared to use the stubby MP-5 K submachine gun lying on the seat beside him, hidden underneath a folded newspaper. Nothing, no one, would be allowed to jeopardize the mission at its present stage.

No, the American was loyal, but he also dealt with other factions on the side, to make his daily bread and a bit more besides. Greed was a sin in God's eyes, but Talmadge had the skills and contacts necessary to complete the job al Qaeda had in mind.

And, more importantly, he had the will.

Whatever had been done to him, turning the soldier bitterly against his native land and people, Muhunnad Hashim was grateful for it. An American so highly trained and worldly wise was vital to this blow against the Great Satan.

And if the gangster scum of China, Canada or some other benighted nation died along the way, what of it? They deserved no less.

Hashim checked his watch, then double-checked the time with his car's dashboard clock. Forty-two minutes had elapsed since Talmadge's phone call, telling Hashim that he was safely on the ground at Winnipeg's airport. Allowing time to claim his hired car and consult a street map, find his way across the river and south from there, Talmadge should be arriving just about...

Now.

Hashim recognized Talmadge despite his baseball cap and mirrored sunglasses, steering a small Ford sedan into a parking space some fifty feet away from where Hashim sat waiting. The American got out, opened his trunk, hoisted a black bag in one hand and closed the lid again. Scanning the lot for any witnesses who might seem overly attentive to his movements, Talmadge crossed the pavement, nearing Hashim's car.

Hashim reached down beside his seat and found the trunk latch, tracking Talmadge all the while by his reflection in the rearview mirror. When the trunk slammed shut, Hashim unlocked the doors and drew the SMG with its concealing newspaper closer beside him, making room for Talmadge.

"I'd begun to think you might be lost," Hashim told the American by way of greeting.

"Traffic slowed me down," Talmadge replied.

It was the closest they had ever come to courtesy, these warriors from two different worlds.

"You have the other gear you need?" Talmadge asked.

"All is ready. You have brought the last component."

"How long for assembly, then?"

"If I begin immediately, with precautions to avoid irradiation…say three hours."

Talmadge checked his watch and nodded. "Fair enough. We don't want any nasty accidents."

"There will be none."

"What kind of timer are you using?" Talmadge asked.

"There is no timer."

"Ah."

Hashim studied the other's face, looking for any intimation of disdain. Americans had never truly grasped the concept of a martyr's love for God and for his people. They revered soldiers who threw themselves upon grenades to save their comrades in the heat of battle, but were shocked that anyone might wrap his body in explosives to ensure destruction of a deadly enemy.

Such hypocrites!

"Do you prefer to follow me, or meet later?" Hashim inquired.

"I'll tag along but keep my distance," Talmadge said. "Watching for tails and all. I also need to reach out to our other friend. You won't want that call on our records."

"No."

"All right, then. Give me five, and I'll be right behind you."

"Yes."

Hashim watched Talmadge go, didn't touch his ignition key until the gruff American was in his car and ready. Then Hashim backed out and navigated through the parking lot to find the exit on McCreary Road.

He had a twenty-minute drive in front of him, to reach the small apartment off St. Vital Park, where his workshop waited for him. There, he had begun construction on a weapon that would humble Washington and teach al Qaeda's enemies around the world that they couldn't ignore the will of God with impunity.

Judgment was coming, and it made Hashim sinfully proud to be a part of it.

TRAILING HASHIM'S VEHICLE east along Wilkes Avenue, Talmadge paid more attention to his rearview mirror than to the sights of Winnipeg around him. He absorbed the major landmarks out of habit, trained to plot escape routes every time he blazed a trail across new territory, but the city didn't interest him.

He was, however, curious about the bomb maker.

Talmadge had known fanatics in his time. Some were the kind who ranted before raging crowds, while others were the quiet sort who wove their webs in secret, plotting the destruction of their enemies without a hint of what was coming. Some weren't averse to suicide, while others chose the men and women who would sacrifice themselves. It took all kinds to keep a world in flames, and Talmadge had served most of them at one time or another.

Until someone made an offer he could not refuse.

Revenge *and* profit. Who, in his right mind, wouldn't have been seduced?

The money was important, but the more he thought about it, Talmadge was convinced he might've done the job for nothing if the opportunity had been presented to him as a work of charity. It was his own good fortune that the men who needed him were also well financed by sultans of petroleum, provided with the best equipment money could obtain.

A shoestring operation would've offered no real prospect of success, and Talmadge wasn't into backing losers. He had been one, had his nose rubbed in it by the officers he'd trusted to stand up for him if need be, and the role of outcast scapegoat didn't suit him.

He preferred the mantle of avenging angel every time.

After the better part of half an hour's driving, Talmadge watched Hashim park in the shadow of a small apartment building, near another river. Talmadge drove past and found a curbside parking space two blocks away. He couldn't see Hashim's place, but he'd know if the police arrived with flashing lights and sirens wailing.

And he'd damned sure know if anything went wrong inside the bomb maker's workshop.

Palming his cell phone, Talmadge tapped a number out from memory and listened to it ring three hundred miles away. His contact had been forewarned to remain at home or take his cell phone with him anywhere he went so that he wouldn't miss a vital call.

Like this one.

Halfway through the third ring came, "Hello?"

Though fluent in English, the contact hadn't lost his accent yet. And never would.

He didn't have the time.

"It's me," Talmadge said. "You alone?"

"Of course."

They always played the game, establishing security parameters, although they never spoke a word on open lines that would alert the NSA or anybody else who might be eavesdropping for fun or profit. Talmadge knew the Feds could pick a million conversations from the air at any given time, sort through them at the speed of light for trigger words or phrases, but he never gave the prying bastards anything to puzzle over.

"Are you ready?" he inquired.

"I am." His contact sounded proud, excited.

"Good. I'll be there soon. Tonight sometime, maybe tomorrow. I'll call when I get into town."

"I'll be here."

"Later, then."

Talmadge broke the connection. He hadn't talked long enough for anyone to triangulate and trace his cell phone, even if they tried. Nothing for damned sure that would lead them to his contact in the States.

No way.

Talmadge wasn't about to jeopardize his mission at this stage. Not when it promised to deliver so much satisfaction, all on top of his substantial fee.

Who said you couldn't eat your cake and have it, too?

Something about that saying nagged at him. Of course, you had to *have* the cake before you *ate* it. How could it be otherwise? But if you turned the thing around...

His rearview mirror showed a blue-and-white patrol car coming up behind him, moving slowly while the driver and his sidekick eyeballed license plates, pedestrians, whatever cops were trained to scrutinize on a routine drive-by.

Talmadge resisted the impulse to slump in his seat or try to hide. Such action was suspicious in itself, and granted cause for them to stop and question him, maybe to search his vehicle. Start out looking for weed or pills and find a well-armed killer when they least expected it.

Talmadge could take them both, no doubt about it, but he didn't have the finished package yet, and any heat he caused here might direct the law to Muhunnad Hashim. The bomb maker was useful, and might be again.

Instead of hiding, then, he took a street map from the

seat beside him, opened it and focused his attention on the printed maze in front of him. He felt, rather than saw, the prowl car slowly pass his vehicle, resisted the temptation to glance over at the officers and smile.

He heard a crackle from the squad car's radio, then it moved on. When it was gone, Talmadge folded the map and settled back to wait, with one hand on the SIG-Sauer pistol in his lap.

*St. Paul, Minnesota*

AFIF MUKHTAR HAD WAITED all his life for just this moment, knowing in his heart exactly how he'd feel. There was excitement, pride, a sense of resignation to his destiny. The one surprise for him was a suggestion of regret over the things he hadn't seen or done.

But God would make all that up to him in Paradise.

Afif Mukhtar hadn't been raised to play a martyr's role in the jihad. His parents, although Muslims, were the soul of moderation, always quick to shake their heads and cluck their tongues when tales of Arab terrorism filled their forty-eight-inch television screen. They had been visibly concerned, some two years earlier, when he—their only child—began to frequent a small mosque in Minneapolis, whose imam was a radical.

In fact, he proved to be the savior of Afif Mukhtar.

Without that good man's guidance, how would Mukhtar know the things that he had learned about America and its oppressive role throughout the world? He never would've found his voice or raised it in protest against the Great Satan.

Mukhtar had been surprised when the imam took him aside and asked him certain questions cleverly designed to test his faith. By then, Mukhtar had found his roots and passed the test with no great difficulty. Half expecting a reward, he had been stunned when the imam instructed him to leave the mosque and never to return.

It was a ploy, of course, as Mukhtar soon discovered. The imam, in his wisdom, suspected that the U.S. government had him under surveillance. There might even be a spy or two inside the mosque. For that reason, if Mukhtar was to prove himself, fulfill the destiny God had charted for him, he had to first deceive the enemy, pretend to be a moderate, perhaps even an infidel.

The first step in his transformation was a quarrel in the mosque, scripted with great precision. Afif Mukhtar "rebelled" against the imam's strident teachings, scuffled with a couple of the regulars and fled the mosque with curses ringing in his ears. Although the imam had predicted an appearance by the FBI, no G-men had been sent to question him.

Mildly annoyed that he had been passed over for interrogation, Mukhtar settled into his new life. His parents were relieved to hear that he had broken the imam's hypnotic spell. They bought him gifts and set him up in a small studio apartment—realtor's code for two rooms barely large enough to turn around in.

And there he waited, bolstered by the imam's promise that some day a man would call upon him and request a service for God. On that day, thought Afif Mukhtar, his life would be complete—and it would end.

He'd been euphoric when the call came through at last,

elated at the prospect of a meeting with the man who would prepare him for his sacrifice. Imagine Mukhtar's shock when that man was not only white, but an American! And more amazing yet, a soldier who had served in Satan's legions, in the war against Iraq!

At first, Mukhtar rebelled against associating with the enemy, but then a late-night call from the imam warned him to mend his ways and humbly yield to God's will. Even an infidel and one-time mortal enemy could serve the cause for reasons of his own, and thereby hasten God's victory.

Afif Mukhtar agreed. His second meeting with the tall American had been more amicable. They had spoken of a plan already in the works, requiring a committed member of the one true faith, willing to sacrifice his life and kill large numbers of the enemy.

Mukhtar had volunteered without a second thought.

Since then, his time at home had mostly been devoted to watching the news on CNN, softly applauding other martyrs who wreaked havoc among their enemies in Baghdad, Israel, Pakistan, Afghanistan—wherever true believers felt the call to stand and fight for their sacred beliefs. Mukhtar knew he would meet those valiant men in Paradise.

And he wouldn't have long to wait.

His parents might be shamed by Mukhtar's action, might even be questioned by the FBI or other agents of the hostile government, but what was that to him? He'd tried to reason with them, all in vain, before God had called him to his special mission. Now, unless his sacrifice somehow persuaded them to resurrect their faith, it was too late.

Mukhtar wasn't concerned about their souls. Each man

and woman made choices in life. Those choices helped determine whether he or she was lost or saved.

Afif Mukhtar had made his choice.

As for his parents, if they chose the path of the infidel, to Hell with them.

*Winnipeg, Manitoba*

GENE TALMADGE TOOK DELIVERY of the completed bomb at 5:19 p.m. He marked the time because it seemed significant to him, a milestone in his life.

First came the call on his cell phone, answered on the first ring. Muhunnad Hashim spoke just three words: "It's ready now."

Talmadge had driven farther east, circled the next block down and doubled back to park outside Hashim's apartment building. The bomb maker emerged ten seconds after Talmadge pulled in to the curb. The suitcase that he carried was a sturdy Halliburton model, slightly larger than the first case, and painted black.

Talmadge opened his trunk and waited while Hashim placed it inside. The slender Arab seemed to have no difficulty with its weight.

The American didn't shake hands or thank Hashim. He simply nodded, then got back into his car and drove away, leaving the bomb maker to watch him from the curb. If any neighbors found their actions strange, life in the district had taught them to mind their own business. Another drug delivery, perhaps, or weapons. What was it to them?

Nothing worth suffering or dying for, when the police seemed not to care.

Talmadge could picture in his mind the contents of the new suitcase. Lead shields, again, screening the weapons-grade material inside. Along with what he'd carried from Vancouver, now there was a trigger mechanism, with a battery and blasting cap embedded in a primary explosive charge—C-4, most likely—that would start the chain reaction leading up to the big bang.

Simple. But it required a craftsman's eyes and hands.

Along with some poor idiot to set it off.

The detonator, Talmadge knew, would have no timer. There was nothing to break down, short out or otherwise go wrong. The handpicked sacrificial goat would walk that package to the target, sit or stand beside it and depress the trigger with a final prayer to Allah on his lips.

When he had put two miles behind him, Talmadge palmed his cell phone once again and dialed another string of numbers from the storehouse in his head. This time, it took two rings before he heard the soft voice of Nasser Asad.

His highest-ranking contact in al Qaeda always sounded calm, regardless of the circumstances. Talmadge tried to match his tone, saying, "It's me."

"Who else?"

"I have the merchandise," Talmadge said. "It's in transit. I've arranged for the delivery."

"No problems, then?"

"A small one," he admitted, "but it's all behind me now."

"The rainy city, yes?" Asad inquired.

Talmadge blinked once, surprised. "That's right. No repercussions, though."

"You're certain?"

"As can be."

"All right, then. Call me when delivery has been completed."

"That's affirmative."

Again, he broke the link before the great ears in the air could get a fix on him. The call might be recorded, but what of it? Any listeners would hear two businessmen discussing…well, business, what else?

It made the world go 'round.

The President said so himself.

Talmadge smiled, briefly, wondering if he could get a subsidy from Congress like the other bastards who polluted the environment. It seemed unlikely, but he'd settle for the satisfaction of a job well done.

Too bad the Army hadn't done the same, when they still had a chance. Instead of recognizing Talmadge's intrinsic value, giving him a little slack when he was clearly in the right, they'd crucified him. Sons of bitches dragged him through the hear-no-evil, see-no-evil farce they called a court-martial, and he was out.

Tough luck.

But it was *his* time now. What went around most definitely *came* around. And this time it would bite his persecutors in their fat, collective ass.

To cover three hundred miles, watching his speed along the way, with rest stops and a crossing at the border, ought to take six hours, more or less. Talmadge was driving, this time, to avoid the slightest possibility of any hassle at an airport, even with a charter flight. It was safer to drive, bull-shit his way across the border with his U.S. passport and a weary guard who didn't really give a damn.

Six hours, give or take, and he would place his package in the martyr's hands. From there on to ignition, it was out of Talmadge's control.

Talmadge was living large, the way they'd taught him at Fort Benning. He was seizing opportunity by the gonads and carrying the battle to his enemies.

Well, to be perfectly correct, somebody else was carrying the battle, but Talmadge had made it possible. He'd wound the doomsday clock and set it ticking down to Armageddon.

With a little help from his friends.

# CHAPTER TEN

*Chinatown, Vancouver*

Chinatown was chaos to most non-Orientals. Never mind the city, be it San Francisco or Los Angeles, Seattle or New York. There was a sense of *otherness* about the shopfronts, with their signs in Cantonese or Mandarin. Sometimes the street signs were illegible to English-only travelers, as well. Strange sights, sounds, smells assailed unwary visitors, led them astray if they weren't in strict command of all their faculties.

Vancouver's Chinatown was south of Hastings Street, bisected on a north-south axis by Main Street. Its major streets bore common names for English-speakers—Georgia, Keefer, Pender, Union, Prior, Gore—but Shanghai Alley also waited to lure those seeking a little something…*different.*

Bolan and Dixon weren't tourists. They hadn't gone for the Chinatown experience, but rather to impress the local triad with a sense that nothing there would ever be the same again unless Bolan received the information he required.

The key to any blitz was speed, but Bolan also needed surgical precision. It wasn't enough for him to simply tear through Chinatown, destroying shops and vehicles at random, injuring or killing passersby on neon-lighted streets. Rather, he needed to inflict the utmost damage on his enemies without endangering civilians—or, at least, without inflicting any needless harm on them himself.

To that end, Bolan left the rental car in a garage at Hastings and Columbia, across the street from Chinatown's official northern border. Vancouver's chill night air explained the overcoats that he and Dixon wore, concealing their equipment for the night ahead. In Bolan's case, a military webbing rig supported most of his hardware, while Dixon made do with the pockets of his coat and slacks.

The air of Chinatown enveloped them as they crossed Hastings Street, southbound on Quebec Street. They inhaled exotic spices and a baffling variety of incense, passing by the open fronts of shops, temples, and studios devoted to the martial arts.

"Damn it," Dixon said, walking with his head down. "I forgot about kung fu. They all know kung fu, right?"

"I doubt it," Bolan said, "but if somebody starts to kick your ass, just shoot him."

"Right. I knew I was forgetting something."

Here, the groceries hung whole, plucked chickens in the windows, dangling by the necks like victims of a lynch mob. Pharmacists sold powdered roots and tiger's penis for what ailed you. Acupuncturists and tattoo artists shared the same floor space. Straight razors glimmered in display windows, beside intricate paper fans.

Bolan believed in thinking big. As his first target, therefore, he had picked the China Gate Casino, located at Main and Union. Owned on paper by a group of smiling front men whose police records in Asia and in Canada were spotless, the casino was in fact controlled by Joseph Lee, and a major cash cow for the 14K Triad.

And it was legal—to a point.

Bolan hadn't researched the China Gate's tax records, since they only told a portion of the story. Income was declared and taxes paid, but no official record could describe the China Gate's role as a money laundry, or begin to estimate the total skimmed each week, year-round, before the gross income was tallied.

Sixty years ago, mob mastermind Meyer Lansky had described legalized gambling as "a license to print money." While not literally true, he caught the essence of an industry that raked in megabillions yearly, its controllers wriggling under and around even the strictest oversight requirements like the oily lampreys that they were.

Outside the China Gate, their faces bathed in garish flashing neon, Bolan told Dixon, "Remember that you're probably on camera no matter where you go. And that includes the restrooms."

As he spoke, Bolan removed a ski mask from his pocket, pulled it down around his ears like a watch cap and left the rest rolled up across his forehead. Dixon donned a matching cap as he replied, "I know. Heard you the first time."

Bolan let that pass and said, "They don't have uniformed security. No rent-a-cops who might see something that they're not supposed to notice in the counting room. Whoever comes against you once we're rolling, armed or otherwise, they're triad members. Watch your back and remember what we're here for."

"Money and leverage," Dixon replied. "No shooting customers."

"*Especially* no shooting customers." Another glance along the busy street, in each direction, and Bolan said, "All right. Let's do it."

CASINOS, IT APPEARED, were pretty much the same in any language. Dixon knew the China Gate was geared primarily for round-eye tourists, to divest them of their hard-earned cash. There were a few Chinese games operating, twangy Asian music on the sound system and incense trying to compete with the tobacco smoke, but if the Chinese staff and superficial decorations were removed, it could've passed for any carpet joint on the Las Vegas Strip, or in Atlantic City.

Smaller than Caesar's Palace, certainly, but Joseph Lee was bagging cash hand over fist, the profits pouring into dirty deals that ranged from sale of bootleg DVDs and blue jeans in Red China to the trade in heroin and human trafficking.

Dixon despised the Chinese Mafia on principle, but once again remembered that his target wasn't Joseph Lee. The triad was a stepping-stone to Eugene Talmadge, one that might prove treacherous and slide out beneath him without warning, leaving Dixon with a broken leg or worse.

Much worse.

His primary assignment in the China Gate was to locate the men's room, go inside and release a grenade. Letting Matt Cooper go his own way, weaving past the gaming tables and the banks of one-armed bandits, Dixon spent a moment searching, then picked out the lighted symbols of a man and woman standing side by side, the caption Washrooms glowing underneath.

Inside the men's room, Dixon chose a stall and closed its door behind him. Hunching low to frustrate any CCV-type spies, he rolled the ski mask over his face, then took two heavy canisters out of his overcoat's deep pockets. Exiting the toilet stall, he pulled the pin on one grenade and tossed the hissing canister into the nearest urinal.

Before it started billowing dark, rancid fumes, he primed the second smoke grenade and left the men's room, moving past an elevated cashier's cage with covered face averted, then reared back and lobbed his burden toward the center of the sprawling room.

Behind him, smoke was wafting from the men's room. Dixon saw it, smiled behind his itchy woolen mask and shouted, "Fire! Get out! The casino's on fire!"

His second canister erupted then, billows of white smoke rising from the floor between a crowded crap table and a roulette wheel, wafted toward the ceiling by the China Gate's extraction fans.

Chaos was his assignment, leaving Cooper to collect the greenbacks, or whatever passed for money in British Columbia. To that end, Cooper gave another whooping cry of "Fire!" and started racing pell-mell through the heart of the casino, shouldering the startled customers aside. As Dixon wove a zigzag course around the room, he shoved and booted patrons toward the nearest exits, all the while bellowing, "Fire! The place is burning down!"

As planned, panic ensued. Dixon was startled, though, to see how many customers first lunged for chips or money on the gaming tables, stuffing loot into their pockets or handbags before they fled toward safety. Under other circumstances, Dixon might've laughed.

But at the moment, he was busy trying to survive.

The triad guards moved to intercept him halfway through his first chaotic circuit of the China Gate's main floor. He didn't know where Cooper was exactly, though he had a vague idea of where the central cashier's cage was located.

No matter. Dixon had to deal with these goons on his own.

Cooper's orders were explicit: "Do your job, and then get out. If you can ditch security in time, meet me at Main and Pender. Otherwise, the fallback rendezvous is Shanghai Alley and Quebec."

Simple, except that now he had five pissed-off hardmen closing in on him, a couple of them armed with saps, all showing bulges underneath their jackets that could only be hardware.

There are no rules, Dixon thought as he stopped dead in his tracks and drew the Smith & Wesson pistol from beneath his coat, holding it down and out of sight against his thigh.

The first sap-wielding thug roared in from his left, aiming a caveman swing at Dixon's head, but Dixon spun and stopped him with a .40-caliber dissuader to the chest. The echo of his shot produced more screams of panic from the milling crowd, and set alarm bells clamoring as if on cue.

The second blackjack artist hesitated, started to rethink his choice of weapons, but he had no time to reach for the pistol slung beneath his arm. Dixon squeezed off another round and watched the blood spray from a mangled shoulder as his target fell.

Get out of here! he thought.

The others would be digging for their guns by now, and he was out of time. Choosing an exit, praying that it was the right one, Dixon ducked his head and ran like hell.

THE CALL CAME through to Joseph Lee at half-past midnight. He immediately recognized the voice, but was surprised by its abbreviated message.

"Call the China Gate."

Just that, a terse command, before the line went dead.

Lee sat and thought about it for a moment. Could it be some kind of trap? If so, what kind? How could it damage him to telephone his own casino? His home lines, swept three times a day by experts, were secure from taps.

What, then?

Suppose his nameless enemies had some arrangement with the government. Suppose they schemed to make him call the China Gate and thus somehow reveal his hidden ownership of the casino. What of it?

He'd simply dial the switchboard's published number, ask for Mr. Ming—a code name for the manager—and see what happened next. If the operator told him there was no one by that name on staff, Lee would apologize, hang up and wait for a call-back from a secure and private line. His own phone log would record only a fleeting call, explainable as a mistake by Lee or one of his household employees.

On the other hand, if anything was wrong at the casino, his inquiry would be answered with a prearranged warning, innocuous to anyone but Lee.

Frowning, he dialed and waited while the distant telephone rang half a dozen times. At last, a harried-sounding operator picked it up and fairly moaned out, "China Gate Casino."

"May I speak to Mr. Ming?" Lee asked, a knot of worry forming in his chest.

The knot became a clutching fist around his heart as she replied, "I'm sorry, sir, but Mr. Ming is not available tonight."

"I understand," Lee said, then he cut the link.

It was the crisis warning. "Not available" meant that the China Gate was in the midst of some emergency light-years beyond a rowdy argument or a pathetic loser's cardiac arrest. It meant a robbery, a fire, an earthquake—the Apocalypse, in brief.

But which, exactly?

What in hell was happening to Lee's casino? To his money?

Lee bolted from his chair and started shouting orders at his staff. He wanted someone at the China Gate to call and tell him what was going on. He wanted soldiers on the street and standing by for orders. He wanted every weapon loaded, every vehicle prepared. He wanted every one of his men on alert for further orders.

And he wanted all of it right now.

His cell phone rang again, while Lee's subordinates were racing off to their appointed posts and tasks. He answered with a sense of grim foreboding.

"Did you call?" his unknown adversary asked.

"The line was busy."

"Call it out of order, maybe I'll believe you."

"You have made a serious mistake," Lee said.

"I look at it the other way around."

"You won't survive this."

"I've heard that before," the caller said. "In case you wondered, I'm just getting started."

Lee's grip tightened dangerously on the telephone. "What do you want?"

"We've been all over that. Remember?"

*Talmadge.* "I do not know where he is. That is the truth, whether or not you—"

"I believe you," the stranger said.

"What?"

"I'm sure you don't know where he is right now," the caller said. "I'm just as sure you have some way to get in touch with him, if necessary."

"Why—?"

"Because," the round-eye interrupted him again, infuriating Lee, "the two of you are doing business. Scratch that. You *were* doing business. Weapons, was it? Maybe China white? You wouldn't crawl in bed with someone if you couldn't get in touch the morning after."

Lee had dealt enough with Westerners by now to know the caller wasn't branding him a homosexual. As calmly as he could, Lee answered, "In Vancouver, I of course have his address and telephone number. You have destroyed his apartment. Therefore—"

"Nice try, but no cigar," the caller said. "He's on the road too much to call Vancouver home. Jakarta, Paris, who knows where he'll be tomorrow?"

"That's my point. I don't—"

"You have a cell or sat phone number for him. Something I can trace. The only question now is what it's worth to you. Knowing whatever deal you had in place with Talmadge has been blown for good, what's your percentage in protecting him?"

"I don't know who you are, or who you represent. I don't know if you are recording this false information to entrap me, but I can assure you—"

"Fine," the caller said. "We'll play it your way. When I call again, you'll be a poorer man. Maybe a little wiser, too."

The line went dead.

Lee bit his tongue to keep from screaming hatred into empty space.


"THIS PLACE," Bolan said, "is supposed to be a cutting plant."

"For drugs?" Dixon asked.

"More specifically, for heroin. It comes in from the Golden Triangle as morphine base and Lee refines it here, then cuts the heroin to stretch his inventory, multiply his take and keep his customers from keeling over on the street first time they take a hit."

"Which flat?" Dixon inquired.

"The penthouse."

Bolan doubted whether anyone had ever used that term before, in reference to their target. First, the building only had six stories. Second, it was one of twenty-five or thirty others, all identical except for fading paint jobs, crammed along the Georgia Viaduct on the extreme southern perimeter of Chinatown. A wide variety of terms might pass through any normal person's mind when viewing the aging tenement, but *penthouse* wasn't one of them.

"Looks like we're using fire escapes again," Dixon said.

"Better than a long hike up and down the inside stairs, with every tenant in the place against us," Bolan said.

"Sounds right."

"Special equipment for this job," Bolan said, passing his companion a small surgical mask and a cheap pair of plastic goggles.

"What's this?"

"Insurance," he explained. "If things get hairy in there—and they could—it may also get dusty. Suck in too much heroin or morphine, and you're DOA. Best-case scenario, I have to carry you back down here with your brain fried."

"Damn. I'm sure this wasn't in the job description."

"You can bail out any time," Bolan reminded him.

"And quit show business?" Dixon snorted through his mask. "Forget it, man. I bought the E ticket."

"Okay. Enjoy the ride."

Ten minutes later they were standing on the fire escape outside a bank of windows that were painted black on the inside, to keep the world from seeing what went on behind the glass. A flaking patch the size of Bolan's thumbnail let him crouch and peer one-eyed into the room beyond, glimpsing a lighted room where men and women wearing masks like his lined both sides of a table filled with beakers and assorted other scientific gear.

"So, how's your love life?" he asked Dixon.

"What?"

"The girls working in there are naked," Bolan said. "Most of the men, too, for that matter. Rules out any chance they're hiding pinches of the stuff under their clothes when they clock out. I don't want it to startle you and get one of us killed."

"My love life's fine," Dixon said, glowering behind his mask.

"Okay. Let's crash this party, then."

He used another flash-bang, pitched it through the nearest blackened window and fell back against the fire escape before it blew. Except for raining glass, most of the thunderclap remained inside the loft, absorbed by startled eardrums.

Bolan cleared the window seconds later, plunging headlong into junkie heaven—or a glimpse of Hell on Earth. The stun grenade had cleared the cutting table, shattering most of the beakers and retorts while sending up a cloud of powder that resembled talc with glitter added for effect. Inside that cloud, Bolan saw figures lurching, staggering, some of them writhing on the floor.

Most of them wore no clothing, which tipped Bolan to the shooter in his dark suit when he suddenly appeared out of the dope screen, brandishing an H&K machine pistol. Bolan gave him three Parabellum manglers to the chest, then swung his Spectre SMG around the room at large, in search of other targets.

A pistol cracked somewhere to Bolan's left, and while the bullet didn't find him, Bolan crouched to spoil the shooter's shaky aim. Dope cloud or not, there was no point in getting careless on the line of fire.

Somewhere behind him, Dixon fired an Uzi burst at someone Bolan couldn't see, immediately followed by the dull sound of a body hitting floorboards.

Two down, if that hadn't been a worker bee.

How many shooters left to go?

One of them came at Bolan through the deadly dust storm, rapid-firing a Beretta with his left hand, while the right gouged at his bleary eyes. The bullets hammered over Bolan's head until he fired a short burst from the floor and put the shooter down.

"Is that it?" Dixon asked him through the settling mist. "That all they've got?"

Bolan kept quiet, willed the green recruit to shut his mouth, but then a triad hardman with a shotgun suddenly came out of nowhere, pumping buckshot through the walls about chest high. Bolan and Dixon hit him with a cross fire, spinning him before he landed supine on the bare, glass-littered floor.

"Okay, is *that* it?" Dixon asked. He sounded peeved.

Bolan said nothing for another moment, but the pale, addictive dust was settling now, and it appeared that they had dealt with everyone who wasn't decked out in a birthday suit.

"Tell them to hit the bricks," Bolan instructed.

Dixon started to speak in Cantonese, moving around the room and booting those—the men, at least—who moved too slowly for his taste. Three minutes, give or take, left them alone with corpses in the loft.

"Is this a mess, or what?" Dixon asked, switching back to English.

"Call it a fire scene," Bolan answered.

"What?"

He palmed a couple of incendiary sticks and primed them, pitching one down toward the west end of the loft, dropping the other near his feet, both sputtering.

"I said, it's time to use the fire escape again."

Dusted with skag from head to foot, Dixon replied, "I see your point," and scrambled through the shattered window into fresh, clean air.


"YOU'LL BE A POORER MAN. Maybe a little wiser, too."

The taunting words came back to Joseph Lee and left a taste of bitter gall inside his mouth. Another four men dead, with something like two million dollars' worth of heroin incinerated by the madman who had killed them.

No, Lee caught himself. His enemy, whatever else the man might be, was clearly not insane. He'd done some homework, linking Lee first to the China Gate Casino, then to his most valuable cutting plant. Where would he strike next time? Lee's home? One of his restaurants? His mistress's apartment?

When the cell phone rang again, Lee snatched it up and checked the Caller ID window. "Private call," the message read. Lee took another shrilling ring to bring his voice under control.

"Hello."

"Do you feel any wiser yet?"

"I wish to stop this," Lee replied.

"And that makes two of us. How do I get in touch with Talmadge?"

"I can't discuss it on the telephone. You understand, I'm sure. When can we meet?"

His caller didn't miss a beat. "There's no time like the present," he replied.

"You know the park at Keefer and Quebec?" Lee asked.

"I'll find it. Two o'clock suit you?"

"I will be there."

"Nice doing business with you," said the round-eye, just before he broke the link.

Lee bellowed for his houseman, started spitting orders at them when they stood before him, giving each a critical assignment with his personal assurance that failure meant death. His honor and the triad's were at stake, together with the crushing loss of revenue he stood to suffer if the raids continued.

Talmadge.

Lee would gladly kill the man himself for bringing so much trouble down upon his head—would kill him, soon, beyond all doubt—but Talmadge wasn't presently within his reach. The cryptic messages Lee left for him on voice mail went unanswered.

Soon.

But first, he would dispose of the impertinent intruders who believed they could make sport of him, embarrass Joseph Lee before his soldiers, the police, the world at large.

That was a grave mistake.

The meeting place he had selected would allow him one glimpse of his enemy before the trap closed. How it went from there depended on the man or men who had incurred his wrath. If they were foolish and surrendered, Lee would take his time, teach them the true meaning of pain. If they were wise and fought against the odds, he still would have the pleasure of presiding at their secret funerals.

And then, the hunt for Eugene Talmadge would begin.

"YOU DON'T THINK this might be a trap?" Dixon asked.

"Think? I'm sure of it," Bolan replied.

"Uh-huh. So, tell me once more why we're actually going."

"We still need a link to Talmadge," Bolan said. "Some way to reach him. This appears to be our only angle of attack."

"A damned fine way of getting killed, you mean."

"That's how it looks to Lee, I'm sure."

"Which part did he get wrong?"

"The part where he walks out alive."

"You're pretty confident," Dixon said. "What do you suppose the odds will be?"

"If Lee brings everybody he can spare? Maybe fifteen, twenty to one," Bolan replied.

"Terrific."

"But I'm thinking you should sit it out."

Dixon froze with a cartridge in one hand, a curved M-P5 K box magazine clutched in the other. "Sit it out? How come? I mean—"

"You had a valid point, before," Bolan explained. "This kind of action isn't in your job description. You're supposed to be *investigating* crimes, not out committing them.

I frankly can't predict how your superiors will take all this, when they read your report."

"I'll have to fudge a bit on that, I think," Dixon replied.

"Better if you just minimize the damage while you can. Tonight will be the worst we've faced, so far."

"Which means you need the help, right?"

Bolan frowned. "I don't know if you're up to it."

"Give me a break! I haven't dropped the ball yet, have I? No. What makes you think I'll screw up now?"

"You've done all right," Bolan allowed, "but you're still green. Tonight, we're cranking up the voltage. When we're done, if we come out of it alive, you shouldn't be expecting any thank-yous from the local law or the RCMP."

"To hell with them," Dixon said. "This is *our* job, right? We follow where it leads."

"You're quoting Washington again."

"I don't see you retiring from the field," he challenged Cooper.

"No. But I've been here before."

"It's how you get experience," Dixon said, hoping that it didn't come out sounding like a whine. "I won't learn anything sitting around, reading about it in tomorrow's newspaper."

"There's nothing more for you to learn," Bolan replied. "A thing like this, you go in killing. Keep it up until you're out of targets. Pray that you're the last one standing."

"So I'm ready, then," he answered, almost cheerfully.

"Why would you want to be?" Bolan asked.

"Let's say I'm sick of pushing papers all day long, pretending that it makes a difference. Maybe I've learned that sometimes it takes dirty hands to get a job done right."

"And can you live with that?"

Dixon responded with a question of his own. "Can you?"

"I've had more practice," Bolan said.

"Okay. That's why I'm here," Dixon said. "Practicing."

"Your choice." The Executioner relented. "Just remember, when it hits the fan, fifteen to one or whatever it is, you're on your own."

Smiling despite the chill he felt, Dixon replied, "I wouldn't have it any other way."

They focused on their weapons, then, reloading magazines, sharing a cleaning kit that Cooper found somewhere inside his deadly bag of tricks. A smell of oil and solvent filled the rental car, almost refreshing after cordite and the chemical wipes they'd used to clean the narco-frosting from their faces, hands and clothing.

Jesus, if the watercooler gang could only see him now. Dixon imagined their expressions, wondered if the macho posturing would melt away, or if the other guys would feel obliged to rival him. And what about Charlene, the only female member of their team? Would all that he'd endured and done repulse her?

Enough.

Daydreaming wouldn't get it done this time. He couldn't simply plot a battle, then go back to filing reams of paper with a mug of coffee steaming on his desk. In just under an hour, they'd be going up against an army dedicated to destroying them.

Fifteen, twenty to one, Cooper had estimated. Maybe

more, if Joseph Lee decided to withdraw his guards from various whorehouses, shooting galleries and any other dirty operation he had running in the neighborhood. Dixon had no idea how many troops the triad leader had at his disposal, for emergencies.

Fifty to one, perhaps.

In which case, Dixon figured he was dead. But he could go down fighting, damn it.

There was always that.

# CHAPTER ELEVEN

The park at Keefer and Quebec had no name posted on a sign, as far as Bolan could discover. That seemed vaguely wrong, somehow, as if the place where he might die should have been labeled at the very least, but he resisted the impulse to dwell on it. After tonight, maybe they'd name it for whatever happened there.

Lee's deadline hadn't allowed Bolan to conduct the reconnaissance that he preferred, examining the ground well in advance of any enemy's arrival, but it was a simple layout anyway. A grassy rectangle with trees and children's play gear covered roughly two square blocks, deserted now in darkness.

Bolan spotted three streetlights that should've helped illuminate the park, but two of them were newly broken, glass still on the sidewalks at their bases, leaving only one light near the intersection to suffice. It cast long shadows from swing sets, pooling darkness underneath the trees that had been planted in strategic rows, permitting the illusion that a visitor to No-Name Park had somehow managed to escape the city's clutches.

"You're backup," Bolan told Tom Dixon as they stood together in the darkness at the tree line. "Lee's expecting me. He knows my voice. I'll keep the meet and see what happens."

Dixon frowned. "And when he kills you with the first shot, then what do I do?"

"The best you can," Bolan replied. "Get out if possible, and call your people in D.C. Tell them that Talmadge got away and may have made his pickup. Anything that they can do to track him, put the wheels in motion."

"I see. You get the glory, being shot to hell in Chinatown, while I take all the blame if Talmadge nukes the White House. Gotcha. Beautiful."

"Look on the bright side," Bolan answered. "Maybe it'll just be FEMA."

"Right. Who'd know the difference? Hey, I was thinking—"

"Time to watch and listen," Bolan cut him off.

The stillness was a blessing, and he didn't want to hear about his sidekick's feelings at the moment. There'd be time enough for that if they both survived the trap and got what they had come for.

Getting out alive was only half of it. If Bolan didn't find a link to Talmadge, it was all in vain, a wasted block of time that simply let their enemy improve his lead.

Dixon touched Bolan's arm, not speaking. Bolan turned in that direction, saw three men in black approaching through the park's trees, stopping inside the tree line at a point some forty yards from where Bolan and Dixon stood. He couldn't tell what kind of weapons they were carrying, but he assumed they'd come prepared.

He caught Dixon's attention, mouthed the words "Watch them," and scanned the spotty woods behind him, seeing no more lurkers there.

It couldn't be that easy, three men hiding in the woods, while Lee came in from streetside. It was too damned simple. If he couldn't plan a better hit than that, Lee never would've made it to a top spot in the 14K Triad.

Two minutes later, Bolan watched a van stop at the curb on Keefer, side door rolling open, shooters pouring out like big-top clowns emerging from a funny car. He counted twelve as they dispersed, some heading for the trees, while others scattered toward surrounding shopfronts, seeking any vantage points they could find.

Fifteen. And Bolan still didn't believe he'd seen them all.

The limousine came next, a stretch that had to have some trouble parking anywhere in Chinatown. It stopped approximately where the van had stood just moments earlier. The shotgun rider exited and held the rear door for his boss. The entourage of bodyguards emerged before Lee showed himself, five stocky shooters fanning out to form a kind of human shield around their master. Lee himself was average height and weight, with nothing to distinguish him from any other resident of Chinatown.

Except that in this place, he held the powers of life and death.

Or *had,* before the Executioner arrived.

"Stay frosty," Bolan whispered, then stepped out of

cover before Dixon could reply. His hands were empty, but available to grab the weapons slung beneath his jacket at the first sign of a double-cross.

Assuming he could see it coming.

Dixon would have to watch the men behind him, and that put a crimp in any plans for Bolan's sidekick to escape if he went down. Dixon might be engaged before the echoes of the first shots died away, and there'd be no escape from that point on, unless he was the last man standing on the field.

Good luck, he thought, and went to face his enemies.

"ONE MAN?"

Lee hadn't meant to speak aloud, in fact had barely whispered, and no one among his bodyguards replied to the question.

It seemed impossible that one man had caused so much trouble for him in Lee's own backyard. Had killed his brother and at least a dozen others, panicked customers at his casino while attracting the police, then trashed his cutting plant and vaporized more than two million dollars' worth of China white.

One man? Impossible.

Lee didn't buy it, and it made him nervous.

"Watch for someone else," he ordered. "This one's not alone."

One of his soldiers raised a two-way radio and spoke into it, then dropped it to his side, leaving his gun hand free.

The round-eye stopped when he was thirty yards in front of Lee's position, separated from him by Lee's ring of bodyguards and what appeared to be a child's sandpit. Knowing that it was time to prove himself, Lee pushed his way between two soldiers, moving to confront his enemy.

"We meet at last," he said, and instantly regretted it, sounding like something from an ancient movie on TV. "It's brave of you to come here, all alone."

"I'm covered," Bolan said. Even now, he sounded confident. "You have the information that I need?"

"You understand," Lee said, "that I cannot allow myself to be perceived as weak. It is…how do you say it? The kiss of death?"

"That's what we say," the stranger answered him. "So you prefer a war to giving up a man who's already betrayed you? Killed your brother?"

Lee stood rock still for a heartbeat, letting that sink in. He guessed it was a lie, the round-eye desperate to save himself by any ploy available. And yet…

"I don't believe you. Why would Talmadge—?"

"He was running for his life," Bolan interrupted. "When your brother tried to stop him, Talmadge put him down."

"You lie."

"One way to check it. When we're finished here, if I'm dead and you're still alive, sort through my weapons. You can likely find them all before the cops get here. Check calibers and have somebody in the ME's office give you a report. The way it sounded, you'll be looking for a 5.56 mm rifle."

Lee's mind swarmed with questions, but he hadn't come to have a conversation with this stranger. For his peace of mind and for his own position in the family, Lee needed to exact revenge.

"You lie to save yourself," he said.

"Whatever. If you weren't negotiating, why'd you come at all? Your goons could do the job while you sit home and light a joss stick for your brother."

"They *will* do the job," Lee said, "under my supervision. I must take a hand in punishing my brother's murderer."

"Too bad he isn't here."

"You'll do."

"Better get to it, then. Time's wasting," Bolan said.

Lee knew better than to show the enemy his back. Instead of turning toward his shooters, he began to speak an order from the corner of his mouth.

But the words never emerged.

One moment, Lee had wrapped his tongue around the words he planned to speak, then he was lying on his back, on grass, one shoulder numb from the impact of a terrific punch.

It seemed impossible that he was shot, the first man down. He hadn't even seen the round-eye draw a weapon, much less fire it. Now Lee wondered if he was about to die.

Around him, other guns were hammering away, ejecting cartridges that pattered on his face and chest like scorching raindrops. Lee tried batting at them with his hands, but only his right arm responded. Nothing from the left but the first shock waves of what he supposed would soon be agony.

One of his soldiers thought to save him, reaching down and clutching Lee's lapel to drag him backward, toward the limousine. His grip, the tugging action, all sent bolts of pain shooting from Lee's left shoulder, down his arm and deep inside his chest.

He gasped, cried out, cursing, but dared not tell his man to stop. If someone didn't move him, he could easily be shot again.

Why were his men still firing, when the round-eye had to be dead by now?

The soldier dragging Lee grunted, a startled woofing sound, then toppled over on his back. One of his twitching feet caught Joseph Lee a solid blow atop his head.

It didn't knock him out, though.

Sprawling in his misery, Lee realized that nothing would be spared him, even at the moment of his death.

COOPER HAD TOLD the triad leader that he was covered.

And what the hell was that about? Had he forgotten his instructions, telling Dixon to clear out if he went down, or did he just assume that Dixon would ignore him. True, he'd mouthed another order when the shooters started moving in, but that wasn't the same as telling him to take them out, or even to cover him.

"Goddamn it!" Dixon muttered to himself, not even loud enough to qualify as whispering. He clutched his mini-Uzi, safety off and index finger on the trigger, knowing that he couldn't leave Cooper and run to save himself.

Thinking that Cooper, damn him, knew it, too.

What was he saying now, about their weapons?

"You can likely find them all before the cops get here. Check calibers and have somebody in the ME's office give you a report."

Thanks for the vote of confidence, Dixon thought. Write me off, why don't you?

He should follow orders, get the hell on out of Dodge while there was time, but Cooper hadn't even made his move yet. At least until that happened, Dixon's feet were rooted where he stood.

And when it came, he nearly missed it. It was that damned fast, a blur of movement and the Glock was there in Cooper's hand, exploding, and the triad boss was pitching over on his back. It startled him that Cooper would've killed the one man who possessed the information they required, but in a no-win situation, he supposed that any move made sense.

Gunfire erupted from Lee's bodyguards, and all his shadow soldiers as they closed in for the kill. Dixon saw Cooper take a headlong dive into some kind of sandbox, planted near a steel merry-go-round, and then he had his hands full.

No more spectator.

He swung first toward the three triad hardmen he'd been assigned to watch, when Cooper went to meet with Joseph Lee. All three had left their cover, firing automatic weapons toward the sandbox, and he raked them with an Uzi burst from left to right that took them absolutely by surprise.

They died that way, startled expressions on their faces, comprehension of their failure stolen from them as they twitched and toppled to the ground. Unless there was an afterlife, they'd never know what happened to them, who had cut them down.

The other gunmen closest to him didn't spot Dixon at first. He guessed that they expected automatic fire from his position, more or less, and with their own attention focused on a target none of them had seen their friends go down. That helped him when he slotted two more shooters at the tree line, on his left this time, and dropped each with a 3- or 4-round burst.

Crouching, hugging the shadows where he could, Dixon moved out to meet the others who were still firing at Cooper in his sandbox.

Was he hit? Already dead? If so, then Dixon's sacrifice was wasted and he should be fleeing for his life, to carry out the soldier's last instructions, warn his DHS superiors and put the country on alert for Talmadge and his dirty bomb.

But if Cooper was still alive…

It was too late to turn back now, in any case. He was exposed, committed to the forward motion that propelled him toward his enemies.

How many? He had given up on counting when he topped twenty, but five of those were down now—make that six, with Joseph Lee. Would losing Lee disorient the others? Maybe throw them off their killing game?

It didn't seem so, as he watched them pouring fire into the sandbox, several of them peppering the play equipment close at hand. Only when Dixon saw a muzzle-flash wink back at them, under the carousel, did it occur to him that Cooper was alive.

Hang on! he thought. I'm coming!

And a stream of Parabellum manglers from his Uzi led the way.


THE SANDBOX WASN'T MUCH, in terms of cover, but it was the best Bolan could manage in the moment. He had scoped it out beforehand, gauged its depth and other measurements when he was checking out the playground gear. And sand was great for stopping bullets—hence its use in sandbags since the nineteenth century.

But Bolan hadn't planned on staying in the sandbox, where he'd be a stationary target for his enemies. His first shot, which had only wounded Joseph Lee, gave him a heartbeat's grace before the triad shooters opened up on him in unison. He'd used that time to leap and slither through the sandbox, giving them a point of reference, then rolled clear and lay prone behind a merry-go-round, whose quarter-inch steel made an even better bullet-stop than sand.

And he was fighting back.

He'd swapped the Glock for his Spectre on the move, the SMG preset to three-round bursts, for maximum effect. Ideally, he could drop seventeen men before he had to reload or switch back to the pistol.

But combat conditions were seldom ideal.

His very first burst, for example, only cut the legs out from beneath a triad shooter, downing him but leaving him alive and in the fight. Before Bolan could finish that job, several others saw his muzzle-flash and started firing at it, bullets spanging off the flat bed of the children's carousel and denting its curved metal handgrips. Bolan huddled low and picked his targets as they came.

Next up, two gunmen charged toward him from Quebec Street, where they had to have worked their way around on foot to box the meeting place. From their position, Bolan was exposed and vulnerable to direct fire, but their nerves and choice of shooting from the hip while sprinting spoiled their aim.

As bullets flew above him, Bolan met the runners with two measured bursts, first to his left, then to the right. His first man seemed to stumble on a tripwire no one else could see, and went down sprawling on his face. The second wobbled through a sloppy pirouette before he crumpled on one side, his skull smacking hard against the concrete curb.

Nine rounds away, and forty-two remaining.

Bolan rolled and crawled, moving around the carousel as gunmen circled after him. The change of scene gave him a view of Lee's black limo, sitting at the curb on Keefer Street. He didn't know if Lee was now inside the car, but if he was, the driver didn't seem in any hurry to transport his wounded boss for trauma care.

Bolan took care of that, flattening three tires on the stretch limo's passenger's side. For now, it was enough to know that he had lamed Lee's ride, and Bolan felt no need to waste more bullets learning if its window glass and doors were bulletproof.

As previously, Bolan's muzzle-flashes drew incoming fire. And once again, he rolled away from it, letting the shooters chase him counterclockwise with the carousel between them. Very soon, though, that would bring him into full view of the gunmen crouched beside the limousine, and that would be his end.

Bolan surprised them all when he popped up from hiding, squeezed the Spectre's trigger three times, rapidly, and then dropped out of sight again.

Three rounds tore through the chest of his most adamant pursuer, slammed him back into the closest man behind him, and they both went down, one dead or dying, his companion smeared with blood and pinned by deadweight.

Bolan's second burst was chinhigh on a third would-be assassin, Parabellum manglers ripping through his neck and vertebrae, nearly decapitating him. He didn't do the headless-chicken run, just folded like a sack of laundry and went down.

The fourth in line was turning, trying to escape or find himself some cover, when the last three bullets stitched across his shoulder blade and armpit, searing through a lung to find his heart, clip the aorta and release a killing flood inside. He fell and slid, reminding Bolan of a baseball player stretching for home plate.

Game over, Bolan thought, and turned in search of other targets, other enemies.

They came at him from Keefer Street, the van riders who had dispersed along its shopfronts, finding shadows there to hide them while they waited for the main event. Now it was here, and they were charging into battle in a ragged skirmish line.

Two dozen rounds remained in the Spectre's magazine as Bolan rose to meet them, dodging toward a tree that offered better cover than the carousel. One of the shooters fell before he had a chance to find a target, and the echo of an SMG along the park's tree line told him that Dixon hadn't fled.

We make some pair, he thought, then found his mark and went to work.

JOSEPH LEE BELIEVED NOW that he would survive his wound, unless the idiots around him let his enemies come close enough to finish him. Hoping he could prevent that, Lee had first called out for someone to evacuate him, then cursed bitterly as bullets flayed his limo's right-hand tires.

Where was the van? Its driver?

Dizziness engulfed Lee for a moment, muffling his ears until the gunfire seemed like distant echoes of a fireworks celebration. Then, a heartbeat later, all the noise and pain came flooding back again and left him trembling, sweating through his bloody clothes. For all Lee knew, he could be quaking through the final moments of his life.

But shoulder wounds alone were rarely fatal, he remembered, even if the person wounded lost use of his arm. What mattered was to stop the bleeding, treat for shock and transport to a hospital as soon as possible!

Lee struggled to sit up, felt hands restraining him, and cursed them. They withdrew, and then came back to help him sit. He leaned against the limo on the driver's side, legs in the street, and wondered when another car would happen by.

He meant to commandeer the next car that he saw, or have one of his men do it, and finally get treatment for his wound. Lee knew that only moments had elapsed since he was shot, but still it felt like hours in his agony, blood soaking through his shirt and jacket, crawling over him as if a colony of insects had arrived to taste his flesh.

Hallucinating now, Lee thought, and slapped himself with his good hand.

"You okay, Boss?" one of his shooters asked.

"Terrific," Lee responded. "Don't I *look* terrific?" Shooting out the hand that he had used to slap himself, Lee clutched the shooter's arm and pulled him closer. "You must get me out of here," he said. *"Right now!"*

His soldier looked confused, responding, "How am I supposed to do that, Boss?"

"I don't care, damn you! Call the van, or drive the limo on its rims. Go steal a car. Do something!"

"Call the van!" his shooter said, as if the thought originated in his own dim brain. "I can do that. Wait here, Boss!"

The soldier lurched erect, turned toward the driver's door, then made a muffled grunting sound and dropped back to his knees. Lee reached for him, gave him a shake, then cried out weakly as the soldier fell across his outstretched legs.

A bullet had exploded through his left eye socket, making him an out-of-balance cyclops with a vague expression of surprise etched on his meaty face.

Now Lee was worse off than before, still wounded, but immobilized by deadweight sprawled across his legs. He couldn't shift the soldier single-handed, and he saw no one else near enough to help him.

Wait. That wasn't right.

He saw no one at all.

Of course, his men were still around him, had to have been, for he could hear their weapons firing, cartridge cases pinging on the asphalt and the concrete sidewalk. But where were they?

And how many did he still have left?

Were there enough to finish off the round-eye and help Lee escape before police arrived?

Lee strained his ears, trying to pick out any siren sounds behind the gunfire, but his ears were numb and ringing. Soon, he knew, a headache would begin to pound behind his eyes, and wouldn't that be perfect? Pain from head to toe, and not a goddamned member of his crew alert enough to make out that he needed help.

It was enough to make a grown man cry.

Or scream.

Lee started bellowing for help, as loud as he could shout. He felt a pang of guilt at losing face, but what else could he do?

Lee called for help in Cantonese and English, switching off, and punctuated it with multilingual swearing. Someone had to hear him, even with the gunfire raging.

Someone would respond.

And in his desperation, Lee had ceased to care who that might be.


BOLAN WAS RUNNING OUT of targets on the killing ground. He took a moment to replace the Spectre's empty magazine and stowed the empty in a pocket, watching Dixon as he prowled among the dead and dying with his mini-Uzi braced in a two-handed grip.

Counting the bodies on the ground was pointless, since he hadn't made an accurate head count before the shooting started. Bolan scanned the battlefield and waited for incoming fire, knowing that any triad shooters still alive and fit for combat had to make their move before police rolled up and swarmed over the scene.

Nothing.

He stood, believing *that* would draw the fire of any lurkers, but no bullets tore his flesh. No gunfire stung his ears.

"I think we're done here," Dixon said.

"Not quite."

The howling had subsided, but its point of origin was fixed in Bolan's mind. He didn't have to travel far, a stroll around the crippled limousine, and there was Joseph Lee, sitting in blood, a dead man in his lap.

"Jesus," Dixon said, coming at him from the other side.

"Not even close," Bolan replied.

They crouched on either side of Lee, watchful for weapons in or near his one good hand. Nothing. The dead man, falling, had propelled his handgun out of reach, and Lee appeared to be unarmed.

"It didn't have to play like this," Bolan said.

"Am I dead yet?" Joseph Lee asked.

"You'll live," Bolan informed him. "If you tell me what I need to know."

Almost incredibly, Lee smiled at that. Giggled. "So much concern about one round-eye. He must be a very naughty boy."

"Something to think about," Bolan suggested. "If you live, and we don't stop him, you'll be doing time as an accomplice to his crimes. You aided and abetted, covered for him. Likely helped him make connections in the first place. All on you, unless you help."

"He's doing something bad, then." Lee still smiled.

"The prosecution of your family won't stop with you," Bolan said. "Canada's a partner in the war on terror. So are Britain and Australia. I can see them rolling up the 14K like an old carpet, beating it to get the bugs and dust out. All on you now. And your boss will know it, while you're sitting safe and sound in prison."

"Maybe not so safe and sound," Dixon said, jumping in.

"Suppose," Lee said, "I just sit here and bleed to death?"

"Not happening," Bolan said. "If I have to, I can drive you to the hospital myself. Sit with you while the doctors work, until the cops arrive."

"Such kindness to a stranger."

"Information, Mr. Lee. That's all we need. He isn't one of yours. He's not even Chinese."

Far off, faint sirens raised their voices like coyotes baying at the moon.

"Hear that?" Bolan inquired. "They're coming for you."

"You must promise to release me, if I tell," Lee said.

"You have my word."

Bolan saw Dixon blinking at him. First confused, then startled, as the meaning of the triad leader's words hit home.

"Come closer, then."

"I hear you fine, from here."

Another giggle. "You're afraid I'll bite you."

"Stranger things have happened."

Sirens closer now. They seemed to help Lee focus.

"Honestly? Your word?"

"I swear."

"Only a phone number," Lee said. "For satellite, I think."

"That's good enough," Bolan told him.

Lee ran down the digits. Bolan memorized them on the spot, while Dixon rummaged through his pockets for a pen and scrap of paper.

"Now, your promise." Lee's eyes held him.

"Fair enough."

He could've dialed the sat phone number, let it ring, but then what? If he rang up now, tipping his hand, Talmadge would simply ditch the phone and with it any hope they had of tracking him. As long as he held on to it, there was a chance of finding him.

"They're getting close," Dixon alerted him.

"I hear them," Bolan said.

He rose and drew the Glock, framed Lee's face in its sights and put a bullet through the triad leader's forehead, providing the release the man had asked for.

"Crazy bastard," Dixon muttered.

"He was cornered," Bolan said, "with no way out except the one he chose."

"What happens if he stiffed us on the number, maybe gave us Pizza Hut instead of Talmadge?"

"Then we order out," said Bolan. "Hold the anchovies."

"I'm serious. What happens now?"

"First thing, we clear away from here," Bolan replied. "And then we get back in the game we came to play."

# CHAPTER TWELVE

*Emerson, Manitoba*

Talmadge approached the border checkpoint slowly in his stolen car, with stolen license plates attached. He'd boosted the new wheels—a respectable Toyota SUV—outside a shopping mall in Winnipeg, after completing his business with Muhunnad Hashim. The plates came from another SUV entirely, swapped for those of his hot car to give John Q. Public the headache. Once his cargo had been transferred, Talmadge performed some fancy footwork in taxi cabs, returned his Canadian rental, and he was ready to roll.

The mercenary was tingling with excitement as he crept behind the other cars backed up to cross the border, but his rearview mirror and a lifetime of experience told him it didn't show externally. To all appearances, he was as cold as ice, without a worry on his mind.

It *was* exciting, though, to think that they could pop him any one of four ways now. The stolen plates, of course. Or, if they looked a little closer, for the car itself. Then, if they had some kind of covert Geiger counter apparatus at the checkpoint, Talmadge wasn't sure whether the lead shields fitted by Hashim could fool sensitive instruments.

Something to think about, and one more reason not to handle the bomb unless he absolutely had to. As in, maybe one more time, when he got rid of it for good.

And the fourth potential snag, of course, was Talmadge himself.

He'd been thinking about it, ever since the raid on his apartment in Vancouver. Briefly glimpsing one of the attackers, Talmadge knew the guy had been a round-eye, and his actions didn't mesh with those of any law-enforcement agency outside Hollywood's illusion factory.

That set him thinking, questioning his first assumption that the hit had targeted his dinner guests. That theory made sense superficially, but once he started taking it apart, it had some gaping holes.

Assuming that the triad had some round-eyed enemies—Russians, Sicilians, Colombians—Talmadge now believed the raid had been peculiar to the point that it was setting off alarm bells. Home invasions were the riskiest of risky business, and while he could think of several outfits that routinely slaughtered families to make a point, he couldn't think of one that would deliberately raid a strange third party's home to kill a well-known mobster.

If the Russians or whoever wanted to kill triad members, they could find targets throughout the city of Vancouver without menacing civilians or unduly tweaking the police. If they were out for Joseph Lee, his brother or some other triad VIP, the shooters would've had the target's address, would've known his favored hangouts, where his mistress lived—in short, the whole damned enchilada.

No.

The more Talmadge considered it, the more he thought that *he* had been the target in Vancouver. That in turn forced him to reconsider suspects and potential motives, scanning back over his private history.

Who could it be?

The shooter Talmadge saw was white, but that meant less than nothing. Africans and Asians could hire hit men any color of the human rainbow, if they chose, and might prefer some misdirection just in case the hit went south on them. There were a couple Third World heavies who might want to take out Talmadge, but intervening years without a move on either of their parts made it unlikely that they suddenly would try to take him out.

Who else?

Someone he'd dealt with recently, but that narrowed the field primarily to members of the 14K who'd bought the farm at his apartment, and to certain Arab groups. He knew damned well the triad hadn't sent a gang of round-eye shooters to his flat, killing their own men in the process by mistake.

Which left the Arabs, and that made no sense at all.

He'd served them well so far, and they were in the middle of their biggest project yet, a blow against the common enemy to which Talmadge had proved his commitment time and time again. There was no reason for al Qaeda to dispose of him at this point, and a raid on his apartment didn't fit their profile.

Not when they could just as easily have killed him when

he met Aman Nadir in Richmond, or when he was waiting for the bomb in Winnipeg. The fact that he was still alive and inching toward the border with his deadly cargo told him that his Arab friends were in the clear.

That only left the other side, and if the Feds were after him in Canada or the United States, wouldn't they come with warrants, flashing lights, tear gas, the whole nine yards?

Maybe.

And maybe not.

Talmadge was frowning when he reached the checkpoint, had to wipe it off his face and give the freckled redhead in the snug blue uniform a smile to make her day. Showed her his U.S. passport that was ninety-five percent legitimate, only the name and address being absolutely false.

She eyeballed it and him, returned his smile, then asked him about meat, fruit or vegetables. She didn't ask him about weapons or explosives, and she most emphatically made no inquiry after any kind of nuclear material.

Talmadge was happy to inform her that he had no veggies in the car.

"Okay," she told him, stepping back. "Have a nice day."

*Washington, D.C.*

TRACING A SAT PHONE WAS more complicated than a landline tap. With landlines, the potential eavesdropper knew where they started, where they went and every point of access in between. These days, in fact, an old-style tap was rarely necessary. There were microphones that could be planted in a subject's telephone itself, and warrants could obtain cooperation from the service carriers. No bugging expert in the world could tell a client if his line was being monitored by telephone company operators.

Cell phones were harder, since they had no lines to tap. But on the upside, every call made from a cell phone was beamed through open air, where anyone could snatch it for themselves if he or she had the equipment and the proper codes. For starters, they would need the cell phone's number and its location. The first part was relatively easy to procure, but pinning down a cell phone on the move required triangulation, which was time-consuming even with computers on the job.

Sat phones were one step up from cell phones, sometimes producing scrambled or encoded calls, but otherwise the principle was more or less the same. Scanners required a starting point—the source phone's ID number and a target signal—that would let them zero in to get a lock. Once that had been achieved, hunters could track the telephone as long as it was turned on, even if transmission had been terminated.

Hal Brognola had the target's ID number, but he didn't have the signal, didn't have the lock.

And so it had become a waiting game.

He hadn't liked the bloodshed in Vancouver, wished it could've been avoided, but at least the casualties were all triad gangsters or their employees in the drug trade. Rattling their cages at a licensed casino had been risky, but the gamble had paid off.

So they had two dozen triad members dead in Canada, the whole place up in arms, rude noises from the RCMP about "overstepping bounds," which could turn into an incident all by itself. Smoothing those feathers would require diplomacy, though Brognola was fairly certain that his counterparts across the border wouldn't miss the thugs that Bolan and his sidekick had removed from circulation without benefit of trial.

Which still left Talmadge on the loose, perhaps already in possession of the weapon that could rock America to its foundations and produce a panic backlash that would make the furor after 9/11 seem like the Age of Aquarius.

But at least they had his sat phone number, thanks to Bolan, and their target had to use it sometime, didn't he? Brognola didn't think that Talmadge meant to plant and detonate the bomb himself, didn't see Bolan's evil twin as any kind of martyr type. That meant he had to have at least one contact in the States somewhere, and he would have to get in touch at least once more.

Unless they had already set the rendezvous.

Unless the contact had another way of reaching Talmadge, or vice versa.

If he switched to landlines, e-mail or the like, they would be back at square one. Lost and going nowhere fast. All Talmadge had to do to lose them was to step inside an Internet café.

"Bastard."

The sound of his own voice brought the big Fed back to the here and now, his office, with its paper-littered desk. He started squaring things away, no system to it really, but the simple action made him feel better.

"You aren't clear yet," he told the empty room, wishing Talmadge could hear him. "It's not over yet. You haven't won. We'll nail you yet, you son of a bitch!"

And having purged himself, Brognola settled back to wait for news from Stony Man.

"THIS WAITING SUCKS," Tom Dixon said.

Lounging beside him in the aircraft hangar, Jack Grimaldi said, "It's in the job description, man."

"That must've been the fine print I forgot to read," Dixon replied.

"It always is, kid. Always is."

Dixon stood up and stretched, then looked around for Cooper, but the former soldier wasn't anywhere in sight. "Where did he go?" Dixon asked.

"Likely catching forty winks up in the Lear," Grimaldi said. "This kind of thing, you get it where you can."

"I can't believe it takes this long to trace a telephone," Dixon complained.

"Technology," Grimaldi said. "It's not all like they make it seem on *CSI* or *SUV*."

"I think that's *SVU*," Dixon corrected him.

"Whatever. Hollywood takes something relatively basic, and they either get it wrong completely or they make it seem like magic, instant-fix time."

"I suppose," Dixon said.

"Look at profiling, for instance," Grimaldi pressed on. "In movies, some hot chick walks through a crime scene, and she's flashing on all kinds of psychic vibes, seeing the killer's point of view and every move he made, reading his thoughts and spitting out some kind of New Age criminology. That's all a lot of crap."

"I figured."

"Same thing, when they show the heroes tracing cell phones," Grimaldi said. "On the tube, they press a button and you see a map, flashing the caller's address nice and bright in thirty seconds, tops. Real life, you have to catch a lot of breaks, starting with number one—he has to use the phone."

"Still, if he's out there, doing business, making contacts, setting up catastrophes, he has to use the phone."

"You'd think so, right?" Grimaldi said. "Unless he has some other way set up to keep in touch with people while he's on the road. For all we know, he ditched his whole life after bailing out of the apartment in Vancouver."

"Then we've lost him," Dixon said. "We've failed."

"You kids today give up too easily."

"So, what's the bright side?" Dixon queried.

Grimaldi began to tick the points off on his fingers. "You and Cooper are alive, and neither of you took a hit. That's one—or maybe two, depending how you look at it. No one but heavies took a hit so far. You didn't get arrested by the Mounties or the local cops. You got the number for his sat phone, even if he hasn't used it yet. You've got a killer team to help you trace it, if and when he does. You've got the Lear and me to take you anywhere you need to go, as soon as Talmadge surfaces. Want more?"

"No, thanks." Dixon was nodding, but he couldn't find his smile. "I just want this thing over with. I want my normal life back."

That made Grimaldi laugh. "Good luck with that," he said.

"What's that supposed to mean?"

"You've crossed a line, kid, and you've seen the other

side. Maybe you can go back, maybe not. Some people at the office may be looking at you differently from now on. Maybe you'll start to get the jobs your watercooler friends can't handle."

"No," Dixon said, almost angrily. "That isn't what I want. I didn't ask for this job."

"Hey, sometimes the job picks *you*," Grimaldi said. "That's how it works."

"Then I'll resign."

"And do what? Sell used cars? Teach junior high? Come on. You've got a taste for it. Said so yourself."

"I said I was *afraid* I might. That's not a good thing."

"Didn't sound afraid to me. And didn't act it last night in the park, from what I hear."

"I couldn't just run off and leave him, could I? Even if he told me to?"

"That's what I mean. You saw a job that needed doing, and you did it. On the downside, though, sometimes there *is* a reason for those orders."

"Leaving men behind to die?"

"If saving them means blowing off your mission, or it costs more lives than you can save. Shit happens."

"Shit is right," Dixon groused. "I feel like I'm in it to my neck and sinking fast."

"Maybe. But you could still walk anytime. Hell, you could quit right now, if you were serious. I think you dig it."

Dixon scowled at that and said the only thing that he could think of. "If you're right, that makes it even worse."

"Somebody has to do the dirty jobs," Grimaldi said.

"All right. Then why can't we get on with it?"

"This is the waiting part," Grimaldi said. "It never goes away."

"But Talmadge doesn't have to wait. He's out there, somewhere, doing what he needs to do."

"You're right," Grimaldi said. "Let's hope he has to do some of it on the telephone."

*Bemidji, Minnesota*

HALFWAY TO HIS FINAL DESTINATION—final for the bomb, at least, if not for *him*—Gene Talmadge stopped for hamburgers and gasoline. The price of both amazed him, and he made a mental note to avoid truckstop diners in the future.

When he had filled his stomach and topped off his gas tank, Talmadge found a reasonably quiet place to park his stolen car and used the sat phone. Two calls that he couldn't very well avoid, for different reasons.

One to make sure that the mission was on track.

And one to make sure he got paid.

He took the second first, dialing the longer of two numbers in his head and waiting through the rings until Nasser Asad's driver gave him a gruff "Hello."

"It's me," Talmadge said. "Put him on."

No names in a long-distance conversation, just in case. Make all those nosy bastards at the NSA work for their keep, at least.

The best part of a minute passed, its slow drag galling Talmadge, before Asad came on the line. "I've been expecting you."

Talmadge swallowed his first response, which would've

flayed Asad for making him hang on an open line so long that it was traceable.

Instead, he simply said, "I need to keep this short. You understand."

"Of course."

"I'm roughly halfway there," he said. Again, no names. "About 230 miles to go before delivery."

"That's excellent. No further problems?"

"Not so far."

"I'm glad to hear it."

"You can go ahead and trigger payment."

"On delivery," Asad reminded him. "As we agreed."

"I'm almost there!"

"A lot can happen in 230 miles."

He didn't like the Arab's tone, the implication.

"Listen up. If you've got something up your sleeve on this, you're making a mistake."

"My sleeve? Oh, yes, I see. There is no trick, my friend. I simply hold to the original agreement, which does not provide for early payment."

"All right, then. It means I'll have to call you afterward. More contact, greater risk."

"I'll take that chance."

Meaning that Talmadge had to risk it, too.

"Your call," he said. And then, "I *will* be paid upon delivery." Not asking any more.

"Of course, my friend."

"Because there will be consequences if that payment doesn't clear."

"We understand each other."

"I hope so."

"Drive safely."

And the line went dead.

Son of a bitch! The rude bastard had cut him off.

A quick glance at his wristwatch told Talmadge that it was just as well. The call had taken too long, for safety's sake. He didn't plan to make that error twice.

His last call to Afif Mukhtar was going to be short and sweet.

The distant telephone rang only once before an eager young voice filled his ear. "Hello!"

"I'll be there in about four hours," Talmadge told him. "Give or take. You'll be at home."

"Yes!"

"Nothing unusual about today, so far?" he asked.

Meaning, had Mukhtar noticed any unmarked vans or strangers lurking in the neighborhood since last they spoke.

"Nothing," the young man said.

"Okay. I'll see you when I see you."

"I'll be here!"

And bouncing off the walls like a demented sugar junkie, from the sound of it.

Martyrs.

Talmadge would never fully understand the rush they got from squandering their lives. But, then again, he didn't have to understand it. All he had to do was make delivery and watch the balance on his bank account to verify one final transfer.

Mission accomplished, but with no high-profile photo ops to spread the word.

Talmadge had always been the quiet type. If not exactly self-effacing, then at least adept at letting others take the blame and catch the hell when anything went wrong.

It wasn't that he didn't know when he was wrong. But why be punished if that punishment could be avoided? It was simply common sense.

He switched off the sat phone and dropped it on the seat beside him. He would only need it one more time, before he dropped it in a river or a lake somewhere.

But in the meantime, he was thinking of new wheels.

*St. Paul, Minnesota*

AFIF MUKHTAR COULDN'T sit still. He longed to run outside his small apartment, cheering in his underwear, but knew that such a celebration would abort the plan and spoil his one clear shot at Paradise.

Of late, the images described by the imam had filled his dreams. Mukhtar had seen the luscious gardens, strolled along the streets of gold, clad in a robe of silk and nothing else. No matter where he went, more nubile virgins waited for him, living but to serve in any way that his imagination could contrive. So far, in those dreams, Mukhtar hadn't sampled any of the kingdom's milk or honey, but he didn't mind. His other appetites had been well satisfied.

On the occasions when he thought about the final act itself, Mukhtar was curious but not truly afraid. He'd made a point of reading about nuclear explosions, their destructive power, and he understood the basic physics of it.

When he triggered the device, within the next few microseconds, there would be a chain reaction that produced the mighty blast. Terrific heat beyond imagining would vaporize his body instantly. Mukhtar supposed there would be pain of some description, but so fleeting that it hardly mattered. Long before he had a chance to scream, he would be gone, the shock waves radiating from ground zero to eradicate his enemies in tens of thousands.

And his soul would be in Paradise, embarked upon a sweet dream that would never end.

Some of the "modern" Muslims in his second mosque had talked about extremism, as if they thought it possible for love of God to be too extreme. They had denied that martyrs earned a place in Paradise, pointing to texts from the Koran that called for peace and love. Mukhtar had smiled and nodded, gone along with them in public, but he hadn't been confused.

He knew his duty and the grand reward awaiting him.

There would be nervousness, of course. Mukhtar knew that was inescapable. En route to carry out his mission, he would have to think about the things that could go wrong and guard against them every step along the way.

He would be driving to the final target, carefully, within the speed limit, avoiding accidents and the delay occasioned by a traffic ticket. On arrival, he would park his car, remove the weapon and proceed as if he were an ordinary citizen transacting business in a standard manner. By that time, if anyone suspected him or tried to stop him, they would be too late. A few yards wouldn't matter in the scheme of things.

Mukhtar could detonate the weapon any time he

wanted to, and still be guaranteed a spot in Paradise. But he would do as he'd been ordered, to the limit of his personal ability.

He ran through various scenarios, rehearsing what to do if anything went wrong.

Suppose he did get stopped for speeding or some other reason, on his drive to reach the target. Mukhtar had a pistol loaded with a clip of Teflon-coated bullets, armor-piercing rounds that the Americans called "cop killers." It would not matter if the officer who stopped him wore a Kevlar vest or not.

Arriving at the target, if police were waiting for him in the parking lot, blocking his path to ground zero—or if security tried to corral him inside—Mukhtar would end it, trigger the device and send the infidels to Hell a minute early.

Done.

It was surprising to discover that he felt no fear.

Death only frightened those who didn't know where they were going afterward, or those who knew that they were headed for their just reward without hope of mercy. For Afif Mukhtar, the great transition held no mystery, no dread. He would be going to a vastly better place.

With all those virgins waiting. Eager. Wanting him.

And he would finally become a man.

A little late, perhaps, but he had waited when his friends—what few he had—were sinning to achieve the earthly pleasure they desired. They had belittled Mukhtar, laughed at him for his decision to abstain.

But he would have the last laugh soon.

And everyone would envy him.

*Vancouver, British Columbia*

"WE'VE GOT HIM," Bolan said.

Dixon and Grimaldi rose from metal folding chairs and faced him. "Where?" the Stony Man pilot asked.

"He made two calls, the first one long enough to trace," Bolan replied. "A mile or so outside Bemidji, Minnesota."

"Never heard of it," Dixon said.

"I have," Grimaldi replied. "About two hundred miles south of the Manitoba border."

"That's the spot," Bolan said. "Talmadge called the dip-lomat, first thing. Somebody kept him waiting long enough to help us out."

"Nasser Asad?" Dixon asked.

"Right. We got the conversation. Possibly enough to boot Asad, if we can prove Talmadge is dirty."

"Boot him?" Dixon challenged. "Why don't we just—?"

"Easy, boy," Grimaldi counseled. "Let's hear where we're going first."

"That's where we hit a snag," Bolan said. "No one mentioned any names of places, but we have Talmadge telling Asad that he has something like 230 miles to go be-fore delivery."

"I'll get a map," Grimaldi said, hustled for it, coming back a moment later with a large-scale folding map of the United States. He spread it on the hangar floor and found Bemidji with a little effort.

"So, 230 miles from here," he said, tapping Bemidji, Minnesota, with a fingertip. "Its safe to rule out Canada, since Talmadge just came down from there."

"And any other place," Dixon said, "that he could've reached by now, without the stop in Minnesota."

"Right," Bolan agreed. "He's going south. Maybe southeast, southwest."

"He's got a thousand towns to choose from," Grimaldi said, "but if he's come looking for a body count, it has to be—"

"The Twin Cities," said Bolan.

"Jesus!" the pilot swore.

"How long to get there?" Bolan asked.

"Let's call it eighteen hundred miles," Grimaldi said. "The Lear can do around five hundred thirty, tops. Allowing for takeoff and landing, four hours would be our best bet."

"Then let's go," Bolan said. "We should get there around the same time as our boy."

"If that is where he's going," Dixon said.

"I'll risk it," Bolan said. "At least we'll be in the right state."

A runway traffic jam delayed them longer than Grimaldi would've liked, but they were airborne twenty minutes later, soaring on a course to the southeast. Bolan knew he was gambling, but right now it was the only game in town.

It made sense, Talmadge heading for the Minnesota anthill that was Minneapolis-St. Paul. Bolan didn't possess the latest census figures, but he knew that the Twin Cities had to be home to some three-quarters of a million people, anyway. And tens of thousands more would work there, making the commute each day from their outlying homes.

Still, there were many larger, more inviting targets to be found in the United States. From Washington, D.C., and

New York City to Miami, Atlanta, Chicago, Dallas-Fort Worth, L.A., San Francisco or Seattle.

Why the Twin Cities?

Bolan tried to adjust his thinking, slip into terrorist mode and work out what al Qaeda's plotters might've had in mind. Minneapolis-St. Paul was located in the American heartland, but so were Chicago and Indianapolis, both with higher potential body counts.

It wasn't just the target, Bolan finally decided, but the contact. Somehow, al Qaeda had secured an agent in the general Twin Cities area, as yet unknown to anyone at DHS, the FBI or Stony Man. An individual who was prepared to die and to take a few hundred thousand Americans with him.

With her?

Bolan dismissed that possibility, in light of ultrafundamentalism's take on women. Hamas might trust a female bomber in a pinch. Al Qaeda or the Taliban? Never.

So they were looking for another man, besides Talmadge. The former Green Beret would guide them to the other, if they found him soon enough.

Brognola had his feelers out already, to the FBI and DHS, to state and local law-enforcement agencies. They would be turning over every rock in the Twin Cities, looking for a handle, anything at all to help the search along.

And in the meanwhile, Bolan had to think about potential targets. Knowing al Qaeda's mentality, it had to be something symbolic, as well as packed with victims. The Twin Towers, in 2001, had symbolized America's global commerce, the very throbbing heart of international capitalism.

What did Minnesota have that could compare?

"Sorry, guys," Grimaldi's voice intruded, "but we've got some stormy weather up ahead. The Midwest's pretty well socked in, in fact. I'll do my best to fly above it, but our ETA just went to hell. Could add three-quarters of an hour to our flight time, if it's really bad."

More time to think, at least, Bolan thought.

But in the meantime, Talmadge would be getting closer to his drop.

And closer to the big bang that could leave America forever changed.

# CHAPTER THIRTEEN

*Coon Rapids, Minnesota*

The storm that had been chasing him for hours finally caught up with Talmadge in a quaintly named suburb of Minneapolis. It broke around him with a thunderclap that could've been God's wrath, long forks of lightning licking underneath the clouds and sometimes reaching down to spark the earth. Rain fell in sheets, rendering windshield wipers useless, but he pushed on anyway, cutting his speed a little as more-cautious drivers parked along the highway's shoulder.

It was perfect weather for replacing stolen wheels.

He found a thriving mall on University Avenue, where Coon Rapids was situated west of the pavement, with suburban Blaine to the east. The mall was in Blaine, its drenched parking lot half filled with cars, but Talmadge guessed none of the shoppers would emerge until the downpour eased a bit.

By that time, he'd be on his way.

He found another SUV he liked—a Blazer, this time—and parked his hot wheels in the slot just beside it. Struggling into a plastic raincoat, he ran around his car and used his jimmy on the Blazer's driver's door. Inside, he popped the locks and sprang the hatch in back before he snapped off the ignition switch and revved it with his rubber-handled screwdriver.

Next job, transferring cargo to the Blazer from the car he was abandoning. That took perhaps a minute, with the Halliburton bomb case heaviest of all his luggage. Talmadge put it in the rear, dumping his own bags in the back seat, just in case of any radiation bleed. He didn't think it was a problem, but he also saw no point in taking needless chances.

Finally, the license plates. Instead of stealing new ones, Talmadge swapped the tags from his hot roller to the Blazer, kept the Blazer's for a later switch at need, and tucked them underneath his luggage.

Ready.

He was rolling free and clear on the five-minute mark, with nothing to suggest anyone had seen him make the swap. There might be cameras in the parking lot—most malls had them these days—but he was counting on the dark day and the driving rain to blur his image on the cheap gear most management bought to save some coin.

It hadn't cost him much in terms of time, either. The storm would be to blame for any tardiness marked down against him, but he didn't have a solid time for meeting Afif Mukhtar. The kid would wait for him at home until he got there, likely worried that he couldn't use the bathroom without missing Talmadge at his door.

He thought of calling, giving Mukhtar an update on his ETA, then thought to hell with it. He'd be there when he got there, making time as best he could. The kid wasn't supposed to do his thing this day, in any case.

Tomorrow was the target date.

Talmadge had marked it on his mental calendar.

D-day, they would have called it in jargon peculiar to the military.

This time around, he simply thought of it as payback time.

He'd been a stickler for the rules when he was on the inside, looking out—and would be still, he guessed, except for how the brass had shafted him. They talked a load of crap about responsibility, honor and duty, but if anything went wrong and risked embarrassing the service, all they thought about was covering their asses and protecting brother officers.

It wasn't as if he'd killed the first lieutenant, after all. Talmadge had caught him dead to rights, attempting rape. No doubt about that whatsoever from what he had seen, or what the victim-corporal had told investigators from the CID. He'd caught the bastard and had called for him to stop before he ever raised a hand in anger.

The lieutenant was the one who'd come out swinging. Reflex took over after that, but he'd stopped short of killing, as he had been trained to do.

Who really cared about a scumbag rapist with a broken jaw and dislocated shoulder? So what if the asshole couldn't get it up again, after a book collapsed his sack and crushed his pubic bone?

That was a good thing, right?

Instead of prosecuting the lieutenant, though, the brass had piled it all on Talmadge, screwed him big time, while the corporal caught a transfer to Butte or Nome or some damned place, with sergeant's stripes to follow if she kept her mouth shut.

Perfect.

The men responsible for crucifying Talmadge likely thought they'd done a good day's work. Maybe they had, from their distorted point of view.

But now a day of reckoning had come. Shoe on the other foot, and all that jazz.

Talmadge turned on the radio and found a rocking band to wail him on his way.

*Airborne over North Dakota*

"I STILL DON'T UNDERSTAND," Dixon said, "how we're going to find Talmadge on the ground."

They were already late, thanks to the storm, and he was feeling green around the gills from all the turbulence. Up front, Grimaldi had his hands full in the cockpit, so Dixon was killing time with Bolan.

"I'm not sure myself," Bolan replied. "We have all kinds of people searching high and low for him down there, around the Twin Cities. Searching discreetly, I should say."

"Meaning they want to find him, but pretend they haven't," Dixon said.

"Something like that."

"He's still ours, then, even though we know he has the bomb."

"We don't know anything," Bolan corrected him. "It's probable."

"Okay. I get that we can't charge Talmadge with treason, since no war has been declared. Got it. But what about the thousand other crimes he's already committed? Even if he's not transporting nuclear material or weapons of mass destruction, we have him for illegal entry into the United States."

"Where he's a citizen," Bolan said.

"Traveling on a false passport, at the very least," Dixon said. "Maybe in a stolen car. With weapons, some of which are banned by state and federal statutes."

"None of that's important," Bolan said. "We want the bomb *and* everyone connected to it. Right?"

"You know Mick Jagger, yes?" Dixon said.

"Never met him personally, no."

"His music. As in you can't always get what you want?"

"We haven't really tried yet," Bolan answered.

"What? We've chased this piece of shit halfway around the world and killed something like half a hundred men trying to find him. If the G-men or a county mountie finds him now, why not just drop the net?"

"Too risky," Bolan said. "We know this is about revenge, at least in part. Talmadge is harboring a grudge against the Army, possibly the country."

"So?"

"So, if he's cornered, given no way out, maybe he'll trigger the device himself. Go out in one hellacious blaze of glory for his own cause, never mind about al Qaeda's."

"Shit!" Dixon hadn't considered that.

"Exactly. And we're in it to our eyeballs if we mess this up."

"So now we're back to surgical excision, I suppose?"

"Ideally," Bolan said. "Find Talmadge. Track him to his contacts. Take them out before they have a chance to make their move."

"Sounds easy."

"Don't I wish," Bolan said.

"Yeah. Me, too." Dixon peered through his rain-lashed window, into clouds as dark as midnight. "This storm's killing us on time."

"It's storming on the ground, too."

"God, I hope so."

Let it pour, he thought, and keep Talmadge from rolling into town before we do.

Wherever he was going with his killer cargo.

As it was, they didn't know if he was headed for St. Paul, for Minneapolis or for any of a couple dozen suburbs. On arrival, he could drive toward any compass point, mingling with thousands on the streets, and keep any prearranged date with his comrade the two of them might've cooked up.

And there was nothing anyone could do about it.

Not unless they caught a lucky break.

Bolan fished in a pocket for his telephone and opened it, though Dixon hadn't heard it ring. "It's me," he said, and waited, frowning. Then, "Okay. Got that. And thanks."

Tucking the phone away, he told Dixon, "We caught a break. Talmadge now has a friend in the Twin Cities who we recognize."

"And that would be...?"

"Nasser Asad," Bolan replied.

"What brings him there?"

"Supposedly, some kind of trade mission. My gut says he's in town to handle any last-minute emergencies—or maybe just because he wants a ringside seat."

"Too close for safety's sake, I'd say," Dixon replied.

"Maybe, but it still works to our advantage."

"What, two birds, one stone?"

"I'm thinking that if Talmadge knows Assad's in town, he might touch base. Just might. It's something we can use against him."

"Maybe. If he makes contact," Dixon said.

"Right," Bolan said, turning to his own small vista on the storm. "A lot of ifs."

*St. Paul, Minnesota*

AFIF MUKHTAR SAT at the window of his small apartment's living room, watching the traffic pass on Fremont Avenue. Beside him on the sofa was a rumpled paper bag. Inside the bag lay the Walther PP pistol he had purchased from a long-haired man who sold guns from his car, at Pig's Eye Park. Mukhtar had fired the weapon only once before, a nervous outing to the green lands of Dakota County, south of Minneapolis-St. Paul, and while he clearly wouldn't rank as any sort of expert marksman, Mukhtar believed that he could manage well enough at close range in emergencies.

He wouldn't need the gun this day, of course. His visitor, although a white man and an infidel, was nonetheless an ally in the cause to which Afif Mukhtar had pledged his life. They might not share a common heritage, but any enemy of the Great Satan was a friend indeed.

He checked his wristwatch, perhaps the fifth time he had done so in the past half hour, and fidgeted, restless, on the sagging sofa cushions. The apartment stank of cats, a prior tenant's thoughtful gift, and it had come with worn-out furniture, a bargain at a monthly rate that tripled what an average worker in his homeland would be paid for working twenty-eight twelve-hour days.

Mukhtar still marveled at the decadence of the United States, but it was working out to his advantage. Even with the anti-Arab feeling that had spread throughout the country since 2001, attacks on local mosques and so forth, Mukhtar still had no major difficulty holding down a job that paid his monthly bills. He led a simple life and waited for the moment when he could emerge from hiding, strike a killing blow against the monster that had tormented his people for so long.

Soon, now. Another day or two, at most.

And then…

He sat bolt upright, his right hand straying to the paper bag beside him. On the street, a dark blue SUV was passing for the second time within two minutes, more or less. The driver was alone and peering carefully at numbers painted on the curb.

Mukhtar was on his feet when the vehicle made its third pass, heading in the opposite direction now. Its driver found a parking space across the street and two doors down, forcing the young man to crane his neck for a clear view. Because they hadn't met before, only discussed their business on the telephone in cryptic terms, he couldn't say if this man was his contact or a visitor for one of his neighbors.

Mukhtar felt his pulse quicken as the man walked around behind his SUV, opened the rear hatch and tailgate and extracted a heavy black suitcase. After he closed the hatch again, the stranger took his bag and crossed the street on a diagonal, moving directly toward Mukhtar's apartment building.

Worried that it might prove to be a trap, he tore the pistol from its crinkled bag, untucked his shirt and slipped the gun into his waistband at the rear, covered by his shirttail. That done, Mukhtar bent and shoved the bag under the sofa, out of sight.

He stood before the door and waited, barely breathing, listening for footsteps on the stairs. They sounded faint and distant, drawing closer as the stranger with the suitcase moved along the corridor in his direction.

The knock was startling, despite his mental preparation for it. Lurching forward, Mukhtar peered through the door's peephole, confirmed that only one man stood there. Swallowing a hard lump in his throat, he fumbled with the three locks, then stepped backward from the open door.

"It is a happy day," the stranger with the suitcase said.

"When God smiles on us," Mukhtar said, completing the pass code. And then, "Come in, please, by all means."

The stocky, solemn man entered his living room, surveyed it with a single sweeping glance and set his suitcase on the floor beside a coffee table.

"Welcome," Mukhtar said. "Would you like coffee? Tea?"

"I'd rather do a run-through on the package," his visitor said, "and make sure you can handle it."

"Yes, please," Mukhtar replied, beaming. "I have been looking forward to it very much."

THE YOUTH SEEMED fairly normal, for a martyr in the making. Talmadge had expected someone with wild eyes, maybe a straggly beard, with sunken cheeks and spindly arms, like something from a refugee camp overseas. But while the young man was indeed quite slender, he still had a healthy look about him, smiling readily, well dressed and groomed. He might've been a college student or somebody's junior secretary, rather than a terrorist about to sacrifice himself for Allah's cause.

It took all kinds.

A glance told Talmadge that he couldn't trust the coffee table with the Halliburton's weight. Instead, he asked the kid to move it, waiting while it was removed into a corner of the Spartan living room. That done, Talmadge sat on the sofa, with his suitcase on the floor in front of him.

"This isn't difficult," he said by way of introduction. "There's no special code to learn, nothing like that. We've kept it nice and simple."

So an idiot could handle it, he thought, but kept that to himself. The kid sat down beside him, close enough to watch, but leaving space between them, so their elbows wouldn't touch, even by accident.

"First thing, open the bag like this," Talmadge instructed, showing Mukhtar the proper way to twist, then press the latching flaps. They popped open with sounds like muffled pistol shots and made the youth flinch a little, though he tried to cover it.

We've got some rabbit here, Talmadge thought, wondering if Mukhtar could find the nerve to finish what he'd started. Still, the Arab's eyes were bright, his attitude suggesting more excitement than fear.

Talmadge opened the suitcase's lid and eased it back onto the floor, revealing what appeared to be a leaden box inside.

"The works are all in there," he said. "Lead shielding all around. There's no reason for you to open it. In fact, you can't, unless you bring in power tools and mess the whole thing up. We clear on that?"

A jerky nod from Mukhtar, but Talmadge waited, making him pronounce the words. "Quite clear. Thank you."

"Okay. You only need to know about two working parts. The first one is right here." As Talmadge spoke, he pointed toward a red switch mounted on the right side of the bomb's lead casing. A red light above it glowed.

"That red light means the bomb's disarmed. It can't go off. All right?"

Another nod. "I understand disarmed," Mukhtar said, assertive, but not snotty with it. Fair enough.

"Push the switch down, the green light there below it should come on, and the red light goes off. That means the bomb is armed. Ready to blow."

"I see."

"No test runs on the arming switch, all right? It's one-time-only. Once you flip the switch, the bomb can't be disarmed. You can't reach in and turn it off. Nobody can. It takes a pro with special tools to go in and disarm it once you flip the switch. Save that for right before the end. Still clear?"

"Of course."

"Okay, we're halfway home. You see, it's easy, like I said. After you arm the weapon, then you close and latch the case again, like this."

Talmadge went through the motions, closed the lid, reset the latches. When he glanced at Mukhtar, the youth nodded.

"Now, once it's armed and latched, the only thing that's left for you to do is blow it, when you reach your target. No trick there. The trigger's built into the handle...there."

He pointed toward a screw positioned on the left side of the case's handle, as he faced it standing upright. It was placed for detonation with the thumb of the right hand, but any lefty could've done it just as well, turning the case around.

"After you arm the bomb and latch the case, that screw protrudes a quarter-inch or so. Nothing too obvious, but it *is* sensitive. Don't leave the case where anyone can handle it or jostle it around, after it's armed. Okay?"

"Okay."

"Questions?"

"It seems straightforward," Mukhtar replied. "It has been tested, I assume?"

"I'm told the trigger has. The big bang, not so much."

"Of course. I understand."

"All right, then, if we're clear on everything," Talmadge said, "I could use that cup of coffee now."

*St. Paul Downtown Airport*

"I'M STARTING OUR APPROACH," Grimaldi said over the Learjet's intercom. "We should be on the ground in twenty minutes, give or take."

The storm had broken somewhere over northern Minnesota, though the clouds still hadn't cleared, and Bolan couldn't see the ground below them from his tiny window streaked with remnants of the thrashing rain. Across the aisle, Tom Dixon cleared his throat and leaned toward Bolan.

"Someone's meeting us, you said?" he asked.

"Supposed to be. Likely the Bureau, unless you've got someone on the ground."

"In Minnesota? I suppose so, but I wouldn't know them. Can we trust the FBI?"

"For information, probably."

Bolan was conscious of the rivalry that simmered between different federal agencies in Washington. It filtered down from jealous, arrogant department heads who craved greater authority, more headlines, and it often hampered operations in the field. Before the 9/11 raids, it had been worst between the FBI and CIA, though ATF and other agencies also complained about the Bureau's tendency to hog glory from cases where its role was marginal at best, and sometimes nonexistent. Since declaration of the war on terror, cutbacks on normal crime fighting, complaints from sister agencies—and from police across the land—had multiplied.

"You don't sound very sure," Dixon said.

"Let's see what they have to say."

Bolan couldn't explain how Hal Brognola and the team

at Stony Man collaborated with the host of rival agencies in Washington. The big Fed had his private contacts, who would help him out whenever possible, while Aaron Kurtzman and his crew had back-door access to a host of protected computer systems, ranging from the FBI and IRS to Langley to the Pentagon, the NSA, and others who were so obscure that Bolan couldn't think of them offhand. Between open cooperation and sporadic data raids, Brognola got the information he required and passed it on as needed to his agents in the field.

Sometimes, like now, he even got a helping hand.

"We're all on the same side, I know," Dixon said. "But I ask you, is this thing about the new bureau a load of crap, or what? I mean, J. Edgar may be dead, but plenty of the brass still seem to think that he's in charge."

"I don't have many dealings with the FBI," Bolan said truthfully.

He'd been a member of the Bureau's ten-most-wanted list, at one point in his life, but that life was behind him now. As far as FBI headquarters was concerned, Mack Bolan was deceased, a bit of ancient history. Some old-timers likely regretted that he hadn't fallen to their guns, but dead was dead.

Bolan felt the jet descending, banking. He was belted in and didn't sweat the turbulence as it resumed with their decreasing altitude. Grimaldi was the best at what he did. Bolan would trust Jack with his life—and had, more times than he could count.

"Ten minutes," said the pilot's disembodied voice.

"And if I never have to fly again," Dixon said, "it will be too soon."

"Be careful what you wish for," Bolan offered. "If we can't find Talmadge, choppy air will be the least of your problems."

"Don't remind me, eh?"

The Learjet's landing gear descended with a solid thunk that Bolan felt through the soles of his feet. Grimaldi took them down through wisps of cloud to gray daylight and tarmac still stained from the last spits of rain. Bolan didn't bother checking out the runway or the terminal as they approached.

Trouble was either waiting for them on the ground, or else it wasn't. There would be news, or there wouldn't. Either way, they had to forge ahead. They'd come too far to turn back now.

A navy-blue sedan with federal license plates was waiting near the hangar when the Learjet taxied to a stop at the commercial end of Holman Field. A standard-issue agent sat behind the wheel, emerging only when the passengers had started to deplane. He waited by the car a moment longer, counting heads, then moved to meet them on the tarmac.

"Agent Mosman, FBI," he said to no one in particular. "Who am I talking to?"

## CHAPTER FOURTEEN

Bolan stepped forward, as the group's spokesman. "Matt Cooper," he replied, flashing credentials printed by the team at Stony Man. "I'm NTK."

"Can't say I've ever heard of that," Mosman responded.

"You still haven't," Bolan said. It was a joke of Aaron Kurtzman's: NTK for Need to Know. Turning to Dixon, Bolan introduced him as an agent of Homeland Security.

"I've heard of that," Mosman said. Facing Jack Grimaldi, he pressed on, "And you?"

"I fly the plane. Jack Armstrong."

Which, as Bolan knew, was lifted from an old-time comic strip, "Jack Armstrong, the All-American Boy."

"Now that we're all acquainted," Bolan said, "I'd like the update we were promised on arrival."

"Can I drop you somewhere?"

"No, thanks. Just the information."

"Right." Mosman's expression flat-lined. He'd apparently exhausted his reserve of small talk. "Turns out that your subject, Eugene Adam Talmadge, crossed the border into Minnesota at 8:19 a.m. Incoming drivers are routinely photographed for checks against our fugitive and terrorism files." ·

"Somebody photographed him, but he wasn't stopped?" Dixon asked, sounding peeved.

"It's not as simple as it sounds," Mosman replied. "The photographs are automatic, digitally stored for subsequent review and biometric scanning. All of that takes place about two hours afterward. That's on a good day, like today. Slow traffic."

"Meaning that you snap a wanted killer's picture, then you let him drive a hundred miles or more before you find out he was wanted in the first place?" Dixon pressed.

"Not *us*," Mosman said. "Not the Bureau. Customs and immigration is part of your DHS program these days. You should know that, Mr. Dixon."

"It's *Agent* Dixon, *Mr.* Mosman."

"Can we move along?" Bolan asked in his best no-bullshit voice.

"Where was I?" Mosman asked himself. And answered, "The photos, right. Okay. The automatic photo system captures vehicles and license tags, as well. So, from the shots of Talmadge, we broadcast his license number—which, of course, turned out to be a plate stolen from Canada, most likely on an SUV he ripped off somewhere else. We used a quiet APB—locate, but don't approach—as per instructions from your, um, the NTK."

"And?" Bolan prodded.

"We got lucky, gentlemen. The ink is barely dry on this

one, but a cop in Blaine—that's north of Minneapolis-St. Paul, a suburb—stumbled on the car he used to cross the border. Sucker dumped it at a shopping mall. We've only had the car for twenty-something minutes, but we're working on the theory that he bagged another set of wheels nearby. Most likely the same parking lot. If we come up with something there, it means another APB."

"Still on the quiet side," Bolan reminded him.

"I get it."

"What about Nasser Asad?" Dixon asked.

"Right. Well, as you may know, that one has full DI coverage. That's diplomatic—"

"Immunity," Dixon finished for him, smiling thinly.

"Yeah. Of course, that only means we can't arrest him. We can watch him all we want, see if he's up to anything like rape or murder, spitting on the sidewalk, this or that. He isn't hiding, so we've got surveillance on him. Right now, it's 24/7."

"Not for much longer," Bolan said.

"Oh, yeah?"

"We'll take over that end of the show."

"Welcome to it. Guy flip-flops from boring to freaky as hell."

"Meaning what?" Bolan asked.

"You know these uptight fundie types. No? Well, let me fill you in. This dude may be all Mr. Islam in the public eye, but when the sun goes down and crowds thin out, he likes a walk on the wild side. Dirty girls, maybe some boys thrown in for the variety. According to his file, he's got connections in the major cities, coast to coast. Cathouses, chicken coops, like that. He likes young stuff and pays top dollar. If the place he's staying doesn't have a house, he orders takeout."

"Last I heard," Dixon said, "that was criminal. Child trafficking's a federal rap, supposedly enforced by...let me think...the FBI."

"I told you, man. He's got DI."

"That's crap. You catch him diddling kids, and State can have him declared persona non grata. It just takes a stroke of the pen."

"Tell it to Washington," Mosman responded sourly. "We've got a hands-off order from the very top. Including State. They either like him very much, or else they're stringing him along to catch a bigger fish. Whatever, we can't touch him."

"Never mind," Bolan said.

"Never mind. Okay. Rewind, erase. It's gone. You want to know his local hangouts, or was all of this for nothing?"

"Hangouts would be good," Bolan said. "And the address where he's staying."

"All right here," Mosman said, as he took a folded sheet of paper from his pocket, passing it to Bolan. Bolan opened it and scanned the list of four addresses.

"Hotel's on the top," Mosman informed him. "Guess you worked that out. The other three are brothels, all protected one way or another. With their prices, I assume the clientele is strictly VIP or freaks with finances. Officially, they don't exist. The local cops can't find them, even though the third one on the list has been in business at the same address for thirteen years."

"We'll check them out," Bolan said.

"Right. Good luck with that." Mosman already had his door open and one leg in the car when he turned back to Bolan. "Did you ever read a novel called Saint Mudd?" he asked.

"Missed it," the Executioner replied.

"It's all about St. Paul, back in the thirties. Opens up saying that in St. Paul, gangsters can fuck in the street while the cops look away."

"The thirties," Bolan said.

"Hey, what's three-quarters of a century, between friends? Money talks. Still the same old St. Paul. Watch your back."

I always do, Bolan thought as the G-man drove away.

AFIF MUKHTAR SAT and stared at the open suitcase. It fairly hypnotized him, in its sinister simplicity.

Time and again, he reached out to the arming switch, caressed it with his fingertips, applying pressure that was *almost* great enough to kill the red light and illuminate the green.

Almost.

It was a childish game, perhaps, but when one's life was measured out in hours, what was the harm?

Mukhtar imagined arming the bomb and latching the bag, walking outside with it and strolling through the streets, surrounded by a swarm of heedless infidels who didn't know Death walked among them, desperate to be released.

He could go anywhere, he realized. It didn't have to be the target that was chosen for him. He could buy a map of the United States and drive toward any compass point until he found a target he preferred, then—

No.

He had pledged both his life and his obedience to God, in the form of God's representatives on Earth. That meant he had to follow orders, trusting in the wisdom of the men who told him where to go and what to do. They had already given him an opportunity to serve his people and God, furnished the key to Paradise. If he tried something on his own, derailed their plans somehow, he might spoil everything.

No glory. No remembrance as a martyr for the cause.

No vestal virgins.

That decided it. He would proceed as ordered and on schedule—but it didn't mean that he couldn't enjoy himself.

After he poked and prodded at the arming switch, Mukhtar stroked the bomb's lead casing. It was painted black, didn't resemble plain gray lead at all, but it still had the oily feel of lead.

How thick? he wondered. Did it really keep the radiation in until the bomb went off, or was he being poisoned even now? Was the white man who had delivered it infected? Would his hair and teeth fall out, his skin blister, his organs swell and burst from their exposure to whatever lay within that drab black casing?

I don't care, he thought. And it was true.

What did it matter if another white man died, along with all the thousands who would die the following day? As for Mukhtar himself, he'd be incinerated, spirit soaring on its way to Paradise, before he felt the first effects of any radiation poisoning.

It was a revelation to discover that he had no fear.

But that was wrong. He *was* afraid of one thing, still. Failure.

If he didn't succeed tomorrow, for whatever reason, would he still be blessed? His imam told him God judged motives, rather than results. Thus, if a martyr died while trying to annihilate his enemies, in God's eyes it was the same as if he'd truly killed them all.

That made a kind of sense to Mukhtar, but how could he be sure?

You'll know tomorrow, said the small voice in his head. Trigger the bomb or die trying, and you'll find out.

But Mukhtar promised himself he wouldn't fail. Once he had armed the bomb, it took only a subtle movement of his thumb to detonate the primer charge inside and start the chain reaction that would slay his enemies by tens of thousands.

Even if police were waiting for him at his target, he could still set off the bomb and get the same result. Unless they found a way to cut him down before his brain transmitted energy enough to move his thumb, the infidels were already defeated.

It was perfect.

But, the small voice nagged him, what if they come sooner? What if they break in tonight?

Would there be time for him to arm the bomb, then latch the case and trigger it before they overwhelmed him with their stun grenades, tear gas and bullets? He was only human, after all.

What if he armed the bomb and slept beside it, at arm's length, to keep from triggering the primer charge by acci-

dent? Would that be safe enough? Transporting it should
be no problem in the morning, if he took his time and followed common-sense security precautions. He would have
a great advantage, then.

And what a thrill, knowing that victory and Paradise
were only a thumb twitch away!

Afif Mukhtar had never seen the old cartoons where
characters argue with themselves over some touchy point,
a devil perched on one shoulder, an angel on the other.
Even if he had, the relevance might have eluded him.

It took him seven minutes to make up his mind. During
that time, his face beaded with perspiration and he trem-
bled with excitement that was almost sexual.

At last, he made his choice, reaching out with a quaking hand and flipping the switch.

The red light died.

Green glowed triumphant as he closed and latched
the case.

CLEARING THE PAPERWORK on yet another rented car took fifteen minutes. It was nearly dark as they rolled north on Highway 52, crossing the Mississippi River near the point where
it turned west, then southward, and became the Minnesota.

"Okay," Dixon asked. "What's the drill? You want to see
Asad at his hotel?"

"Talmadge won't meet him there," Bolan replied. "Too
many witnesses."

"So, what? We wait outside, relieve the Bureau guys and
follow him around?"

"Sounds like a waste of time and gasoline," Bolan said.

"So, our strategy is…what, again?"

"Talmadge will pick a place where anyone who sees him with the diplomat won't talk about it later. Someplace where discretion's guaranteed."

"One of the houses. What did Mosman call them?"

"Chicken coops." Bolan pronounced it with distaste.

"Sick sons of bitches," Dixon muttered. "If I really thought the cops protected places where you…where they… Shit! Can you believe it?"

"I believe some people will do anything for money," Bolan said. "You know it, too. A house can't operate for thirteen years without protection."

"Sons of bitches!" Dixon said again.

"The way to hurt them is to hit them in the wallet," Bolan stated. "But that's another mission, for another time."

"The bomb. Right," Dixon said. "I'm not forgetting that."

"Of course, we might get lucky. Hit a two-fer."

"How's that?" Dixon asked.

"We're both agreed Nasser Asad is backing Talmadge and al Qaeda, right?"

"I'd say so," Dixon answered. "Why else would he be in St. Paul now? It's not like any diplomatic action comes to the Twin Cities."

"And it's safe to say he won't be staying for the fireworks show," Bolan continued.

"Right. No martyrs in the silk-suit crowd."

"So he'll hook up with Talmadge soon, likely sometime tonight. And where?"

"One of the goddamned chicken coops," Dixon said, nearly sure of it.

"That's my guess, too."

"Okay, but still. We can't watch four of them at once, now that you sent the G-men home."

"You're right," Bolan said. "We can't *watch* them. But suppose we shut a couple of them down before Asad checks in. Narrow his options for a night of fun and frolic on the town."

"It could go either way," Dixon suggested. "Either funnel him to where we want him, or disrupt a meet they scheduled in advance and put him in the wind."

"If that happens, he'll have to get in touch with Talmadge," Bolan said.

And Dixon saw the brilliance of it then. "By phone." He almost sighed.

"And we've already got the soldier's sat phone covered."

Dixon could've sworn that Cooper smiled there, for a second, but he couldn't prove it. "Sweet," he said. "Where do we start?"

"We may as well work from the top of Mosman's list," Bolan replied.

"Suits me."

Dixon had no idea where they were going, though he'd briefly scanned the G-man's list of addresses. Unlike Nasser Asad's hotel, the so-called chicken coops didn't have names. No great surprise in that, since they could hardly advertise their twisted menu to the neighbors.

He remembered street addresses, but it was his first time in St. Paul and Dixon didn't know his way around. Now that he thought about it, Cooper always drove the car, and it had turned out just as well for both of them, so far, that he did so.

No problem, Dixon thought. But if we ever wind up in D.C., I'm telling him to let me drive.

He almost laughed at that, but caught himself and settled for the mere ghost of a smile instead. They were so far beyond the laughing zone right now that Dixon couldn't quite remember what it felt like to be cheerful without strings attached.

Since meeting Cooper, he'd been laughing at the damnedest things, assailed by feelings so removed from what his normal life had been that Dixon sometimes felt he might be losing it.

He didn't know how Cooper lived this way, year-round, but maybe he'd misunderstood the man. Maybe this kind of mission was as rare for Cooper as it was—had been—for him.

No, that was wrong. He hadn't misinterpreted the stranger's comments that much, and he knew from Cooper's swift response in killing situations that he wasn't out of practice. But if this was normal for him, Dixon asked himself, where was the action happening?

Okay, he understood that there were wars all over the planet but he and Cooper had been hunting people, killing people, in Vancouver. Now, the hunt had moved to Minnesota, in the U.S.A., and Dixon had to ask himself, if this shit happened very often, who was covering it up?

Dixon believed that he was relatively well-informed, thanks to a list of carefully selected newspapers and all the foxy newsladies at CNN. Despite that fact, he hadn't been apprised of any recent unsolved massacres in North America, beyond the same old gang-banging that hardly even registered.

What kind of stories were reporters in Vancouver feeding local residents right now, about the triad killings there?

What would reporters say the next day, about St. Paul's chicken coops, protected by police until a pair of wildmen blew in out of nowhere and went crazy?

Guess I'll have to wait and see, he thought while settling back to enjoy the ride.

TALMADGE ALLOWED HIMSELF one Bushmills Irish whiskey—neat, as they would say across the water—and he took his time enjoying it. The bar itself was Irish, warm and cozy, dark wood paneling and Guinness stout on tap for those who wanted a real taste of the old country.

Talmadge wasn't Irish, but he had a sneaking admiration for the people and their spirit. They'd been fighting British squatters for the best part of four hundred years, taking the war home to their enemies whenever possible, and even in the days of fragile cease-fires they still held the line on their demands for freedom.

In his own decades of military servitude, if anyone had asked him, Talmadge would've mouthed the party line on Irish terrorism and the methods Britain ought to use combating it. Now he rooted for the IRA to keep its weapons, stand and fight.

What a difference a day made.

And all because of a stab in the back.

He rerouted his thoughts, focused on his meeting with Nasser Asad in…what? Two hours, now, and counting. Talmadge had been startled, or the next thing to it, when Asad had called him on his sat phone to announce that he was in St. Paul. In fact, Talmadge had thought Asad would probably take care to put some neutral space between himself and the United States, before the next day's big event.

There was no question that he'd leave St. Paul before H-hour, but his presence here and now raised pressing questions in the former soldier's mind.

Why fly in on the eve of Armageddon, after all?

To pay Talmadge in person, for the first time, when they'd always used wire transfers in the past? Unlikely.

To congratulate Talmadge on having pulled off the whole thing? A phone call would suffice, most likely after the event.

To silence Talmadge personally, when a hit team could've done the job with no risk to Asad? A big, emphatic "No."

Why, then?

Talmadge could only think of one reason, and it had only the most tenuous of links to rationality. He thought, perhaps, the Saudi wanted to involve himself more personally in the deed, either for later bragging rights among his oil-sheikh buddies, or—more probably—to satisfy some private need.

He wanted to be close, to flirt with martyrdom.

The joke would be on all of them, however, if their pigeon got excited playing with his brand-new toy and set it off ahead of schedule. Like this night, for instance, while Asad was getting dressed at his hotel and Talmadge dawdled over whiskey with a pair of strangers flanking him on barstools.

*I should stand him up,* Talmadge thought. *Book on out*

of town and let them wire the money like before. Get out before something goes wrong.

Like in Vancouver.

He took another sip of whiskey and savored the fire on his tongue, scorching a path to his stomach drop by drop. Another six or eight of those, and he would be relaxed enough to ride the fallout cloud on high and wait to see where he came down.

But getting hammered on a business trip to unfamiliar turf wasn't the best idea he'd ever had.

It would be over soon, nothing but smoke and ash this time tomorrow, and whatever followed afterward. By that time, Talmadge would be far outside the lines of fire from either side. Maybe not safe, exactly, in the long-term scheme of things, but certainly safer.

It was about the best a fighting man could hope for in this goddamned crazy world.

And then he had a thought.

How would it be, he wondered, if he set it up to let Nasser Asad take his fair share of the blame for what was coming? His fair share and then some, maybe?

All the diplomatic immunity in the world wouldn't cover the Saudi's ass in that case. Congress would revoke treaties, amend the Constitution and write new statutes to fry the man responsible for touching off a dirty nuke on U.S. soil.

Of course, in Talmadge's scenario, Asad wouldn't be standing trial. He might give fingerprints and DNA, but only at the local morgue. And that facility, if it survived tomorrow morning, would be swamped with work until Doomsday.

Make that the next Doomsday.

It wouldn't be so difficult. Just meet Asad as planned, then take him out, along with any bodyguards he brought along. Dress up the scene so that even a local cop, working in the shadow of disaster, couldn't miss Asad's connection to the main event.

Simple.

Al Qaeda might see through it, given time, but tracking down Talmadge to punish him would be no easy task. After the following morning, every AQ man on file with any agency on earth would be pursued until he died or broke down and surrendered. There would be no golf course photo-op with some administration big-wig saying that he wasn't too concerned about bin Laden or his gang.

After tomorrow, talk like that could get a politician lynched in broad daylight, on Pennsylvania Avenue.

Talmadge looked down into his empty whiskey glass and smiled, then raised a finger to the bartender and said, "I'll have one for the road."

THE FIRST TARGET on Agent Mosman's list, after Nasser Asad's hotel, was on the north bank of the Mississippi River, just off Shepard Road. It was a big, old house, likely an antebellum monument to someone's money that had been refurbished to keep up with modern times.

But now, another was coming to the neighborhood.

Mosman hadn't provided floor plans for the chicken coops, hadn't been asked for them, but Bolan got a fair idea of the layout from driving past and circling twice around the block. It was three stories tall and handsome in a Norman Bates or Freddy Kreuger kind of way. In fact, he thought it looked like what it was.

A house of horrors.

What he couldn't see, but only guess at, was the most important part.

"What do you think about security?" Dixon asked.

"Don't expect alarms," Bolan replied, "unless they only flash or ring inside the house. These folks don't want to rouse the neighbors, and they definitely don't want the police snooping around."

"Shooters?"

"Say weapons, and you may be closer to it," Bolan answered. "If they've been protected in the past, they likely won't have soldiers camped out on the premises. Some strong-arm help, for sure, in case someone gets too excited and goes ape. With any luck, shooting won't be their first impulse."

"And wiring?" Dixon asked.

"Count on it. I'd expect CCTV all over, both for prowlers and blackmail potential. Audio recordings, too, most likely."

"Blackmail? Serves the lousy bastards right."

"They can afford it," Bolan said. "And I imagine that's a backup system, not for use against the regulars unless they suffer an attack of conscience and decide to blow the whistle. The proprietors will make more over time, from steady customers, than they could net from any one-time bustout scam."

"This ever make you sick, sometimes?" Dixon asked.

"Sure. Try every day. Kids are the worst."

"And yet you don't seem angry."

"Anger has its uses in the moment, heat of combat, but it has no place in planning. Anger, hatred, love—the whole range of emotions cloud your judgment if you're working on logistics and your life is on the line."

"Just business, eh, Godfather?"

Bolan shook his head. "It's never strictly business, but it has to be professional, or I'd be dead by now, a thousand times over. Soldiers who charge ahead without a second thought make great heroes, but all their decorations wind up being posthumous."

"I'm not sure I can turn it off like that," Dixon said. "Not about the kids."

"Then you should definitely wait outside," Bolan suggested. "Watch the car."

"You're kidding, right?"

Bolan had parked their ride, switched off the lights and engine. Now he turned and studied Dixon by a distant streetlamp's light. The man from DHS was staring back at him, as if Bolan had slapped his face.

"I'm deadly serious," Bolan replied. "We may not find a dozen hit men waiting for us in that place, but you can bet your life it won't be the Three Stooges, either. We'll be trespassing on turf whose occupants have everything to lose, and then some, if their cover's blown. They may come straight at us, or use the kids as shields. But either way, if you're a starter in this game, you need to keep your mind straight. I don't want to die, or see those children die, because you couldn't check your righteous anger at the door."

Dixon seemed to deflate a little, easing back into his

seat. "Okay. You're right. I read you, five-by-five. Just don't make me the damned valet, all right?"

"If you can handle it, you're in. If not…"

"I'll handle it."

"One other thing to keep in mind," Bolan said. "I assume they've got some heavy-duty soundproofing inside there, for the neighbors' sake and so the action from one party room won't bleed into another. Spoil the moment, as it were."

"Makes sense," Dixon replied through gritted teeth.

"But I would *not* expect the walls, the doors or ceilings to be bulletproof," Bolan continued. "If we have to use our weapons, keep that fact in mind. We don't know where the kids are, going in. It's not a free-fire zone."

"I get it. Aim and squeeze."

"Better if we don't have to shoot at all," Bolan corrected him. "Remember, what we're doing here is looking for Nasser Asad, and narrowing his options if he hasn't picked a playpen for the night yet. I'd prefer to roust the coop and have the neighbors call police without a bloodbath. Party lights on top of squad cars are the surest way to make Asad keep moving."

"Or," Dixon replied, "he might just bag it for the night. That way, we miss him altogether."

"It's a possibility," Bolan agreed, "but he's in town to meet with Talmadge somewhere. Otherwise, the trip's a waste."

"We could go back to the hotel and track Asad."

"Too late," Bolan said, reaching for his gym bag with the Spectre SMG inside. "We're here now, and it's party time."

# CHAPTER FIFTEEN

Stay cool, Dixon thought. Don't go off half-cocked.

That almost made him snigger, but he swallowed it and followed Cooper up the stone path from the sidewalk, to the front door of the chicken coop. He stood with one hand underneath his jacket, on the mini-Uzi's pistol grip, while Cooper rang the bell.

It took almost a minute for the door to open. He supposed someone had scanned them in the meantime, maybe with a covert CCTV setup or a hidden peephole. Either way, the doorman met them with a cautious smile and said, "Good evening, gentlemen."

The words seemed out of place in that mouth, coming from that round, slightly misshapen face. It was a boxer's face, maybe a street fighter's, but not a butler's.

"We're here for the party," Bolan told him.

"Ah, of course." The nearly lipless mouth twitched with an almost smile. "Your invitations, please?"

Dixon could feel the first knot forming in his gut, but

his companion said, "Right here," and pulled his SMG, jabbing its muzzle underneath the doorman's chin, shoving his way inside.

He scoped the entryway they stood in and the spacious parlor just beyond. No children were in evidence, but Dixon saw a thirty-something woman standing several yards behind the doorman, just about to run.

"I wouldn't," he advised her, showing off the Uzi for effect.

She froze, silent and wide-eyed, while the doorman, standing with his head pushed backward, said, "Youse guys are makin' a mistake."

"The drive was longer than I thought," Bolan said. "We're already back in Brooklyn."

"Funny," the doorman said. "Youse could die laughin'."

"Speaking of dying," Bolan told him, "if you want to keep this ugly melon on your shoulders, we need information."

"Fuck de botha youse."

More pressure on the weapon's muzzle cranked his head back at an angle that could only hurt. Dixon covered the woman, wondering if he could really shoot her. Then he thought about the kids and knew it wouldn't be a problem.

"One more time," Bolan said. "Your choice."

"Blow me," the doorman told him.

The single shot was muffled slightly by the doorman's pudgy throat, but there was no disguising its effect. Roughly a quarter of the Brooklyn bouncer's cranium took flight, dragging a comet's tail of blood and brains behind it. He was dead before he hit the floor, but still kept twitching anyway.

The woman wound up toward a squeal, then saw two submachine guns pointed at her face and kept it in. "What do you wanna know?" she asked them in a mousy voice.

"How many kids? How many johns?" Bolan demanded.

"Nine and two," she said. "Slow night, so far."

"More muscle?"

"Coming in at nine," she answered.

Dixon checked his watch. They still had close to forty minutes.

"Right," Bolan said. "Take us to your customers. The first surprise will be your last."

She led them to a staircase, and from there up to the second floor. A hallway with dim lighting led them past two doors. Their guide stopped at a third and knocked, then called out, "Mr. Smith? Excuse me, sir."

Such courtesy for scum, Dixon thought. He stood ready, covering the hallway and the woman, all at once. Enough rounds in his weapon to wreak bloody havoc, if it came to that.

After what seemed a long time, someone fumbled with the door and opened it a crack. Bolan gave it a solid kick and slammed it back into the scumbag's face. The guy was nearly out when Bolan stepped across his body, dragged the woman after him. He spared a glance for Dixon, on his way.

"I'm good here," Dixon told him, standing ready in the hallway with his SMG.

He didn't want to go inside that room. Most definitely didn't want to see whatever had been happening atop its rumpled bed.

He thought of walking over there and giving "Mr. Smith" a round between his eyes—or better, in the groin—but Dixon mastered the impulse.

"You live because I let you," Dixon muttered to the fallen pedophile. "How fucking weird is that?"

Bolan returned a long five minutes later, with the woman at his side. They walked another two doors down, another door across the hall. This time, the john was waiting for them, peeking through a crack to see what the disturbance was about. Before he had a chance to slam it, Bolan threw himself against the door and charged inside.

Dixon stood back and listened to the beating, wished he could've joined in, but he couldn't face the rest of it. After the thrashing, there was whispered conversation, but he didn't try to eavesdrop.

There was only so much he could see or know and keep his mind intact.

Bolan returned a moment later, with the silent woman trailing. When he asked again, she swore to him that he had met the only current customers.

"Okay," he said, stepping across the corridor to pull the handle on a square alarm box set into the paneling. "Fire drill."

TALMADGE COULD FEEL his second shot of whiskey, but it had no impact on his driving. He was still rock steady at the wheel, thinking ahead to where he'd ditch the latest stolen car and find another one.

No problem, Talmadge thought. I've got all night.

He had the address for his meeting with Nasser Asad and

understood that it would be a semiprivate place, maybe some covert business going on around them while they talked. He didn't care about the Saudi's predilections, had no interest whatsoever in his private life or thoughts. They meant nothing to Talmadge, less than nothing, just so long as he got paid.

So long as their joint venture served a common goal.

Talmadge was early for the sit-down, even after killing time over his second whiskey. Driving now, he held it just a mile or so above the posted limit, letting other drivers pass and flip him off. Ignore them. Let the impatient bastards clear his path, draw off the traffic cops, while Talmadge took his own sweet time.

Thinking about his plan—his new plan—Talmadge had decided that Asad was doing him a favor, dragging him across town to a whorehouse stocked with children under twelve. He'd seen the same thing elsewhere, in the Far East, and had passed it by.

But not this time.

Nasser Asad had picked the perfect place in which to die.

If the police showed up and found him in the chicken coop, there went the Saudi's rep, such as it was. And on the flip side, if the mob proprietors got rid of him, he'd likely disappear without a trace into one of the state's reputed thousand lakes, or maybe take his last ride in a double-decker coffin at the nearest syndicate-connected mortuary.

Either way, al Qaeda would have trouble finding him, more trouble linking his demise to Talmadge. And if they came looking for him, asking questions...well, they had to find him first.

Talmadge would be on guard, the same as always. He had lived that way since he was old enough to sign enlistment papers, and he couldn't break the habit now. Not when he finally was able to retire.

The money. Get the money first, he told himself.

Damned right.

Before he made a move against his Saudi paymaster, Talmadge would either get the money in his hand or phone the bank himself for confirmation. He deserved a bonus, for a dicey job well done, but he would definitely settle for the payoff they'd agreed to in advance.

On that, and what he'd banked beforehand, Talmadge reckoned he could live luxuriously in his chosen tropic hideaway for ten, maybe twelve years.

And after that?

Hell, after that, he'd see what happened next.

The thing about this night was getting through it, without giving up his final payment or making new enemies. The guys who ran the chicken coop might be pissed off, but Talmadge didn't know them, and before they had a chance to find out who he was, the next day's big event would knock them and the country for a loop.

The dashboard clock told him that he had half an hour yet before he was supposed to meet Asad. There was no point in showing early, which would only leave him waiting for Asad and killing time among the freaks.

No, thanks.

Talmadge was ready, braced to take whatever he might see, before he made his move, but nothing said he had to draw it out, show up ahead of time and mingle with the perverts.

Talmadge would be fashionably late—five minutes, give or take—and once the money had changed hands...

He smiled at his reflection in the rearview mirror, checking out the face of Death.

THE SECOND TARGET WASN'T on the riverfront. It was literally on the wrong side of the tracks, planted on Acker Street, midway between the Minnesota Transportation Museum and Oakland Cemetery.

Bolan drove past with Dixon, checking out the house. It was a smaller place than their first target, single story, maybe four bedrooms. It wouldn't do a volume business, but the prices charged would keep it in the profit column.

Bolan pictured burning down the place and knew it wasn't in the cards. Maybe another place, another time.

"Same drill as last time?" Dixon asked him.

"Might as well," Bolan replied as he was scouting for a parking place.

"Up here," Dixon said, pointing.

"Thanks."

He parked, killed lights and engine, reached back for his bag of tools as Dixon asked, "You think somebody's tipped them off?"

Bolan had thought about it, knew no one had phoned directly from their last stop, but he couldn't say about the cops or the attorneys who'd be circling around the last joint's staff by now. Assuming that the coops were all connected, as they had to be, the word was bound to spread in time.

How soon? How far?

"We'll just do what we can," Bolan replied, and stepped out of the car.

"Just thought it couldn't hurt to ask," Dixon said, joining him.

"You're right," he said. "Let's do a change-up."

"How's that work?" Dixon asked.

"Go in from the back this time. Come out the front."

"Sounds fair."

His around-the-block reconnaissance had shown Bolan an alleyway behind the Acker Street houses, a runway for the garbage trucks to make their pickups once or twice a week, unseen. Fenced yards fronted the alley, crumbly asphalt underfoot. They counted gates and houses, coming in behind their target.

"This one?" Dixon asked him.

"Right."

The gate was padlocked from the inside, but the wooden fence was nothing insurmountable. Approximately six feet tall, no razor wire or broken glass on top. Bolan went up on tiptoes, checking for security devices, then decided that he'd have to take the chance.

Front-line defenses in the suburbs wouldn't be the lethal kind. No electrified fences to fry dogs or children and bring out the cops. Most definitely no Claymores or frag grenades on trip wires.

"Can you climb it?" he asked Dixon.

"Are you kidding?"

Bolan took that for an answer and went over in a single fluid motion, landing in a crouch beyond the fence. He half expected motion sensors linked to floodlights, but the spacious yard stayed dark. Of course, that didn't mean that no alarms were going off inside the house.

Dixon landed beside him, staggered just a bit, then found his balance. "Easy," he told Bolan, whispering.

"It may not stay that way," Bolan replied.

"It doesn't sound like anybody hit the panic button."

"Let's find out."

He started for the back door, moving over close-cropped grass, beneath shade trees. When he was halfway there, the door opened and two hardmen stepped onto the concrete stoop.

"You assholes picked the wrong house to come creepin'," said the bruiser on their left.

His partner studied them a second longer, then declared, "They're pretty damned well-dressed for burglars."

"Yeah."

It clicked, then, and the heavies reached for hardware under their respective jackets, stopping short when they saw submachine guns pointed at their chests.

"Oh, shit," one of them said.

"Jesus!" the other one agreed.

"You've got two ways to go," Bolan said. "Pitch the iron, no tricks, or give it your best shot."

The two hardmen shared a glance, a silent question passed between them, then the hulk on Bolan's left said, "Guess we're finished, either way."

"Your call," Bolan replied. "If that was what we wanted, you'd be dead by now."

Off to his right, Dixon muttered, "Dead is what they ought to be."

"What's that?" the second shooter asked.

"Nothing," Dixon said.

"So, this ain't a hit?"

"You're going out of business," Bolan told him. "No one says you have to go out in a body bag. Your choice."

"These guys ain't cops," one heavy told the other.

"Nah. They ain't."

"The cops are coming," Bolan said. "The only question now is whether you'll be breathing when they get here."

"I don't understand this shit," the taller of the two goons said.

"We're going to meet the johns," Bolan said. "You can be our doormats or our guides. Decide."

He saw it coming, tension in their faces and their shoulders, both men going for their hidden pistols after all. He stitched them, left to right, Dixon reversing it with six or eight rounds from his Uzi.

"Come on!" Bolan snapped. "Time's wasting!"


AHMED ZERO LISTENED to the shower running, checked his watch and saw that they were late as usual. Rather, Nasser Asad was late. Zero believed that habitual tardiness was a symptom of shameful arrogance. Children were punished for it in his country, while adults of wealth and influence made punctuality a point of pride.

This night, however, he was just as glad to be delayed.

Zero didn't enjoy meeting with mercenaries, more particularly with the hired American whom Nasser treated as an equal when they spoke. He still suspected the American was plotting to betray them somehow, but his thoughts meant nothing to Asad, so Zero kept them to himself.

Above all else, he hated meeting *anyone* in the vile houses that Asad was prone to patronize. His master's lust for children, while not banned by a specific text of the Koran, revolted Zero. It made him feel unclean by mere association with the pig who called himself a man.

But what could Zero do?

At home, Asad made no great secret of the children whom he kept in his *seraglio*. His powerful associates, oil sheikhs and so-called statesmen, either turned a blind eye to his predilections or indulged themselves on those occasions when they were invited to his home. Zero kept track of names and faces, often wishing he could sell their stories to the Western press and thus humiliate them.

But his duty to God came first.

Nasser Asad and the important Saudis who surrounded him—some of them, anyway—were also staunch supporters of al Qaeda in its time of trial. Their money, for the most part, had supported pilot training for the martyrs of September 11, the African embassy bombings and the later attacks in London.

To Ahmed Zero, victory took precedence over the private sins of those whom he was forced to serve. Destroying Israel and her allies, most particularly the United States, was what he lived for. God, in his wisdom, might surprise the defilers of children when they died, refusing them admission at the gates of Paradise, but that wasn't for Zero to say.

Meanwhile, he swallowed his revulsion and contempt,

maintained a bland expression on his face and did as he was told.

This night they would be visiting a sty that Zero had selected for his master, from half a dozen operating in the nest of decadence called Minneapolis-St. Paul. Two of the houses he had judged as too remote, demanding long drives out into the country, wasting time and complicating Asad's meeting with the mercenary. One catered to pederasts alone, while Asad's taste ran more to young females. Two others, after drive-by visual inspection, struck Zero as seedy, even for establishments where children could be bought and sold.

His final choice was twenty minutes from Asad's hotel, by car, and offered fairly adequate security. Local police, he understood, were "on the pad"—meaning that criminals had managed to seduce and bribe them, as was true throughout the world, in Zero's personal experience. He had walked through the place himself that very afternoon, while Asad got a haircut and massage at the hotel. Zero imagined that it reeked of vile corruption.

And he knew Asad would love it.

Someday, when al Qaeda was victorious and there was time to purge the party of its filthy hangers-on, Zero planned to volunteer for the elimination squad. With any luck, he might be chosen to eradicate Asad and others like him, who had soiled the holy war with their perversions.

Then again, perhaps *he* would be one of those eliminated on that day. No one knew better than Ahmed Zero the risks involved in plotting against rich and influential men.

While waiting for that day, whatever it might bring him,

Zero did his job like any faithful bodyguard, chauffeur and errand boy. He carried weapons with impunity and was prepared to use them in Asad's defense, though it hadn't so far been necessary.

At the moment, he was literally dressed to kill. Beneath his tailored suit jacket, made roomy to conceal his hardware, Zero wore a .44 Magnum Colt Anaconda revolver beneath his left arm and a Walther P-88 on his right hip. His third gun, a .380-caliber Colt Mark IV automatic, occupied an ankle holster on the inside of his left leg, ready for a cross-hand draw. Between them, the pistols gave Zero twenty-nine shots before he was forced to reload.

It ought to be enough.

He only needed one shot for the mercenary, after all.

Of course, Asad hadn't approved Zero's suggestion that they kill the brash American instead of paying him. Asad suggested that they might need Talmadge later, for another mission, but that answer struck Zero as being disingenuous.

While Talmadge lived, he was a danger to al Qaeda. Mercenaries were notorious for switching sides to serve the highest bidder, and he'd seen too much, had met too many people of importance to the cause. If the Americans or British didn't buy him back, Talmadge himself could use his knowledge as a weapon for blackmail. He might even threaten the relationship between Saudi Arabia and the United States itself.

Or, maybe not.

Some time ago, a documentary had aired the links between the Saudi ruling clique and 9/11. It was screened throughout the U.S. and the world at large, but somehow most Americans had managed to ignore it, reelecting those same politicians who had buried the original reports of Saudi culpability immediately after the September strikes.

Would it be any different today, now that six years had passed? Wouldn't the sheep be even more complacent now? Their apathy was monumental, their attention span perhaps the shortest in the universe.

Al Qaeda had attacked the heart of their homeland, but after the initial vengeance spasm in Afghanistan, most citizens of the United States went back to life and business as usual. They gorged themselves on chocolates, read gossip magazines and huddled on the couch before their television sets. The world around them was on fire, but they cared only for red-carpet photo ops, reports of "baby bumps" in Hollywood and gaunt "survivors" squatting on some godforsaken island—with a camera, of course.

With that in mind, Zero decided that it likely made no difference if Eugene Talmadge lived or died, but that was all beside the point. He was a danger to al Qaeda and therefore should be killed on principle.

In fact, thought Ahmed Zero, he might go ahead and find a way to do it, even if Nasser Asad did not approve. *Particularly* if Asad did not approve.

For the first time in weeks, a smile lit Zero's swarthy face. This night, he thought, might not be wasted after all.

Tom Dixon's final thought, before he followed Bolan past the leaking bodies and across the bloody threshold, was: too bad nobody thought of using sound suppressors.

It wasn't his department, granted, but he knew that half

a dozen neighbors would be reaching for their telephones right now, complaining to police about the rattle of machine-gun fire. A neighborhood like this, the cops would take them seriously. Squad cars would be rolling within three, four minutes, tops.

"Time's wasting," Bolan said, and he was right.

Inside the coop, they found a dowdy-looking woman fumbling with the kitchen telephone and talked her out of it. Hard-bitten mother figures seemed to be the rule so far, with brothels catering to child molesters. Dixon didn't know if they were meant to help the customers relax or make the children feel at home, but the examples he'd met so far reminded him of extras from a poor, low-budget women's-prison film.

Bolan went through the same drill as before, asking if there was any other muscle in the place, then ordering the woman to conduct them on a hasty tour of the house. This time, they only found one customer, and it was Dixon's privilege to knock the balding fat man on his flabby ass, while Bolan went to calm the object of his warped affection.

Dixon wished that he could stop somewhere and take a long, hot shower with the harshest soap available, but they were on the clock, no sign of Talmadge or Nasser Asad in any of the cheaply furnished rooms.

Sirens were whooping in the middle distance by the time they got back to the kitchen with their tour guide. She was crying, shooting little sidelong glances at the dead goons on the back doorstep, and begging for her worthless life. Dixon imagined that he could've shot her without los-

ing tons of sleep, but he was still relieved when his partner found a pair of handcuffs somewhere—in his pocket?
where did he come up with all this gear?—and left her
manacled to the refrigerator.

"How many kids?" Dixon asked, as they crossed the
dark backyard. He'd made a point of looking elsewhere
when the children left their rooms, preferring not to see
them in their present circumstances.

"Six," Bolan replied. "I think they'll be okay."

Again, Dixon felt the pressing urge to scrub his mission,
double back and find the monsters who had put the chicken
coops in play. It couldn't be a real crime, Dixon thought,
to simply hunt them down and shoot them on the spot,
wherever they were found. Could it?

Jogging along the alley toward their car, he wondered
what would happen if they lost Talmadge and didn't find
the bomb in time. How many of the pigs responsible for
the perversity he'd seen that night would be eradicated by
the blast or its fallout?

They reached the car and scrambled into it. They were
rolling, just another pair of party guys out for a drive, when
cop cars started racing past them in the opposite direction.
Three, four, five of them Dixon counted by the time they'd
traveled half a mile.

"You think they'll be okay?" he asked Bolan.

"I do. In time."

"Some fucking people, man."

"I know."

"Okay, what's next?"

"Two down," Bolan said. "Two more left to go."

Dixon removed his Uzi's magazine, began reloading it. "So bring 'em on," he said.

BOLAN WAS WORRIED about Dixon, wondering if he could keep himself together in the face of all he'd seen and done, that night and in the past two days. He hadn't been exactly green when they got started, but he wasn't bloodred, either.

The children made it worse, of course. It was no secret in law enforcement that officers assigned to deal with child abuse, pornography and prostitution often burned out earlier than those detailed to vice, narcotics, even homicide. Many were parents, saw their own children reflected in the victims' faces, and it broke their spirit. Others gave in to the rage, sooner or later, and couldn't be trusted in the same room with suspects they arrested.

All of which proved they were human—but it also clogged the slowly turning wheels of justice with complaints of rough interrogations, searches that exceeded the parameters of lawful warrants, this and that. Sometimes the bad guys were freed because an overzealous officer had crossed the line.

That kind of thing could drive a cop to drink—or, in the worst cases, to eat his gun. Bolan had known such officers, the good ones who, despite their best intentions and their courage on the firing line in battle, couldn't face the grim parade of children suffering from wounds or malnutrition, psychological or sexual abuse.

And damn it, absolutely none of that was relevant to Bolan's mission in St. Paul.

It was a bonus that he got to bust some child molesters,

put a couple of them in the ground and send some others off to jail, but Bolan's eyes and mind were focused on his primary objective with a fierce intensity.

Unless he found the bomb that Talmadge had delivered to some unknown contact in St. Paul, it wouldn't matter what became of ten or twenty children. No one would remember them, or their abusers, if the extremists wiped St. Paul off the map.

As cruel as it sounded, even to the Executioner, there were much more important things at stake right now.

Thousands of children and their parents would be killed outright or suffer long, slow deaths from radiation poisoning unless he found the bomb and managed to prevent its detonation.

If he couldn't manage that, whatever else he did along the way was wasted time and effort.

"Where's the third place?" Dixon asked him when they'd been five minutes on the road.

"Northeast of here," Bolan replied. "Out by the Hillcrest golf course."

"Money, then," Dixon said.

"I imagine so."

"Bastards."

"It's not the neighborhood," Bolan said. "Just one house."

"And people running it," Dixon replied, his face turned toward the neon night beyond his window. "Dirty cops that let it stay in business. Feds that turn a blind eye to the trafficking across state lines. The politicians who accept mob contributions. Voters who keep swallowing their bullshit, reelecting them to office. Man, it's everybody."

I hope not, Bolan thought, but he didn't bother arguing. Dixon was overdosing on emotion at the moment, grieving for the children, for himself and for society at large. It was a feeling well-known to the Executioner, and one he'd never fully put behind him.

But he covered well, and didn't let emotion guide his actions.

Almost never.

"If Asad is going out tonight," Bolan said, "then we've narrowed down the field."

"And if he doesn't?" Dixon asked.

"We've still got his hotel. If we strike out the next two stops, then we'll go back and see him there. Get in a little heart-to-heart."

"Just so he doesn't get away."

Bolan had thought of that, as well. The possibility that Talmadge's contact might change his mind and bail instead of meeting with the former Green Beret. In that case, they could only hope to catch him on the fly, before he was beyond their reach.

But Bolan wasn't giving up on Plan A yet.

They still had two more chicken coops to bust, and if they didn't find their man at either one of them, Plan B was waiting.

If they weren't too late to make it work.

If it wasn't too late for all concerned.

# CHAPTER SIXTEEN

Talmadge drove past the house where he'd been told to meet Nasser Asad, then doubled back and parked as close to it as possible. He wasn't shocked to find a house of prostitution operating in a residential neighborhood, but it surprised him that a kiddy brothel could exist without a semblance of exterior security.

Oh, well. He guessed the fix was in and let it go at that. Grease made the world go 'round.

Leaving his car, he double-checked the SIG-Sauer P-226 inside his belt, heavy and reassuring at his hip. He could've worn his raincoat, taken in the Steyer AUG, but Talmadge didn't want to spook Asad. Just get his money or a confirmation of the transfer, do his other business and get out.

A small thrill of excitement shivered down his spine as Talmadge rang the bell and waited for admittance. His new take on the meeting made him happy. Maybe it would be a good night, after all.

The doorman bore a strong resemblance to Lurch, from the old *Addams Family* show, except that he was bald and wore a patch over his left eye. Beautiful. Talmadge supposed he'd have to kill the giant, too, and found he didn't mind a bit.

The more the merrier, in fact.

Inside, he smelled a hint of incense and a stronger whiff of coffee brewing. Almost like a normal home, except for the hostess who greeted him and asked his preference. Talmadge repeated what he'd told the giant on the door.

"I'm here to meet Nasser Asad."

"Why, yes. Of course."

She led him down a short hall to a barely sunken living room, a half step down to reach the altered level. There, Asad was lounging on a love seat built for two, while Ahmed Zero stood against a wet bar on the far side of the room.

Talmadge was glad they hadn't brought the kids out yet. Or had Asad come early, done his thing before Talmadge arrived? It seemed unlikely from the look of him, his hair and suit, but who could say?

There'd been a time when Talmadge would've fumed and fretted over what went on in joints like this. He would've downed a beer or three and blustered about going after them himself, but when he'd actually had the chance—in Thailand, and again at Subic Bay—it never seriously crossed his mind.

By that time, he'd come to accept that there were freaks of all descriptions in the world, and they would do their thing no matter what he thought about it. There was nothing he could do about it, thus no point in getting all worked up for no good reason.

Now, here he was, collecting his retirement payoff in a kiddy brothel. In St. Paul, of all places. Would wonders never cease?

"Hello, my friend!" Asad called out to him, with no attempt to rise from the love seat. "It's good to see you one last time. Come sit beside me, please."

Talmadge veered toward Asad, keeping an eye on Ahmed Zero as he went. Killing the two of them would be more difficult if they were twenty feet apart, but he supposed that only Zero would be armed.

Zero, and maybe Lurch. How many others were tucked away that Talmadge couldn't see?

There's only one way to find out, he thought, and plastered on his finest smile.

He sat beside Asad, inhaled the Saudi's perfume, shook his soft and finely manicured hand. "I'm glad to be here," Talmadge told him. Only half a lie.

Asad leaned close enough for Talmadge to smell cloves or something like it on his breath. "And the delivery?" he asked. "Did that go well?"

"No problems," Talmadge said. "The handoff went as planned. Our boy's all set to go."

"Tomorrow, yes?"

"That's right. Unless he screws it up tonight." The sudden look on his companion's face almost made Talmadge laugh aloud. Instead, he said, "Just kidding."

"Ah. Americans. Your sense of humor."

"Keeps us going," Talmadge said, "when things get tough."

"But not, I think, after tomorrow, yes?" the Saudi prodded.

"That will be a hard one to make jokes about," Talmadge agreed. He tried to picture Leno, Letterman, whoever, cracking wise about a nuclear explosion in the heart of Minnesota. By this time tomorrow, would they even be alive? Would there be any television for the drones to watch?

Talmadge cleared his throat and said, "About my final payment…"

"Ah, of course."

Talmadge eased back the right side of his jacket, halfway to the SIG-Sauer, still watching Ahmed Zero while Asad withdrew a folded piece of paper from an inside pocket, handing it to Talmadge.

"Printed within the hour, from my laptop," Asad said.

Talmadge unfolded it and saw what seemed to be a confirmation of deposit to his numbered bank account in George Town, Cayman Islands. He counted off the zeroes, none missing, and noted that identifiers for Asad's account of origin had been blacked out.

"You don't mind if I call and check," he said, not really asking.

"But of course not," said the Saudi paymaster.

Talmadge retrieved his sat phone with his left hand, switched it on and thumbed his bank's number from speed dial. They were staffed around the clock, specifically for inquiries from distant time zones, checking up on transfers like this one.

He got an operator on the second ring, read off his nine-digit account number from memory and waited twenty seconds while the drone in George Town tapped computer keys. At last, the faceless operator said, "Yes, sir, I show a wire deposit made to your account at 20:15, local time. And the amount is—"

"Thank you," Talmadge said. He broke the link and pocketed the phone, then told Asad, "All square."

"How gratifying," the Arab said. "May I offer you a glass of—?"

"Nothing, thanks," Talmadge said. Showing them the pistol as he said, "our business here is done."

BOLAN CHECKED OUT the vehicles parked at the curb around the target house, while he was looking for an open slot nearby. They weren't luxury cars, no stretch limos to make the neighbors gape and phone their friends, but any of them could belong to men with extra cash on hand for certain outlawed luxuries.

What kinds of cars did child molesters drive? They were like anybody else, in Bolan's personal experience. No special style or color they preferred. It was a money thing. The wealthy ones had better wheels than those on tighter budgets, but they also wouldn't park their top-end rides were John Q. Middleclass would find their presence overly suspicious, maybe drop a dime to the police.

Self-preservation was an instinct finely honed in predators who operated on the wrong side of the law. They watched cop shows like everybody else, and learned from the mistakes of fictional bad guys.

Bolan parked near a hydrant, trusting they'd be in and out before a random prowl car came around to ticket him. It wouldn't be a tow job, anyway, and by the time some lower-ranking magistrate issued a warrant for the rental's driver, he'd be history.

In one way or another.

"Ready, there?" he asked Dixon.

"Third time's the charm," the man from DHS replied.

I hope so, Bolan thought, but didn't voice it.

They crossed to the far side of the street diagonally, weapons hidden under jackets. From a distance, they could pass for salesmen, or a working husband bringing someone from the office home to meet his wife and kids. He scoped the house of suffering and shame located three doors farther west, and wondered what the neighbors thought about it. Did they question the parade of men who came and went in hourly cycles? Were they ever curious at all, or had suburban apathy completely blinded them to evil in their midst?

No matter. Either way, it ended here. This night.

The brothel's yard was freshly mowed. Bolan could smell it as he led Dixon along the sidewalk, turning up the concrete walk that led to the front door. He rang the bell, while Dixon stepped aside. A small precaution, just in case the peephole was the only method of surveillance on the porch.

Chimes tolled inside the house, and Bolan waited, listening for footsteps, ready when a shadow blocked the faint light from the peephole. Latches clicked and rattled, then the door swung inward to reveal a hulking cyclops in a rumpled suit.

"What can I do you for?" the doorman asked, eyeballing Dixon on the sidelines with his one good orb.

"We're here to meet Nasser Asad," Bolan said, trying out his hole card.

"More, huh?" said the cyclops. "No one told me it was a convention."

As the doorman stepped aside to let them pass, a gunshot, thunderously loud, echoed from somewhere in the house. The big man whipped around to look in that direction, then swung back to face the new arrivals. When he saw the SMGs they leveled at him, angry color stained his craggy face.

"What the hell is this?" he challenged, blocking Bolan's entry to the house, his huge hands opening and closing like a wrestler's in the ring.

"We're going in there," Bolan told him. "Now."

Though obviously torn between emergencies, the hulk stayed where he was and said, "I don't think so."

"Your call," Bolan replied before he shot the cyclops in the chest.

AHMED ZERO WAS FAST enough to save himself from the first shot. He'd sipped his lemon-lime soda, watched as Talmadge spoke to someone on the telephone, not really listening. He wasn't there to eavesdrop on Asad and the American, but rather to protect Asad from any danger in the house.

That might include Asad's own mercenary, and Zero was watching when Talmadge replaced his cell phone in a pocket with his left hand, then reached underneath his jacket with the right. At the first glint of gunmetal, Zero dropped his glass and drew the big Colt Anaconda from its shoulder harness, thrusting out its six-inch barrel toward the Yank.

Talmadge already had a pistol in his hand, pointed half-way between Asad and Zero. While he puzzled over choice of targets, Zero thumbed the Anaconda's hammer back and fired his first shot, its report as loud as cannon fire within the living room.

He missed, haste and the big gun's recoil ruining his aim. His bullet drilled the wall between Asad and Talmadge, causing both of them to flinch in opposite directions as it smacked through plaster and kept going into other rooms.

Zero was angling for a clear shot at his target, Talmadge almost ready to return fire, when an automatic weapon stuttered from the general direction of the foyer. Startled, Zero let his focus stray just long enough for Talmadge to squeeze off a shot that nicked the left sleeve of his jacket.

Cursing, he fired another wasted Magnum round, then threw himself across the wet bar, glasses flying, bouncing when they hit the carpet underfoot. Zero came down on two or three of them and felt them crack beneath his sudden weight, their jagged fangs tearing through fabric, into flesh.

The pain lanced through his hip and outer thigh. No major arteries or veins endangered, but the clear, cruel blades were still inside him, grinding when he turned from his left side onto his back.

Zero clenched his teeth around the pain and flinched when the next shot exploded in the living room, but that one seemed to send no slug in his direction.

Could it be Nasser Asad? Had Talmadge killed him?

In which case, the only thing that Ahmed Zero could accomplish was revenge. If he was up to it.

With almost Herculean will, he struggled to all fours. The effort cost him blood and agony, but Zero made it. As for rising to his feet, that seemed to be a task beyond his power at the moment. Only when he heard the sound of scuffling feet, circling around the wet bar, did he thrust with both legs, clutching at the wall with his free hand.

And he was on his feet, shoulders against the wall to help him balance, tracking with the Anaconda while his free hand awkwardly retrieved the Walther pistol from its holster on his hip. The draw, cross hand and backward, made him stagger, but he held the Colt before him in a hand that wobbled just enough to make him seem tipsy.

But where was Talmadge?

There'd been footsteps. Had he fled the room, leaving Zero behind?

Ahmed Zero saw Nasser Asad sprawled on the love seat, leaking crimson from a bullet hole above his glazed left eye. The gunshot had been fired from such close range that powder had tattooed the corpse's forehead, while the exit wound in back released a deluge onto velvet cushions.

Where was Talmadge? "Over here," the mercenary said, rising on Zero's left.

Zero swiveled in that direction, both guns firing, but he was too late. A double tap from the American's pistol punched through his eye socket and cheek, dropping the gunman into darkness without end.

OKAY, DIXON THOUGHT. This sucks.

He didn't know if word had gone around somehow, after the first two raids, or if this chicken coop was somehow special, rating extra guards, but from the moment they had shot the one-eyed bouncer on the door, it had been hell on wheels.

Dixon still didn't know who'd started shooting first, before they even pulled their SMGs outside, and at the rate that he was moving, he might never know. Some joker with a shotgun—sounded like a 10-gauge where he was, on the receiving end—had pinned him down beside some stairs, barely a dozen feet inside the joint's front door.

And Dixon saw that getting out of there would be a bitch.

Mindful of Cooper's early warnings, children in the rooms they couldn't see directly, Dixon couldn't act on his impulse to simply hose the stairs with Uzi fire and hope he hit something or someone.

He needed better strategy, and needed it right then.

And while he thought about it, Cooper had already vanished, lost somewhere within the house.

While he was crouching, plotting, by the stairs, more shooting echoed through the house from guns he couldn't see.

One of them sounded like a cannon, louder even than the shotgun that had pinned him down, but Dixon only heard it two, three times. He reckoned it was fifty-fifty that the shooter had been killed, or else had shifted to another weapon that was quieter, maybe with less recoil.

Who cared?

Another shotgun blast boomed out above him, buckshot peppering the banister and stairs, snapping the newel post like balsa wood and leaving strips of carpet from the stairs drooping like tentacles of some moth-eaten squid.

If he couldn't see the shooter, Dixon had to draw him out. But how? With bait, of course. And that meant him.

Scanning the area around him, Dixon saw the same things that he'd seen already: walls, more carpet, stairs, and underneath the stairs, some kind of cupboard. He'd ignored it earlier, knowing the last thing that he meant to do was hide inside some kind of cubbyhole, but now he had the germ of an idea.

He snaked forward, opened the cupboard door and saw that there was ample room for him inside if he sat with knees against his chest. No problem there, but how would he persuade the shotgun man to come downstairs and into range?

He fired a short burst toward the ceiling, up there, hoping there were no kids in the attic, and called out before the echoes faded, "It's been fun, asshole, but I've got things to do."

Another shotgun blast came instantly, ripping through several of the upright banister support posts like a chain saw's blade, but Dixon was already moving, bundling himself inside the almost hidden cupboard with the mini-Uzi almost underneath his chin, aimed at the bottom of the stairs three feet in front of him.

Dixon had barely braced himself and gripped his weapon when he heard swift footsteps on the stairs above, descending. They were too heavy by far to be a child's, and Dixon told himself that he and Cooper were the only innocent adults inside the chicken coop.

He held the mini-Uzi's trigger down and let it rip, tracking his unseen target down the stairs. Its buzz-saw noise was ear numbing inside the tiny storage space, and hot brass spewed into his face, rebounding from his forehead, cheeks and chin.

He took it, fired until the little weapon's magazine was spent, tracking the downward progress of his target as the guy first ran, then stumbled, finally tumbling down the stairs to puddle at the bottom in a heap. Dixon rolled out, forgot about the Uzi's empty clip in his excitement, then remembered it too late and drew his pistol to confront the shotgun man.

No need.

The guy was dead as hell, with eight or nine wounds visible, and one of those beneath his chin. Dixon holstered his Smith & Wesson, swapped the Uzi's clip out for a fresh one, then reached down and grabbed the dead man's shotgun.

Twelve-gauge. Go figure.

Dixon checked the gun as best he could without unloading it and starting off from scratch. It had a live round in the chamber, and thumb pressure on the first round in the under-barrel magazine met stiff resistance, indicating that the tube was either full or nearly so. Dixon supposed the shooter had to have been reloading when he'd made his play and tricked the guy downstairs.

All's fair, he thought, and went to find the action, following the sounds of gunfire through the chicken coop.

TALMADGE WAS LOOKING for a back door when the skanky-looking mistress of the house popped up in front of him, waving a pistol in his face. It was a lady's gun, shiny, maybe a .25 or .32, but either one could drop him if she put a slug in the right place. Skill or a lucky accident could take him down right now, unless he watched himself.

"Hey, hey," he chided her, keeping the SIG well down beside his right leg. "What's this all about?"

"Cut out the crap, okay?" she answered. "This is all your fault, yours and the raghead's. You're not going anywhere."

"Hold on! You think I brought those shooters with me?"

"I don't give a shit who brought them," she replied through smoker's teeth, clenched tightly. "You're the one I caught. You've ruined everything, and now you're going down."

"Maybe," Talmadge said. As he spoke, he ducked and sidestepped, raised the Smith and fired all in a single fluid motion. "Maybe not."

His .40-caliber slug struck her somewhere below her left breast, batting the slender woman backward and away. She lost the shiny pistol without ever firing it and landed on her back, a rag doll cast aside by someone who'd grown tired of her.

Talmadge was about to leave her there, continue looking for that exit, when a male voice, close behind him, said, "You won't get out that way."

"Why not?" asked Talmadge, turning oh-so-slowly to confront his latest adversary.

The opposition—six feet tall, athletic build, armed with a Spectre SMG from Italy—replied, "It isn't in your stars."

"I don't believe in that crap," Talmadge told him.

"Call it intuition, then."

"I'd rather trust in luck."

"It's all run out," the stranger said.

"Do I know you?" Talmadge asked, frowning. "You

don't look like one of the pathetic clowns who run this place."

"We haven't met," the shooter said, "but I've been working on it for a while."

A light bulb suddenly went on, inside his head. "Vancouver?" Talmadge queried. "Was that you?"

"I had some help. That was round two."

"Looks like I missed round one."

"Jakarta. You were gone before we got there."

"Shame. We could've settled this last week." He had a firm grip on the SIG-Sauer, ready to use it, but the cold stare of the Spectre made him hesitate. "You mind me asking what it is that's made you go to all that trouble?"

"You don't know?" the stranger asked.

Talmadge had an idea, but jumping to conclusions was an easy way to break one's neck.

"Some kind of grudge?" he offered. "Payback? I'm a merc. I must've stepped on someone's toes along the way."

"No payback," said the gunman. "It's prevention."

There it was.

"Sorry, but I don't follow you," he lied.

"The bomb," his adversary said. "I need to know who has it, what he plans to do with it. The whole thing, here and now."

Talmadge surprised himself by laughing. "What, that's all? I'm just supposed to give it up because you say so? And then you'll let me walk, I guess?"

The shooter held his SMG rock steady. "Guess again," he said.

"Oh, so you plan to kill me, but I'm still supposed to

help you? Why would I do that? Out of the goodness of my heart?"

"Maybe because you took an oath and served this country once, with honor. You were good at what you did, maybe the best. And you were proud."

"Still am," Talmadge replied. "I'm just not proud of Uncle Sam."

"You got the shaft. I understand that," said his enemy. "I've read your file."

"Ah, so this is official, then."

"You can't go forward with it, Talmadge. It's too much. The payback's disproportionate. It's My Lai, times ten thousand."

Talmadge flared at that. "You want to talk about war crimes? Our boys commit them every day, on orders from the top, but if they're caught, the same brass hangs them out to dry. It wasn't even that, in my case. If you've read the file— the real file—you already know that. Christ, I stopped a crime in progress. Saved a fellow soldier from a fate that some consider worse than death. My great reward? Suspended prison time and a dishonorable discharge. How's that sound to you?"

"It sounds like something you should tell the media," his nemesis replied. "Go for the ones who screwed you over, not a city full of innocent civilians."

"Innocent?" Talmadge jeered. "Let me guess. Two wrongs don't make a right, eh?"

"It was true, last time I checked."

"Well, look again, pardner. These innocents you're so concerned about keep voting in a pack of scumbags who send men and women off to war for nothing but their own political advancement. Lying bastards, every one of them. You want to know the truth? My one regret about this deal is that our package won't be going to the White House."

"So, why not tell me where it *is* going? Who's the delivery boy?"

"How do you know it's not a girl?" Talmadge asked.

"Working for al Qaeda?" said the stranger. "Not a chance in hell. They might let her make coffee, but the martyr shop's a boys' club."

"Good guess," Talmadge said, "but you're too damned late. The parcel's on its way. Can't stop it now."

"Maybe. But I've stopped you, at least."

"Think so?"

"The only question is, will you be leaving here in hand-cuffs or a body bag."

"I guess they never taught you overconfidence can get you killed," Talmadge replied. "If you were really smart, you'd leave this place right now, get in your car and drive like hell. North, east, or west. Just fucking go."

"Not yet. We've still got business here."

"Okay, your call," Talmadge said. "Do you want it like the movies, counting down from three."

"This isn't Hollywood," the stranger said.

"You're right, it's—"

Even as he threw himself aside, raising the SIG-Sauer to fire, Talmadge was wondering if he could make it. When the muzzle-flashes started winking at him, bullets ripping through his abdomen and rib cage, he had his answer.

No way.

No damned way at all.

"SORRY I'M LATE," Dixon said, coming up behind him.

Bolan glanced at him, saw he was carrying a shotgun now, the mini-Uzi slung over his shoulder.

"It's a loaner," Dixon explained, shrugging.

"We're pretty much done here," Bolan replied.

"Talmadge." The man from DHS stood over him. "I guess he didn't spill?"

"We talked," Bolan said, "but it wasn't helpful."

"Shit! I found Nasser Asad back there," Dixon explained, cocking a thumb over his shoulder, toward the living room. "Somebody plugged him in the head. Same thing for Ahmed Zero. Could've been our boy here, but I guess we'll never know."

Three targets dead, and Bolan had nothing to show for it but gun smoke in the air. *Looks like you blew it,* nagged the small voice in his head.

He crouched beside Talmadge and started going through the dead man's pockets, scattering their contents on the floor around him.

"Can I help you find something?" Dixon asked.

"I'll know it if I find it," Bolan said.

"Sure. Okay. But the police—"

He found it in the inside pocket of the soldier's bloody sport coat. Just a glossy tourist pamphlet, printed and distributed in tens of thousands every year. He held it up for Dixon to peruse.

"Mall of America? So, what? Maybe… Oh, shit! You don't think…?"

Dixon saw the phone number that Talmadge had inscribed across the top edge of the pamphlet's foremost page. He'd used a ballpoint, written carefully, but blood had smeared the last two digits slightly.

"Can you read that?" Dixon asked him. "Can you?"

"Yes," Bolan replied. "And now, we need someone to trace it."

## CHAPTER SEVENTEEN

Martyrdom can be exhausting business.

Despite his best intentions starting out, Afif Mukhtar hadn't managed to sleep at all the night before his great transition into Paradise. Each time he'd closed his eyes, he had imagined prowlers entering his flat, stealing the case from underneath his very nose and making off with it to parts unknown.

It wasn't so much that he feared the thieves would accidentally detonate the bomb, but rather that they'd carry it somewhere outside the city, to some cabin in the wilderness, where only they and some raccoons or deer would be incinerated by the blast.

Each time the vision came to him, Mukhtar leaped upright, brandishing his Walther PP pistol at an empty room. The shadows mocked him, but the fact that he was wrong each time did nothing to relax him.

Sunrise was a relief, although it found him weary, footsteps dragging. In the bathroom mirror, Mukhtar saw a face that had apparently aged five years overnight. His olive skin had turned a sallow brindle color that suggested jaundice, but he had no need of medical attention.

In a few more hours, he would have no need of anything at all.

Waking with the sunrise, four hours remained before he had full access to the target. He'd allowed an hour's driving time, which meant he had three hours left to kill before he packed the bomb into his car and left his flat behind forever.

Mukhtar wouldn't miss it, but it still felt strange.

He made breakfast, ate a double helping of scrambled eggs, toast with marmalade and strong black coffee on the side. On *CSI* the lab detectives would review the contents of his stomach to determine how he spent his morning, but the local officers would have nothing to work with once he pressed the little button on the handle of his case.

Nothing at all.

It didn't bother Mukhtar that the infidels might never know his name. As long as God recognized his sacrifice and honored it, all else was immaterial.

Since he had armed the bomb the previous night and couldn't switch it off again, Mukhtar gave it a wide berth in the morning. He would take no chances with it, either in his flat or in the car, in transit. He'd already stripped the ratty bedspread from the bed, planning to wrap and pad the case after he placed it in the car.

He would be careful not to wrap it too well, though, in case the bedspread pressed against the trigger button and it went off prematurely.

How could he have known there'd be so many worries in the last few hours of his life?

Mukhtar felt that he should be breezing through those final hours, focused on his goal and nothing else. Instead, he found himself consumed by a hyperawareness to frivolous details that vexed him immensely and ruined his mood.

Mukhtar could feel the wrinkles in his stockings, and the kitchen faucet dripped annoyingly. The tag inside his chosen shirt felt rough against his skin, and when he changed shirts the next one felt worse. He couldn't find a comfortable place to put the Walther, in his pants. It either made his pockets bulge and pressed into his thigh, or dragged his belt down, with his shirttail dangling at the back.

At last, when he could stand no more of pacing through his rooms, he put the pistol in a paper bag, wrapped it inside the bedspread, took the case, and walked out to his car, leaving the flat unlocked behind him as he left. What difference did it make if thieves broke in and stole his belongings now?

During his sleepless night, Mukhtar had planned exactly how to place the bomb inside his car. The trunk was out: too hot and too much chance of sliding, with the trigger armed. The back seat, likewise, was a fatal accident waiting to happen. If he had to hit the brakes in an emergency, the case could tip and fall, striking the trigger on the front seats or the floorboard.

No.

The perfect method was to drape the bedspread on the back seat and the floor behind the driver's seat, open, then set the case on top of it, the trigger button on its handle facing inward, where a minor jostling offered no prospect of impact with a solid object. Once the case was situated properly, fold the bedspread around and over it—again, leaving the trigger bare. Thus padded, wedged tightly between the seats, the bomb would only be disturbed in transit if he rolled the car.

Sparing a final glance for the building where he'd· spent the last year of his life, Afif Mukhtar pulled out into the empty street and motored toward his date with destiny.

He felt a sudden urge to shop.

Afif Mukhtar was going to the mall.

THE TRACE WAS RELATIVELY simple once they had a phone number. It got Bolan a name and local address, plus the make, model and license number of a five-year-old sedan.

Afif Mukhtar, a Palestinian whose parents emigrated to the States from Jordan back in 1983, when he was nine months old. All three of them were U.S. citizens, and nothing indicated that the parents had made any moves to contradict the oaths they took before a federal judge in 1988.

Something had happened to their son, though.

He was in the fast lane of a one-way road to Hell.

"So, now the G-men take him, right?" Dixon asked after Bolan shared the ID on their target.

"Wrong. A SWAT team crashing in could make him trigger the device. Even with NEST on standby, we can't take the chance."

"You mean *we're* going over there to roust him?"

"No," Bolan replied. "Plainclothes already checked his

neighborhood. There's no sign of his car. Smart money says he's on his way."

"There are a hundred ways to stop his car. Set up an early-bird sobriety checkpoint, or—"

"Anything with uniforms attached to it would only make him hit the trigger."

"Damn it! Have I mentioned that I hate this job?"

"Hard to believe," Bolan replied. "You're so good at it."

"Here it comes," Dixon said. "Soap before the bar."

Bolan made no attempt to sugarcoat it. "We can get there first and try to spot him coming in. If we do everything just right, we have a chance to drop him when his guard's down. Maybe he won't trigger it."

"Maybe. Your confidence is overwhelming, man."

"No guarantees," Bolan reminded him. "We knew that going in."

They were already rolling south on U.S. Highway 35 from the Twin Cities, down to Bloomington, while Bolan ran through his knowledge of the target. Most of it came from the pamphlet he'd found on Gene Talmadge's corpse.

While not the largest mall on Earth—or even in the States—the Mall of America sprawled over 4.2 million square feet. Its three levels harbored some 520 stores, fifty restaurants, fourteen theaters and seven nightclubs, altogether employing more than twelve thousand persons. Four million shoppers visited the mall in an average year, leaving their vehicles either in the open parking lots to the north and south, or in the seven-story parking garages to east and west.

Afif Mukhtar could drop his car in any one of twenty thousand parking spaces, then set off his bomb right there, or carry it inside the mall proper to find ground zero. Either way, finding that needle in a haystack promised to be one of Bolan's toughest challenges to date.

Maybe his last.

Look on the bright side, Bolan told himself, and smiled. If he and Dixon split the difference, they only had to check ten thousand parking spaces each, before they went inside the mall. By that time, if their man hadn't decided to eat every item offered in the mall's food court, he should've found his spot and blown them all to kingdom come.

Terrific.

"Did you think of something funny?" Dixon asked him.

"Funny?"

"You were smiling there."

"That's just my sunny disposition."

"Right. Because we're happy warriors. Listen, Cooper, is there anybody who can help us out with this?"

"Jack's working on it."

"Right. Okay. Sorry I asked."

Grimaldi had been circling in a chopper for the past three-quarters of an hour, watching the approaches to the mall. They knew that Mukhtar's Saturn Ion Quad Coupe was silver, likely faded after four long Minnesota winters. Back in Washington, Brognola had pulled strings to get one of the NSA's spy satellites retasked to scan for makes—and license plates, if possible.

At least they had a shot.

"If you're giving up and want to bail," he cautioned Dixon, "jump out now. I don't have time to stop."

"And miss the big finale? Not a chance."

Another moment passed, then Dixon said, "Speaking of chances, did you have your friend with the computers calculate our odds?"

"It slipped my mind," Bolan said.

"Yeah. I wouldn't want to hear them, either."

Bolan *had* done certain basic calculations on his own, however. Four million shoppers per year meant an average of eleven thousand per day. Toss in twelve-thousand-plus employees, and they had twenty-three thousand dead at ground zero, before the heat and shock waves spread, before the fallout planted lethal time bombs in the cells of thousands more.

Something to think about. Incentive, as it were.

But there was nothing they could do until they found their man.

Tom Dixon hadn't planned to die this way. If anyone had asked him how and where he planned to kick the bucket, bite the dust or buy the farm, he never would've mentioned nuclear explosions.

And he damned sure wouldn't have envisioned being vaporized outside a Minnesota shopping mall.

He knew Matt Cooper's rule about defeatist thinking, and he generally shared that sentiment, but for the life of him he couldn't see a happy ending to their grim little adventure.

Even if they found Afif Mukhtar somehow, a minnow swimming in the ocean, Dixon saw no realistic hope of killing or disarming him before he had a chance to trigger his payload.

And once he hit the panic button, they were history.

Instead of fretting over that, he tried to think about what happened after the explosion, when the smoke and fallout cleared. It would be too damned late for NEST—the Nuclear Emergency Search Team—to lend a hand. Maybe the new, improved FEMA could get its act together this time without bungling every step along the way and making matters worse.

Someone would ultimately trace the bomb back to al Qaeda. Dixon reckoned that the White House and at least a handful of the Pentagon's brass hats had to know the score already. They'd be huddled in a room somewhere, plotting retaliation.

Against whom?

It made no difference to Dixon which countries the President invaded after he was dead, but the response could start a deadly chain reaction if they didn't get it right the first time. Any kind of knee-jerk action, executed without solid proof of guilt, could set the whole damned world on fire.

That wasn't really what al Qaeda wanted. Was it?

Were the old men squatting in their caves and hovels so damned crazed with hatred and religious madness that they'd rather have no world than one whose map included the United States and Israel?

Were they really, truly crazy, after all?

I could've been a fat, lazy insurance salesman, Dixon thought. In L.A., or in Omaha.

But that wouldn't have saved him, either, if the world went up in flames. Better to go out in a flash, at ground zero, than linger for a year with radiation poisoning, losing his teeth and hair, watching his flesh rot slowly on his bones.

They were already in the shit, and Dixon couldn't see

a clear way out of it. Okay, Cooper had Jack flying traffic watch, and his mysterious connections had retasked some satellite to help them out, but when did anything like that work out, except in movies?

Better than nothing, he supposed.

But not by much.

The mini-Uzi, sitting in a bag between his feet, was fully loaded. Not that he would get a chance to use it, if the play went down. He couldn't spray the bomber and his suitcase or whatever with a damned machine gun, maybe blow the primer charge himself instead of letting Mukhtar do it.

No. That wouldn't do at all.

They passed a billboard for the mall, six miles ahead.

Dixon sat back and closed his eyes, wishing he could remember how to pray.

AFIF MUKHTAR CURSED bitterly as traffic slowed his progress, then muttered a terse apology to God for his sin. He had to maintain proper decorum, even at the point of death. Especially then, since his final feelings, thoughts and words might weigh more heavily on judgment's scales.

But could he lose his place in Paradise, if he went through with his heroic martyrdom as planned? The imam had encouraged him to think it was a lock, sewn up, as long as he was blown apart in God's service, fighting for the holy cause.

But what if he was wrong?

Men made mistakes, and Mukhtar recognized the broad range of Islamic thought in modern times. While fundamentalists maintained their pressure for jihad, others preached liberal philosophies, some even hailing the

American invasion of Iraq as a blessing. It would be tragic if Mukhtar selected the wrong path to Paradise, only to find himself excluded at the end.

Ridiculous!

He understood his duty, and the reasons why the imam couldn't do the job himself. Each man was chosen for a reason, for a different role. Some had the ultimate honor of martyrdom, while others were forced to watch from the sidelines, recruiting and encouraging new front-line warriors.

No doubt, if the imam could sacrifice himself, he would.

Would he?

Mukhtar said another prayer of expiation for that most unworthy thought. He only had his present fast-track shot at Paradise because his imam had been good enough to pick him from the crowd, bestow that blessing with a firm hand on his shoulder and a whispered word.

Mukhtar had visited his target half a dozen times, rehearsing the specific moves that he would make today. He couldn't guarantee a certain parking space, of course, but his arrival when the mall was barely open ought to let him have his choice of parking lots, at least. Because he wouldn't see the sun again after he passed inside the mall, unless it shone in Paradise, he chose the northern outdoor parking lot. The last walk through fresh air would brace him, do him good.

Inside the mall, he had surveyed the shops and other offerings, deciding that he didn't want to haul a heavy suitcase on the escalators. Anyway, a ground-floor blast would drop the upper floors. Unlike conventional explosives, no one in the giant mall would be protected when he pressed the trigger.

Mukhtar passed a billboard telling him that he had only one mile to go before he reached his destination. He switched on the radio, for a distraction, but the mindless jabber and discordant sounds that passed for music only inflamed his mounting anger and frustration.

He had thought of driving to the mall last night, when it was closed, to find the perfect parking spot and be there waiting when it opened in the morning, but he'd feared that mall security or the police would challenge him. His goal wasn't to simply flatten a gigantic shopping center and a couple of night watchmen.

Mukhtar wanted customers, employees, passersby. He wanted thousands, *tens* of thousands, at ground zero when he triggered the device. He longed to see their vapid faces in the split second before they all melted together into nothingness, before the shock wave swept them all away.

He tried the radio again and got a Spanish-language station this time, all guitars and drums, with male singers who sounded more like women. How he missed the haunting rhythms of his native Palestine!

Of course, Mukhtar had never been there, knew it only from the second- and third-hand accounts of others, but he loved it still. And what he did today would ultimately help his outcast people to reclaim their homeland.

Wouldn't it?

Holding that thought, Mukhtar switched on his turn signal and drifted toward the lane that would deliver him, with several thousand other drivers and their vehicles, to his selected target zone.

*Washington, D.C.*

THE WAITING SUCKED.

As long as he'd been in the business, mounting stake-outs and surveillance, sweating out the hostage situations, waiting for some target to resurface after weeks or months in hiding, Hal Brognola still chafed at the inaction. He hated sitting on his hands.

Waiting five hundred or a thousand miles away was even worse. If he'd been at the scene in Minneapolis-St. Paul, at least he could've paced the floor with men and women who were caught up in the action, bitched and moaned with them about the steady march of passing time.

Except, he thought, there were no men and women on alert in the Twin Cities. Only Bolan, Tom Dixon and two or three FBI agents had any idea what was happening, what *could* happen any minute now, to turn their lives upside down or erase them forever.

Brognola wasn't pacing, wouldn't give in to the urge transmitted by his weary brain to jangling nerve synapses. There was literally nothing he could do at this point, but to wait for certain information and transmit it, if and when it came to him.

Not if. God, make it *when*.

And not too late.

Jack Grimaldi and the satellite were circling, searching for Afif Mukhtar. Whether they'd find him in time remained to be seen. Failure might not be an option on this job, but it was still a distinct possibility.

Brognola's hand stretched out in the direction of the

Stony Man hotline, but iron will retrieved it. Everybody at the Farm was working overtime, no slackers. Every one of them was briefed and understood the cataclysmic stakes involved. If they could tell Hal anything, they would, without his prodding or incessant questions keeping them from what they had to do.

The good news was he had his best agent in place.

That was the bad news, too.

If anything went wrong, he would be losing Bolan, no two ways about it. And the world after this day might be a place where warriors like the Executioner were needed more than ever, if the country or the human race was going to survive.

Somewhere in Washington, a crisis team was poring over Midwestern maps and weather reports, quietly preparing for the worst-case scenario. If all went well, most U.S. residents would never know they'd had another covert brush with death.

If anything went wrong, the dead and dying wouldn't care.

Beyond D-day and its grim aftermath, there'd be calls for an investigation in the House, the Senate, anywhere a group of politicians could sit down and try to benefit from the disaster by sacrificing scapegoats.

And Brognola, when they learned his name, his role, would wind up near the top of everyone's hit list.

He didn't fear the inquisition, was nearly immune to personal embarrassment in public life, and he had long ago decided that some secrets would go with him to his grave. A threat of jail, if he refused to testify, meant nothing to him—though he hoped it wouldn't come to that.

The phone rang, jarring Brognola out of a daydream where he crawled through slimy tunnels with the cast of TV's *Prison Break*. He spent a heartbeat singling out which telephone it was, then snatched up the receiver for his line to Stony Man.

"Tell me," he snapped into the mouthpiece.

*Bloomington, Minnesota*

"ALMOST THERE," Dixon said as if Bolan couldn't read the signs himself. "Shouldn't be long now."

Bolan wrote it off to nerves without replying. He was grappling with a case of that himself, although he'd had a good deal more experience at coping with the symptoms.

There were always nerves before a battle, before any operation where the stakes were life-or-death. The fact that Bolan's failure might doom tens of thousands, maybe millions, helped to elevate his blood pressure, but there were also tricks to staying calm.

It had to be worse for Dixon, he decided. First time in the field, and he'd not only faced the possibility of death, killed men he'd never met before to save himself, but now there was also the chance that he'd be standing at or near ground zero when a suitcase bomb went off.

Pressure? You bet.

The rookie hadn't cracked, and Bolan still couldn't be sure exactly how he felt about recent events. It wasn't something Bolan had to worry over. If they made it through the day alive, he'd likely never see Dixon again. But he was still concerned about the way Dixon seemed torn between loving and hating the dark side of his profession. If he didn't find a balance—

Then it's someone else's problem, Bolan told himself.

If he was really all that troubled about Dixon's long-term fitness for his job, Bolan could always have a quiet word with Brognola and pass the burden on that way. No sweat.

Right now, he had to focus on Afif Mukhtar, his lethal cargo and the target that was now only three-quarters of a mile ahead.

"Where do we start?" Dixon asked. "If your guys don't call, I mean."

That was the very question Bolan had been pondering before his mind got sidetracked. Where to start? Two parking lots and two enclosed garages. Twenty thousand slots for vehicles, maybe one-third of them concealed from airborne eyes.

Where do we start?

"I haven't got a clue," he answered honestly. "Without a tip, figure we spend an hour, minimum, just looking for his car."

"Longer than that, I'd bet."

"Or we can bag that part of it and just go straight inside," Bolan suggested.

"Not much better," Dixon answered. "Even if we split up, we've got three floors, six hundred different businesses, plus washrooms and employees-only areas. God knows how many thousand faces passing by."

"So, what else can we do?" Bolan asked.

"I was thinking, maybe turn around and drive like hell until the wheels fall off or we run out of gas."

"Sorry. It's not an option."

"No. But still, something to think about."

Bolan had thought about it, sure. What firefighter had ever run into a burning building without thinking he should stay outside? What soldier ever threw himself on top of a grenade in combat, without asking, What in hell is wrong with me?

"It brings us back to duty," Bolan said at last. "Once you take that upon yourself, it's a responsibility. There's no back door."

"Soldiers surrender all the time," Dixon reminded him, half-joking.

"Surrender doesn't mean running away. Our opposition isn't a legitimate combatant, and he's not dictating terms. He's going for the kill shot, here and now."

"Hey, don't mind me," Dixon said. "It's this crazy living, breathing thing I've grown attached to. Anyway, I got a nice new shotgun out of it. You want to do some hunting when we're finished here?"

"Let's take it one hunt at a time," Bolan suggested. "If we—"

His sat phone rang and Bolan snatched it up.

"I'm listening," he said.

Brognola's distant voice told him, "North parking lot! We found the bastard!"

"On my way," Bolan replied.

## CHAPTER EIGHTEEN

Afif Mukhtar remembered his turn signal at the last moment, jolted by the thought of a police officer stopping him within sight of his goal. He had the Walther PP pistol on the seat beside him, within reach if an emergency arose, but he saw no patrol cars waiting for him up ahead.

Would they disguise themselves? Their vehicles? If agents of the Great Satan knew he was coming, would they hide so cleverly, or would they shield his target with a wall of flashing lights and guns?

It didn't matter now.

As Mukhtar nosed his Saturn into the north parking lot, he realized that he had won. Whatever happened next, from that point onward, he could detonate the bomb at any time and still inflict great damage on his enemies. Whether they shot him by his car and Mukhtar pressed the trigger as he fell, or if he stood inside the teeming mall, the end result would be the same. He craved the more dramatic gesture, for his own sake, but since none of those who heard him would survive to tell the tale in any case, what difference did it make?

Mukhtar began the tedious process of looking for a parking space. He'd thought that coming early to the mall would make it easier, but others in their thousands obviously had the same idea. The lot wasn't full yet, by any means, but Mukhtar wanted something close to the main entrance, if it was available.

He started cruising, cursing underneath his breath, forgetting the apologies to God in his mounting anger. His watch and dashboard clock agreed that the mall had only been open for thirteen minutes. How could so many shoppers be inside already, buying things the average Palestinian at home would never see, much less afford?

They would be punished this day for their long years of extravagance, while others suffered poverty in silence.

The space he found at last was still nearly one hundred yards from the main doors, but Mukhtar took what he could get. Nosing his car into the slot, he scraped the Saturn's front-left fender on the bumper of an SUV already parked in the next space. That made him curse again, imagining the ugly scratches, the expense of fixing them, then he remembered that there would be no repair work on his car or on the one he'd struck. None of it had the slightest meaning anymore.

And in that moment, with that thought, Afif Mukhtar felt truly free.

He could do anything within the next few moments. Strip off his clothes, if he wanted to, and run into the mall stark naked—though the notion mortified him. He could shoot some of the infidels inside and watch them squirm, before he triggered the device and put them all out of their misery.

He could do anything but walk away from it alive.

This is the end, he thought. And just as quickly, heard the voice of his imam, inside his head, reply, And the beginning of eternity in Paradise.

So let it be.

He backed out of the parking space and tried again, more careful this time. When he had the Saturn squared away, had switched the engine off, Mukhtar sat rock still in the driver's seat for yet another moment, checking out the lot for watchers. Enemies.

Reaching across the seat, he palmed his pistol, double-checked that he had set its safety in the Off position, then slipped the pistol underneath his belt on the right side, for a right-handed draw. Mukhtar would hold the suitcase bomb in his left hand, thumb poised above the trigger at all times until he detonated it, and still be free to fire on any adversaries who revealed themselves to him.

That done, he reached between his legs and found the lever that released the driver's seat. Pushing with both heels on the floorboard, he edged forward to the point where he felt cramped behind the steering wheel. It snagged his pistol as he slid out of the car, but Mukhtar quickly put it back in place.

Patting his pocket to make sure he had the keys, Mukhtar then closed the driver's door and opened up the left-hand rear. With extra room, now that the driver's seat had moved, the case wobbled at Mukhtar's touch. He peeled the bedspread from it carefully, avoiding any contact whatsoever with the trigger built into its handle.

Perfect.

Now that the case was clear, Mukhtar reached in and lifted it, drawing it slowly from the car and into bright sunlight.

The *real* sunrise would come in ten or fifteen minutes.

It would be the dawning of a bright new day.

"RIGHT HERE!" Dixon said, pointing. "Turn in here!"

"I see it," Bolan told him. "Get a grip."

"What, you aren't worried? Scared?"

"I didn't say that."

"So, you *are* nervous?"

"I don't let it take over," Bolan said. "It just gets in the way."

"I hear you. I'm not letting anything take over, man. I'm chilling. Cold as ice."

Both of his legs were jiggling, and the fingers of his left hand drummed the seat beside him.

"I can see that," Bolan said. "Just keep an eye out for that Saturn, will you?"

"Roger that. What do they look like?"

Bolan grimaced as he turned into the mall's north parking lot. "A small sedan. Silver or gray." He rattled off the plate number again.

A throbbing sound somewhere above him told Bolan that Jack Grimaldi was on station in the air. Craning his neck to catch a quick glimpse of the chopper, Bolan saw that it was circling, searching, closer to the mall.

"Jack hasn't found him yet," Dixon said.

"No."

Their hit had come from farther out, the NSA's spy satellite. It seemed incredible, but Brognola and Stony Man's techs all confirmed the hit on Mukhtar's ride as he'd entered the parking lot.

"Can't they just tell us where he parked the goddamned car?" Dixon asked.

"If they can, they will," Bolan replied. "Meanwhile, keep looking."

Unless Grimaldi or the Farm came through again, their only recourse was to cruise the rows, one at a time, until they spotted Mukhtar's small economy sedan or spied the man himself. Brognola's call had come five minutes earlier, so there was still a decent chance they'd find their target in the parking lot, instead of in the mall proper.

"We get this close, then miss him," Dixon said, "I'm gonna be pissed off."

"But not for long," Bolan said, feeling a hysterical impulse to laugh, which quickly faded.

"He's joking now," Dixon advised some silent and invisible third person. "*Now* he's joking."

Bolan's palms were welded to the steering wheel with sweat. The tension felt like static electricity running beneath his skin. His pulse thumped in his ears, reminding him of a stopwatch marking time.

He started searching near the mall's main entrance, operating on the knowledge that he'd never seen a person leave a car out on the fringes of a parking lot unless the lot was full.

Mukhtar would try to minimize his personal exposure in the lot. He would be thinking ambush, watching for a trap, and—

Bolan reached out to grab the two-way radio that lay beside his sat phone, in the console slot between himself and Dixon. He pressed the button for transmission.

"Striker to the whirlybird. Come in!"

"You got the bird, Sarge. Over."

"Don't come in too close," he cautioned. "Spook this guy, and we've got Hiroshima. Over."

"I hear you, Striker. Rising as we speak. You know, more altitude means less chance that I'll spot our boy. Over."

"Affirmative. Do what you can with caution. Out."

"Can't catch a break, I guess," Dixon said.

"We already caught one when they tipped us to this lot."

"Unless they're wrong," the man from DHS replied. "Remember all those WMDs? They had a year to spot those babies, not five minutes. And what happens?"

"I remember," Bolan told him. "This is now."

"I'm watching," Dixon said. "I've got my eye right on the— Shit! Is that our boy?"

Dixon was pointing one row over as they passed. Bolan had time to crane his neck and glimpse a man with dark hair, olive skin, an Army-surplus jacket over blue jeans. He was standing by a car that might have been silver or gray, but with a bulky pickup in between them, Bolan couldn't swear to it.

"Let's check it out," he said, accelerating to the far end of his row.

A heavy bleach-blonde slowed them down, dragging a

stroller from the tailgate of her SUV while balancing a baby on one hip and snapping at a two- or three-year-old who ran around her in frenetic circles, treating Mommy as a maypole.

Bolan edged around her, Dixon cursing fluently while she ignored them, marvelously self-involved. When they were clear, Bolan stood on the gas and raced past the remaining cars in his row, cranked a hard right on the steering wheel and turned into the row where he had seen a man who might be his intended target. One who might be on his way to end the world as Bolan knew it.

"There he is!" Dixon said. "Jesus, is it him?"

"Hang on," Bolan replied, "and we'll find out."

THE HELICOPTER'S SOUND disturbed Afif Mukhtar. He stood beside his car and turned to sweep the sky, almost unconsciously reaching for the pistol beneath his windbreaker.

He saw the helicopter hovering above the far side of the parking lot, perhaps three hundred yards away from him. When Mukhtar's eyes locked on to it, the chopper was ascending. It didn't appear to be involved in any kind of systematic search.

Still…

Was it even possible that Mukhtar's enemies had somehow tracked him to his target? If they knew that he existed, knew his name, address, his mission, wouldn't he already be in custody or dead? Why would they let him get this far before they dropped the net?

Mukhtar remembered that the Mall of America was a tourist attraction, drawing busloads of infidels each day to squander their money inside. Perhaps it also featured in some flying tours of the city—which, if he was honest, had few other landmarks anyone would pay to see. Or was the helicopter owned by one of the Twin Cities' television stations, flying traffic watch?

That notion pleased Afif Mukhtar. It gladdened him to think that thousands of unholy infidels outside the blast zone might observe it on their television screens and tremble. Better still, if it was taped—and if the helicopter somehow managed to survive the blast—the images would be broadcast time and again on every major network in the world.

He started to relax, but not too much.

The most important part of his mission, his martyrdom, still lay ahead of him.

Afif Mukhtar hadn't yet earned his ticket into Paradise.

Hefting the case in his left hand, he found it heavier than he remembered it. Of course, he'd carried it outside that morning in his right hand, which was slightly stronger than the left. He estimated that the case weighed thirty kilos, possibly a little more. A grain of sand, in the eternal scheme of things, and yet it held such power.

Mukhtar considered switching hands, but since he couldn't shoot well with his left, he dropped that plan. With only sixty yards or so to walk, what did it matter if his shoulder felt some strain? Within ten minutes, none of it would matter in the least.

Mukhtar looked around one last time and was vaguely conscious of a car approaching from behind him, at the far end of his row.

More infidels arriving to indulge themselves, only to be surprised that they had come shopping on Judgment Day.

Off to his right, two rows of vehicles between them, Mukhtar saw a blond woman proceeding in the same direction. She was pushing an elaborate baby carriage, while a second child trod almost on her heels, chanting monotonous singsong gibberish. Was it a boy or girl, beneath that ginger hair?

In any case, the woman snapped at it, "Will you be quiet, Terry!"

Motherhood.

Mukhtar thanked God for the thousandth time that he was born a male, without the curse of bearing children, tending them and—

Rubber squealed behind him, tires gripping the pavement as a driver hit his brakes. Mukhtar swiveled his head and saw the same car he'd glimpsed seconds earlier, now stopped dead in the middle of their row. Two men in the front seat sat watching him, then flung their doors open on either side.

Sobbing a curse, Mukhtar whipped out his pistol, dodged between the nearest cars on his right and sprinted toward the target.

Toward his fate.


DIXON STUMBLED, cursing, on his way out of the car, but caught himself before he fell. His skull was throbbing with a headache that had come from nowhere, sucker punching him behind his eyes. He heard his pounding heartbeat in his ears and felt it in his fingers, where he clutched the mini-Uzi in a death grip.

Cooper had grabbed the shotgun from him, when their car screeched to a halt and both of them bailed out. He hadn't argued, didn't really care which weapon he was holding when the world went blinding white around him and the flesh was melted from his bones.

He'd grown accustomed to the little submachine gun, anyway. With any luck, maybe he'd get a chance to stitch Mukhtar with half a magazine before the nuke went off and dusted all of them.

They blew it with the stealth approach, though, revving in and squealing rubber on the stop, alerting him. In Cooper's place, Dixon supposed he might've run the little bastard down, but that would put the bomb directly underneath their car, assuming that the impact didn't trigger it.

Now he was running, having made them with a startled backward glance, and Dixon guessed that he could blow the primer charge at any point, unless the bomb was on some kind of timer set-up. In which case, they would likely need some kind of genius to disarm it, even if they killed Mukhtar and grabbed the case.

They had a basic no-win situation on their hands, as far as he could see, but Dixon still kept running after Mukhtar, finger on the trigger of his SMG and ready, but no firing yet.

It wasn't safe to simply drop him, Cooper had explained in haste, because the bag he carried might be fitted with some kind of dead-man's switch. Release the handle, for example, and the whole thing blew. Of course, that also meant that if Mukhtar should drop his burden accidentally, on a mad chase through the parking lot, they were as good as dead.

There's no good way to go, he thought, before the small voice in his head added, except the opposite direction.

But it was too damned late for that.

Forget about the honor talk and any stain of cowardice, since Cooper would be dead and couldn't smear him anyway. The sad fact was that Dixon had already come too far. Although he had the power, physically, to turn and run away, he couldn't gain safe distance from the bomb now, even if he took the rental car and drove like hell.

He was within the blast zone now.

Ground Zero, here we come.

He wondered for a heartbeat if they'd find his shadow scorched on asphalt, as the shadows of some Hiroshima victims had been etched on walls, but then he realized the whole damned parking lot would be obliterated, turned into a smoking, poisoned crater lined with sand and asphalt melted into ugly glass.

No shadow, either, Dixon thought. Now I'm a lost boy, just like Peter Pan.

And he'd be flying in another minute, on the wind.

As ashes.

Cooper was breaking to his left, around one of those grotesque pickup trucks with four doors and a double set of wheels in back. At the same time, he pointed Dixon to the right, trying to flank Mukhtar.

But they would have to catch him first.

A pistol shot rang out, and Dixon saw the pickup's windshield sprout a spiderweb pattern of cracks. It served the owner right, he thought, for buying such an arrogant and ugly vehicle.

Cooper didn't return fire with the 12-gauge, so Dixon held his own, clutching the SMG against his chest as he advanced more cautiously. One slow step at a time. He couldn't see Mukhtar now, and it troubled him.

In seconds, he might not see anything at all.

"Dixon!" Bolan called out to him. "Tell him we need to talk!"

AFIF MUKHTAR WAS STARTLED when the gunman spoke, called out to his companion with instructions. After several seconds of delay, the one called Dixon spoke, repeating what the other one—his boss, apparently—had said in English.

Mukhtar bit his lip to keep from laughing at these ignorant Americans. The impulse died when he imagined others swarming all over the parking lot with bullhorns, guns, bulletproof vests.

Not that the vest would save them when he pressed the trigger on his loaded suitcase.

*Do it now!*

Something delayed him, though. Perhaps it was the vain hope that if more police and FBI agents arrived, he could destroy them all. They might have blocked him from the mall's interior, but he could still inflict great damage on his enemies and on their city.

"Try again!" the first gunman demanded.

His companion did as he was told, telling Mukhtar once more in Arabic that he should speak to them. There was a hesitancy in the other's voice, a tightness born of fear.

This time, anger replaced the near-hysteric mirth Mukhtar had felt a moment earlier. Without showing himself, he called back to the men who hunted him, "What are you saying? Don't you speak English?"

Muffled curses from the translator made Mukhtar smile. When neither of them instantly responded, he told them, "Speak, then, since you've sacrificed yourselves to come this far. What will we talk about?"

"That bomb you're carrying," the first one answered. "I don't think you really want to do this."

"But of course I do," Mukhtar replied.

"You've been deceived. There's no shortcut to Paradise. Certainly not by killing thousands who've done nothing to you, people who you've never met."

"I don't need to meet my enemies," Mukhtar said, watching carefully to make sure neither of the men advanced while they were talking. "They hate God and my people. They must be destroyed."

"Who taught you that?"

Mukhtar sidestepped the trap. "I see it for myself on CNN and read it in the newspaper. Surveillance on imams and mosques. Racial profiling. Your planes bomb Muslims countries only, if they won't agree to your demands."

"Mukhtar—"

"I know the definition of a terrorist," he interrupted, simmering. "The State Department calls it anyone who uses violence or threats to influence government policy. Is not the President himself a terrorist? What do you say?"

The translator replied, "I say you ought to take that bomb and shove it—"

"Dixon!" the other snapped, and silenced his companion.

Then, to Mukhtar, he said, "Neither one of us can change the world. But we can start deescalating, here and now."

"You mean I should give up without a fight and let you win. Surrender to America. Accept your word as law."

"If you want to debate our foreign policy, let's do it," the gunman said. "If you have demands—"

"My one demand is that you die," Mukhtar retorted. "One press of the button, and I get my wish."

"You've got your twenty-second birthday coming up next month," the nameless stranger said, reminding him. "Wouldn't you like to celebrate it?"

"In a prison cell, where I will sit until I die?" Mukhtar responded, mocking. "Or until you execute me for resisting U.S. tyranny?"

"There's no death penalty unless you kill someone, Mukhtar."

"You'd rather have me rot in jail for fifty years than go to my reward in Paradise. How typical! Think only of yourself, the country, what you want."

"How are you any different?" asked the one called Dixon. "Here you are, committing suicide and killing thousands more besides, because some half-baked preacher told you it's a good idea. What kind of sense does that make, asshole?"

"Dixon!" the other barked.

"No! Screw that! This guy is a mass-murderer wanna-be. He doesn't get to hide behind some philosophical debate of right and wrong. He wants to kill people. That's wrong."

Through clenched teeth, Mukhtar asked, "And have you never killed, Dixon? Be honest, now."

"Give me a shot, I'll kill you in a second," Dixon said.

"Then take your shot," Mukhtar replied. "What is it you Americans all love to say? Stand up and take it like a man."

And Mukhtar rose as he was speaking, careful not to let the other shooter see him, with a van between them. He held the heavy suitcase in his left hand, pistol in his right.

Some twenty feet away, the stranger known as Dixon rose, clutching a small machine pistol. Mukhtar triggered two rounds before the other man could fire, and saw at least one of them strike him in the chest. Dixon went over backward, spraying bullets at the sky.

Surprised and pleased that all his shooting practice had paid off, Mukhtar turned toward the vehicle where Dixon's comrade was concealed.

"And you?" he asked. "Will you come out and face me like a real American? Show me that might makes right!"

BOLAN WAS MOVING when the shots exploded, braced and ready as he could be for the world to end if Dixon hit Mukhtar and made him drop the case, *if* it was fitted with a dead-man's switch.

But there was no explosion and no whoop of triumph from the DHS agent. Instead, while he was circling around a van with dueling naked Viking women painted on its sides, he heard Afif Mukhtar.

"And you?" the Palestinian called out to him. "Will you come out and face me like a real American? Show me that might makes right!"

Words couldn't goad him into hasty, reckless action. Bolan didn't care what Mukhtar said or thought about him, what he said or thought about America. This was a death game, and it wasn't played with words.

The shotgun Dixon had expropriated from a corpse was a Beretta Model 1201 FP with rifle sights, a pistol grip, six rounds inside its magazine and one more in the chamber. It was also semiautomatic and could fire all seven shots before the first spent casing hit the ground.

With double-aught loads, that meant Bolan could send five dozen .33-caliber pellets hurtling downrange in roughly two seconds. The Beretta's twenty-inch barrel and full choke assured him of minimal spread at any range inside of twenty feet.

"Where are you?" Mukhtar taunted him. "You want to stop me? Now you have a chance."

He had been listening beyond the propaganda drivel, hoping to glean something from his enemy, and so he had. One press of the button, Mukhtar had informed them, and *I get my wish*.

Not a dead-man's switch, then—unless he was lying.

That made it a gamble, the stakes all-or-nothing. Bolan didn't love the odds, but he would play the only cards he had.

As if he had a choice.

Mukhtar called out to him once more, as Bolan reached the right-rear quarter of the van. "Are you a coward? Won't you face me?"

His position meant that he would have to fire left-handed, moving out around the van. It shouldn't be a problem, but he knew Mukhtar was waiting for him, with his pistol ready.

Facing which way?

He stepped into the clear, sighting along the shotgun's barrel. Mukhtar had his back to Bolan, but he heard or felt him, turning smoothly with his pistol raised and tracking.

Both men fired together, Mukhtar's bullet hammering against the custom van, while Bolan's buckshot charge ripped through the joint of his left shoulder. Bolan fired a second blast, same striking point, with Mukhtar airborne, then a third round to the middle of his chest before he hit the pavement on his back.

The Palestinian was dead, no doubt about it, with his left arm nearly severed at the shoulder and his rib cage shattered, all the vital organs mangled where they lay inside it. He lay stretched out in a spreading pool of crimson, with his eyes open, locked on his last view of the Minnesota sky.

Or maybe Paradise?

It made no difference to Bolan what became of Mukhtar's soul. If it was punished or rewarded, if it went nowhere at all, the end result was all the same to him.

He had been sent to stop the mind and body from performing heinous deeds, not to surmise about the afterlife. If Mukhtar started wreaking havoc on some other plane, it would be someone else's problem.

Bolan heard Grimaldi circling overhead and raised a hand to signal that the field was clear. Next thing, he crouched beside the black case and peered at it until he found the trigger button on its handle. Having done that, it was safe—or relatively so—for him to lift the case and take it with him when he went to find Tom Dixon.

"Jesus," Dixon asked him, wheezing through a chest wound, "did you have to bring that with you?"

"It's my first-aid kit," Bolan replied.

"I guess you got him, then?"

"He's done," Bolan said.

"So am I, I think," Dixon informed him.

"No. You're tougher than you think."

"I don't feel tough right now."

"An ambulance is on the way. Stay frosty now."

"No problem," Dixon said. "I'm cold as ice."

Bolan knelt beside him, listening to sirens in the distance, drawing closer with their banshee wails like vengeful spirits coming to a feast of death.

"Hang on," he said. And then, again, for emphasis, "Hang on, damn it."

# EPILOGUE

Dixon hung on.

Grimaldi had been making calls in the helicopter to various emergency responders. By the time Bolan reached Dixon, the Stony Man pilot had summoned agents of the FBI, local police, two ambulance crews and the nearest Nuclear Emergency Search Team.

In no special order, the ambulance teams were for Dixon and Mukhtar, the latter a patient in need of no red lights or sirens. Police would seal the scene and hold at bay the crowd of rubberneckers from the mall and environs who had already started to gather. G-men would take overall charge of the case as a terrorist matter. NEST would be transporting—and hopefully—disarming Mukhtar's bomb.

Such an assemblage of authority would normally have Bolan on the move, but he was ready this time with a pocketful of impressive credentials to dazzle all comers. For this occasion, he produced a laminated card identifying Matthew Cooper as an agent of the CIA, approved since 9/11 to pursue its foreign cases onto U.S. soil.

And everybody bought it, more or less.

The cops, or course, were miffed at Feds of any pedigree who showed up on their turf without a please, thank-you or by-your-leave. Nonetheless, under Homeland Security arrangements, they had no choice but to swallow their complaints and get on board, unless they wanted to be frozen out completely—and, no small incentive in itself, risk losing federal funds.

The FBI, predictably, sent out a squad of clean-cut eager beavers. Aside from taking over Bolan's case—for which the Bureau would, of course, assume full credit now that it had been resolved—the agent in charge also had plans to debrief Bolan at the nearest federal building. He was ready to pull rank, maybe slap on the cuffs, until a call from Washington left him red-faced and muttering distractedly about a "breach of jurisdictional propriety."

Bolan was standing by when EMTs put Dixon on a gurney and stowed him in their ambulance. He might have followed the vehicle to the hospital, but there were questions to be answered—or evaded—at the shooting scene, and he knew news hawks would be gathering around the young DHS agent soon.

And speaking of the media, they were descending in swarms, like ants at a picnic or flies in an outhouse. Bolan wasn't worried at the moment, since police and county deputies had been dragooned to block off all streets granting access to the mall. They stopped short of evacuation, reasoning that it would only cause more panic and confuse an already chaotic situation, but they were not letting anybody in or out until the scene had been secured, processed and cleared.

In his abbreviated interview with FBI agents, Bolan didn't refer to any of the raids on local chicken coops. He'd leave the G-men to connect Nasser Asad and Ahmed Zero to the bomb if they were able, or to wait for Tom Dixon to give an edited account of their adventures covering the past few days. Bolan trusted that Dixon, if he lived to grant an interview, would be sufficiently discreet. When he was finished there, at least to Bolan's satisfaction, he produced the sat phone, thumbed a speed-dial number, spoke two words and settled in to wait.

Grimaldi didn't keep him waiting long. Some fifteen seconds later, tops, the chopper was back, settling without a hint of difficulty in the middle of the nearest blocked-off street. Bolan turned his back on frowning cops and Feds, jogged to the chopper and ducked underneath its spinning rotors to reach the cockpit. A moment later, he was buckled into the copilot's seat and they were lifting off.

"How's Dixon?" Grimaldi asked.

"Chest wound," Bolan said. "He was talking, but it could go either way."

"Too bad."

"He took one for the team," Bolan replied. "We might still be dancing with Mukhtar down there, otherwise."

"Be nice if he could walk away from this one, even so," Grimaldi answered.

"Yeah," Bolan agreed. "It would."

"No hospital, I guess?"

"Too many cameras. We'll leave him to the medics and let DHS look after him."

"They'll be high-profile after this," Grimaldi said.

"Could be, unless they hand off to the Bureau and the Company."

"What's that? A bureaucrat who shuns the public eye? Don't bet your life on it."

"Okay, I won't."

And that was one thing Bolan could control.

He'd bet his life again one day, and likely soon. But when he did, it wouldn't be on something trivial, or on a sure thing like the average D.C. bureaucrat's craving for fame. He might as well lay odds against tomorrow's sunrise and be done with it.

The sun would rise tomorrow over the Twin Cities, and while most locals would know by then that they had lived through some kind of unspecified emergency, few would ever realize its nature or how close they'd come to being literally blown away. If and when the records were finally declassified, say fifty or a hundred years down the line, only a handful of Twin City residents alive today would make the effort necessary to obtain the heavily redacted copies.

And they'd learn nothing that Washington—meaning the White House and the State Department—didn't want to share.

Freedom of Information Act? Forget about it.

"Where to, then?" Grimaldi asked.

"Someplace where I can ditch the hardware," Bolan said, "and maybe catch a little R & R. Some sleep, at least."

"Your wish," Grimaldi said, "is my command."

*Arlington National Cemetery*

BOLAN CAME FAIRLY OFTEN to this resting place of ordinary men and heroes, laid out side by side with markers giving no more information than the occupants, if living, would've offered to their captors if they had been prisoners of war.

Which, in a sense, they were.

The markers told no stories, wouldn't hint which of the fallen had been loving husbands, fathers, brothers, sons, or which had been the kind of men you really didn't want to be around when he was drunk or angry. There were no brief sketches of the battles that had claimed their lives—or, for the veterans who'd fallen later, in civilian life—or the events that brought them to this place at last. Among the dead from battles dating back to Lexington and Concord lay a U.S. President, a murdered civil rights leader and others whose lives had been remarkable in their own way. The graveyard drew four million visitors each year, on average.

The same as the Mall of America.

This day, Mack Bolan hadn't come to visit any certain grave, or to commune with fellow warriors generally. He had an appointment with one of the living instead.

Brognola found him gazing at the headstone of a private first-class neither one of them had ever heard of, killed in Normandy on June 8, 1944.

"He made it through D-day," Bolan said.

"So did you."

"Looks like it," Bolan granted. "How's the fallout?"

"Puns like that should be illegal," Brognola said. "Anyway, if you've been reading any newspapers or watching network coverage, you know we've got a lid on it."

"How's Dixon?"

"Critical but stable. DHS is in the middle of a pissing contest with the Bureau over who debriefs him when he's able to respond."

"Doesn't Homeland Security outrank the FBI?" Bolan asked.

"Theoretically, they run the antiterror shooting match, but the Patriot Act left the Bureau independent in fact, still answering to the attorney general. It's like a Hoover hangover. Nobody likes to rile the G-men."

"*You* don't mind," Bolan reminded him.

"I was a G-man," Brognola replied. "I have a knack for pushing buttons over there."

"You do," Bolan agreed. "No comeback from the Saudis, yet?"

"Officially, State's raised no beef about Asad or his batboy. Riyadh's embarrassed that the pair of them died where they did—which has been covered by the media, in case you missed it. On the down-low, I'm advised that presidential messages to Saudi's honchos have suggested that they screen their diplomats more carefully in future."

"Nothing but a wrist slap," Bolan said. "Again."

He wasn't forgetting that all but two of the 9/11 hijackers were Saudis, financed in large part by oil money straight from their homeland. If they hadn't all been dead, they would've been on Bolan's hit parade. Brognola had exerted serious persuasion at the time to keep Bolan from carrying the battle further up the food chain, to Riyadh itself.

"The Man does what he can," Brognola said.

"Politically, you mean."

"For politicians, what else is there?"

Bolan frowned and shook his head. "There should be something."

"Anyway," Brognola said, "you saved the day. Again."

"We plugged the dike, Dixon and me," Bolan corrected him. "For now. We saved *one* day."

"That's how we take it," the big Fed acknowledged. "One day at a time."

"Sounds like a twelve-step program, not a strategy for winning."

"Is there any difference between the two?"

"Well, if you put it that way."

"You know how it goes," Brognola said. "Hell, *you* taught *me* this game. We play the cards we're dealt and take whatever hands we can. On good days, we break even."

"There's a time coming," Bolan said, "when that may not be enough."

"Maybe, by then, we'll have a new deck," Brognola said. "Or new dealers."

"Maybe." Bolan didn't feel or sound convinced.

"You didn't ask about al Qaeda."

"If anyone had bagged the big cheese," Bolan said, "that *would* have been on CNN."

"Still looking," Brognola confirmed. "These days, the theory is that he's in Pakistan, sheltered by what the Pentagon describes as 'friendly tribes.' Nobody seems to know exactly who or where they are."

"We could go in and have a look around," Bolan suggested.

"We?"

"I'd need a translator," Bolan said.

"I believe we'll pass on that. Thanks, all the same."

"Clean slate," Bolan said. "What's the bad?"

"That brings us back to oil and politics."

"And isn't that a shame?"

"Not ours to reason why, you know?"

"I keep remembering what happened to the Light Brigade," Bolan said, picking up on Brognola's poetic reference.

"I try not to remember it," Brognola said.

"Lessons of history and all."

"We're learning all the time. Applying what we learn may take a little longer, but we're getting there. Just like the tortoise. Slow and steady."

"Trouble is," Bolan said, "that we may not have the time. The hare in this fable is rabid, and he's biting everybody he can reach."

"We'll get him," Brognola said. "We'll get all of them."

"Such confidence."

"I call it optimism. Either way, it keeps me sane. Saner."

"Good luck with that."

"So, what's your trick?" Brognola asked.

"No trick to it," Bolan told his oldest living friend. "I just keep keeping on."

"Don't tell me," Brognola began.

And Bolan finished for him. "That's it. One day at a time."